STONEWALL INN MYSTERIES

KEITH KAHLA, GENERAL EDITOR

BY LEV RAPHAEL

Nick Hoffman Mysteries

Let's Get Criminal
The Edith Wharton Murders
The Death of a Constant Lover
Little Miss Evil

Fiction

Dancing on Tisha B'av
Winter Eyes

Nonfiction

Edith Wharton's Prisoners of Shame
Journeys & Arrivals

Coauthored with Gershen Kaufman

Stick Up for Yourself!
Dynamics of Power
Coming Out of Shame

THE DEATH OF A CONSTANT LOVER

A NICK HOFFMAN MYSTERY

LEV RAPHAEL

St. Martin's Press ✹ New York

Library of Congress Cataloging-in-Publication Data

Raphael, Lev.
    The death of a constant lover: a Nick Hoffman mystery /
Lev Raphael.
        p.   cm.
    ISBN 0-8027-3326-3 (hc)
    ISBN 0-312-26496-8 (pbk)
    I. Title
PS3568.A5988D36   1999
813'.54—dc21   98-42836
                                                          CIP

First published in the United States by Walker Publishing
Company, Inc.

First Stonewall Inn Mysteries Edition: May 2000

10 9 8 7 6 5 4 3 2 1

To the tireless staff at

GK Consulting, Inc.

*The world is full of banks and rivers
running between them, of men and
women crossing bridges and fords,
unaware of the consequences, not looking
back or beneath their feet, and with no
loose change for the boatman.*

—*Arturo Pérez-Reverte*, The Club Dumas

Acknowledgments

My thanks go to Carole and Mike Steinberg for their hospitality north of Northport, where I did important work on this book. Howard Anderson of Michigan State University helpfully explained various academic procedures, giving me models I could work with in developing what happens to Nick. Information on Quebecois expressions was supplied by Wendy Thomas, Luc Pesant, and René Jolicoeur of the Canadian Heritage Information Network, and by Bob Newland of Fanfare Books in Stratford, Ontario. Yohannes Mochtar supplied some helpful facts about Indonesia, but any mistakes here are my own, and Lucille is not a relative of his, fictionally or otherwise.

THE DEATH OF A CONSTANT LOVER

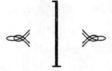

It was Stefan's idea that I eat lunch now and then by the Administration Building bridge—despite the murder. Well, actually, it was *because* of the murder.

Two years ago, the body of my officemate Perry Cross had turned up in the Michigan River, snagged on some rocks right near the bridge. It wasn't a diving accident.

At the part of the shallow river where they had found Cross's body, artfully scattered boulders created a tiny rapids, and ducks gathered year-round to be fed by children and their parents. The sloping lawns on either side of the river were always full of contented-looking students when the weather was even remotely warm enough: reading, tanning, eating, dreaming. An inviting terrace lined with benches stretched along the south bank, down three wide granite steps from the walk paralleling the river.

All kinds of things showed up in the Michigan River: notebooks, beer cans, sneakers, condoms. But there'd never been a body before.

And even after two years, Cross's murder was still very much alive at SUM's verdant Michiganapolis campus. You could often

2 | LEV RAPHAEL

see students stopped on the wide bridge with its rounded steel rails, pointing down to where they thought Cross's body had been found. Some leaned far over the rail as if pretending to plunge to a battered, wet death. It was ghoulish playacting that got uglier when they shrieked or laughed and made loud jokes or choking noises, then staggered away from the rail crying, "Help! Help!"

The murder hadn't done my career at the State University of Michigan any good, even though I wasn't the killer. Since I'd been involved in a scandalous death, I was perceived as having brought shades of *Hard Copy* to the hallowed halls of SUM, which meant bad publicity for my college, my department, and me. I knew I would have trouble getting tenure next year with that kind of baggage; as they say in politics, I was tainted. Even worse, I hadn't written a new book since I'd gotten to SUM four years earlier, so I wasn't considered productive enough.

But that wasn't my only problem. In some kind of weird delayed reaction to the murder, I had found myself dreaming about Cross's death more and more, and over the last two years I'd increasingly avoided the bridge and that general part of campus. I took roundabout detours that ate up my time.

When he found out, Stefan was immediately concerned.

"Nick, you can't be terrorized by the past."

"Are you kidding? Gibbon said that history was basically a list of the crimes, follies, and misfortunes of mankind. Sounds scary to me!"

He ignored that. "Go have lunch there—make it a regular thing."

I gulped. "Lunch? Why stop with lunch? How about breakfast at the Michiganapolis morgue?"

"It'll start with your staying away from the bridge, then you'll want to avoid your office, and then—"

"Wait a minute," I snapped. "Avoiding your office is what half the professors around here do, and you know it. That's not a sign of trauma, it's a sign of laziness. They hate their students and don't want to talk to them! There's no way that could ever happen to me."

Stefan relented a little. And since he looks like a stockier, shorter version of Ben Cross, who played the Jewish runner in *Chariots of Fire*, Stefan's relenting face is really something.

But I didn't let it distract me. "Come on—are you *really* afraid that I'll turn into Miss Havisham, withered and covered with dust, and go up in flames, just because I won't cross the Administration Building Bridge, or even come to it?"

Wisely, Stefan didn't answer. He did what quiet people do so well: He listened. Sometimes it's helpful, sometimes it's annoying. Right then I was annoyed.

"Hey—it was a complete shock for me, okay?" I said. "Corpses have no place on our campus. This isn't Rwanda—this is Michiganapolis."

He shrugged. "*Et in Arcadia Ego.*"

"Latin? Isn't it bad enough you quote stuff at me in *French*, and that your accent is perfect?" I was very touchy about my French, since my parents were Belgian Jews, and they hadn't succeeded in raising me fully bilingual. To me, that would have meant being able to argue as well in French as in English, to gobble angrily way down in my throat the way my father did, those rare times he lost his temper.

Patiently, Stefan said, "*Et in Arcadia Ego* means death is in paradise, too."

"Jeez, Stefan, I know what it means—I saw *Brideshead Revisited*, remember that was me sitting next to you in the living room? Hey," I said, suddenly distracted. "Now we know why Lady Marchmain looked so miserable and pinched in that series.

Claire Bloom was living with Philip Roth then! That would give anyone a case of the grims."

Stefan's grin faded after a moment, and it was my turn to relent. "Okay, I won't put it off. I'll go have lunch at the Bridge of Death. And don't look at me like that! It's what students are calling the bridge. I didn't make that up."

Stefan was right, but it bothered me that he wasn't nearly as shaken by the murder as I was, even though I understood why. Stefan's parents were Holocaust survivors, and his glimpses of the horror they'd endured outweighed any tragedy that could enter our lives. My cousin Sharon, who lives in New York, had put it well: "Nick, Stefan expects the world to be horrible, but you have a comic vision of life. Murders don't fit." That was it exactly. I couldn't figure out how to make sense of the killing that had erupted so close to me, so I had avoided dealing with it, or tried to, by avoiding the bridge.

But that wasn't an option anymore, with Stefan herding me back to reality like the tireless sheepdog he could be.

I figured I could try eating lunch at the terrace by the bridge at least once every few weeks, when the weather permitted. You know, become my own Pavlov's dog by associating food with the bridge, though nobody would have to clean up after me. Stefan was right: How else was I going to overcome my phobia about what had once been my favorite spot on SUM's idyllic campus?

Unlike Stefan, who'd taken longer to appreciate SUM, I'd fallen in love at once with its spectacular, lush 6,000-acre campus, justly famous for its gardens, trees, and landscaping. No building on campus is over six stories, so the nineteenth-century Romanesque sandstone halls with turrets forming the original campus aren't overwhelmed or even mocked by the brooding, columned granite piles of the 1920s or the brick boxes of the 1950s with decorative turquoise panels above and below the windows.

And no matter how different the buildings, they're intimately connected in an appealing, inviting whole by the curving roads and walks twining through the vast array of trees, many of them a century old: glorious weeping willows, maples, oaks, blue spruce, and Scotch pine. There are also lush flowering cherries, apples, dogwoods, hawthorns, magnolias, and redbuds. In addition, the horticulture department maintains acres of lilac and forsythia, countless courtyard gardens, and dazzling ornamental beds of tulips, hyacinths, iris, gladioli, petunias.

At the center of campus, the ill-fated bridge is one of several wide concrete spans crossing the meandering, shallow Michigan River to connect the northern and southern parts of the university's gigantic Michiganapolis campus. The northern section, where SUM's oldest buildings crowd together, abuts one of the city's main shopping areas, the Mile. That street of shops and bars cordons off the campus from faculty and student neighborhoods farther north.

In the much larger southern part of SUM's campus, newer buildings are spread farther apart as if dropped by an absent-minded giant, and separated by vast parking lots, fields, and experimental farms. SUM was founded in the mid–nineteenth century as an agricultural college of several small buildings (including my department's crumbling home, Parker Hall), mushrooming in the 1920s and again in the Eisenhower years to become one of the nation's largest schools. It currently housed close to 50,000 students, or "customers," as our idiotic new president liked to say and I suppose we were lucky he hadn't instituted drive-through classes yet.

Thousands of students crossed the bridge every day, many of them at lunchtime, but despite the crowds, I did not feel safe on my return, though I was trying to. There I was on the first warm day of spring in my fourth year at SUM, clutching my lunch in one hand in an SUM bookstore crimson-and-gray plastic bag, making my way from Parker Hall, trying not to feel flushed or nervous. I couldn't help wishing Stefan were there to remind me that my avoidance of the bridge didn't make sense. But since there were other things I preferred not to think about that day, going to the bridge was better than hiding under our bed at home.

And it was blessedly warm and sunny. Michiganapolis is one of the cloudiest cities in the country—because of its position between two Great Lakes, I think. So what might be picturesque winters with snow and crackling fires are often spoiled by the endless weeks of dense gray sky. It had been a typically dismal winter here, with layers and layers of cloud cover.

But spring was early and especially warm. Dangerously warm, longtime residents were saying knowingly. I didn't pay attention to their dire parentheses about the greenhouse effect. I was determined to enjoy the color, the warmth, the freedom.

On my way over to the bridge I ran into Betty and Bill Malatesta, the two brightest and friendliest graduate students in my department, English, American Studies, and Rhetoric (EAR). For as long as I'd been there, they had both been publishing articles, presenting conference papers, making themselves the stars of the Ph.D. program. They were cheerful, sexy, and attractive—a sort of intellectual Bogey and Bacall.

Today, as usual, they were dressed in funky black.

"Great day for strolling!" they chirped, almost in unison. Then Bill, who loved lightbulb jokes, asked me, "How many SUM administrators does it take to change a lightbulb?"

I shrugged.

"None! Because first they have to form a committee and write a report about reinventing the university that goes to another committee where nothing happens."

"Not bad," I said.

"How many women's studies majors? None, because they're suing the bulb for sexual harassment."

Before I could groan, he rushed on: "How many football coaches? None! Their strategy is defensive—make the bulb come to *you*!"

I laughed now, but the hilarity stopped when Bill said seriously, "I want to talk to you about one of the new TAs in the department. I'll come by during your office hours."

And without telling me who he was talking about, they said good-bye and moved on. What was that all about? Though tempted, I couldn't stand there all day wondering, so I continued toward the bridge.

I saw our college's dean, cruel-eyed Magnus Bullerschmidt, make his stately way across campus. He was tremendously fat, and the weight made him seem like a turbaned despot in a 1940s movie, ordering casual mayhem from his peacock throne.

As I walked farther along, I kept my eyes down, hoping trouble wouldn't find me, but suddenly I saw a grotesque flash of red. Blood red.

Getting closer to the bridge, I could see an open cardboard box of Holy Bibles with improbably garish and cheap-looking leatherette red covers. In the whirling dense crowd of students, those covers were like a fiery distress call—or a warning.

"They're back," I thought wearily. The preachers were back. I stopped where I was.

Every spring, SUM was hit by a blight of these thin and fevered preachers, who passed out Bibles at most of the campus crossroads and bridges, occasionally bursting into tirades as if they were singing waiters at a religious restaurant. The preachers were as dreary and startling as the enormous, strident crows that had become as common a spring sight on campus as the squirrels and raccoons.

Today the lurid box by the bridge was guarded by a meager-fleshed young man in a crumpled blue suit, his forehead a flaming relief map of pimples that made the red binding an even more unfortunate choice. As students and faculty passed, he stabbed Bibles at them with the spring of a malevolent troll. Though the day was cool, he looked hot and sweaty—fired up by his mission, no doubt. He must have been expecting some kind of martyrdom, since people like him were often heckled on campus, and sometimes threatened. Maybe he'd even been reading the letters in the student newspaper, where the presence of preachers on campus was attacked or defended in the kind of intemperate language the paper loved because it generated controversy.

The preachers descending on campus were strange and geeky clones: all of them in plain, unattractive suits and haircuts that made them look like rejects from the *Lawrence Welk Show*, each one with false thunder in his voice. Doling out their Holy Bibles, they sometimes hectored students to "Save yourself!" as if Michiganapolis were as steeped in moral degradation and evil as New York, Los Angeles—or Ann Arbor. Whenever I walked past them, I had an image of myself as trapped in some weird kind of carnival with barkers offering salvation instead of rides or teddy bears.

I didn't understand why they were even allowed on campus, but I guessed that university officials simply wanted to avoid an argument with the local religious right.

I stood and watched the action. Most students crossing by today's preacher on the Administration Building bridge bent away from him or darted past his outstretched hand, but some seemed pathetically eager to receive any kind of gift, and he blessed all of those. I could imagine their loneliness or confusion. Many students at SUM came from Michigan towns barely half the size of the university and felt hopelessly overwhelmed and disconnected (which was probably why the administration cut counseling services every year).

Two EAR colleagues passed me, locked in conversation: boring Carter Savery and grim, miserable Iris Bell. I'd never seen them together before—what could they possibly have in common? Iris was perpetually complaining about being underrecognized in EAR, and Carter was as blandly self-satisfied as Jabba the Hutt. Neither of them paid me any attention in the department.

I let them get a good distance ahead of me before I finally approached the bridge. I veered away from the young man and his box so that I wouldn't get a bloody-looking Bible thrust at me. And so that I wouldn't have to feel embarrassed by saying "No, thanks" or something equally inadequate to the occasion. When people ring my doorbell at home to share what they claim is the word of God, that's different: I always tell them I'm offended by their invasion of my privacy. It satisfies me to leave them nonplussed. But here at the bridge—an open, public place—I felt constrained. And I was a faculty member—*my* nutty outbursts were supposed to be saved for departmental meetings.

Safely across, I took a seat on the edge of one of the wide steps of the terrace that was just west of the bridge. I wasn't teaching today, and it was dress-down Friday anyway, so I had jeans on and didn't have to worry about getting dirty.

The preachers gave me the creeps; they made me feel that we here at the university were nothing more than a bunch of campers huddled over a dwindling fire, trying to pretend the hungry wolves weren't just beyond the edge of light.

And their presence made me worry about SUM.

See, no one was really in charge at the university right then, so we were a little like a former Soviet republic, drifting while various power centers prepared themselves to compete for control. The provost had left after a sexual harassment scandal, and there was fierce competition on campus to fill the plum position, even though there was a pro forma national search going on. My own chair, Coral Greathouse, was a front-runner in this race.

There'd also been a shake-up on the Board of Trustees, and our moronic president, Webb Littleterry, was continuing to provide uninspired, uninvolved leadership. That wasn't surprising, since he was SUM's former football coach, and his election to the board had proven the scornful observation in some quarters that SUM wasn't much more than a football program with a university attached. If only it were a winning program. . . .

I tried to relax into the day, tried to enjoy the life all around me here: toddlers waving and flapping at the ducks, gamely flinging bits of bread; students taking time off from classes to just sit and drink pop, chat, catch some rays; other students coming with more elaborate plans for picnics that included Frisbees, board games, and puppies. It was a combination park and town square, and if you stayed there long enough, you were bound to run into people you knew.

Juno Dromgoole, the rowdy visiting professor of Canadian studies, dashed across the bridge toward Parker Hall, her chic black leather briefcase clutched under one arm like a large purse. Headed in the other direction was Polly Flockhart, an annoying neighbor of ours who was a secretary in the History Department.

From the bridge now came what sounded like fierce quotations from Revelation or a Stephen King novel. I tried to block out the noise and the image of that angry pimpled face so that I could enjoy my thermos of Kenyan coffee and my smoked turkey breast on focaccia.

The shouting died down a little.

"Dr. Hoffman, hi! Want some company?"

I looked up and grinned at Angie Sandoval, a former student of mine now majoring in criminal justice. She had helped me enormously each time I'd been unavoidably involved in murder at SUM. Perry Cross's death was just the beginning: A year later murder stalked the Edith Wharton conference I had organized (under duress) at SUM. Buildings don't burn down around me or anything like that, but I'm not exactly the luckiest man on campus.

"Sure, Angie. Sit down." I moved over on my step and she joined me, pulled out a can of Vernor's, Michigan's own ginger ale, from her pink knapsack, and popped it open for a slug.

I owed a lot to Angie. She had clued me in to the importance of the county medical examiner in a criminal investigation, and she'd also explained that SUM's campus police weren't at all like security guards at a bank. They were *real* police, with all crimes at SUM under their jurisdiction, just as if it were a small town. And wasn't it?

Short, slim, apple-cheeked, with curly dark hair and a heart-shaped face, Angie was eager and bright and helpful. Whenever I'd run into her on campus this past year, I'd been surprised at how glad I was. Surprised, too, that I found myself thinking that if I had a daughter, I'd want her to be like Angie. I'd never before felt fatherly about any of my students. But then I'd also never been just over forty, either, and thus more than twice the age of most of my students.

I asked Angie about her classes, and we chatted about them, enjoying the partly sunny day as hundreds of lunchtime idlers eddied and flowed around us. Suddenly, there was renewed shouting on the bridge. A bicyclist speeding by was yelling at the preacher, "The Bible is bullshit!"

"You'll burn in hell!" the pimply young man roared. *"Burn in hell!"*

There were mocking cheers from students crossing the bridge, and a few catcalls.

Angie sighed and drank some more pop. I wasn't sure if she

was religious or not, so I didn't say anything. I wasn't in the mood to be lectured about moral decay by someone barely out of her teens, no matter how pleasant her personality.

"I hate the way things have changed around here," she said. "Everybody's mega pissed off! Like, nonstop."

"You've got that right." Now it was my turn to sigh.

The murders I'd been mixed up in had been among faculty and were unusual, since faculty members are more given to character assassination than the real thing. But the student body at SUM had seen intolerance of all kinds become commonplace, and violence was no longer rare.

Angie and I chewed over the recent troubles on campus for a while.

A black student had been set upon by a handful of white students on a dark campus path at night. They beat and kicked him and called him "nigger." The rumor was that he'd been found facedown with his pants around his ankles and had either been raped or almost raped, but the student had vehemently denied it before taking a semester's leave.

The tiny office of the Muslim Students League at the Union had been broken into, trashed, and spray-painted with slogans like "Go Back to Iraq!" A car parked at Hillel, where Jewish students met, had been set on fire, and the gas tank exploded, causing thousands of dollars of damage to the building. Campus Young Republicans had received phoned death threats, as had members of SUM of US, SUM's queer student group. Assaults were up, bicycle thefts were up, and more thefts and flashers were reported in the library.

As a bibliographer, I found that particularly distressing, because it was bound to give students the wrong idea about research.

"It's like everybody's just waiting for a chance," Angie said, "to let go."

"Maybe it's a plan," I suggested.

"What?"

"Maybe we're the target of a hostile takeover by the University of Michigan—and they're doing everything they can to drive down the value of our stock."

Angie smiled dutifully but said, "I don't think this campus needs any help looking bad."

She was right, and I thought the atmosphere among students was even influencing faculty. My new officemate, Lucille Mochtar, a minority hire, was generating some ugly comments from other faculty members. Mochtar had been hired right out of Berkeley's graduate school at an amazing salary, without any publications. But she was part black, part Indonesian, and SUM pursued her with desperation and briefcases full of cash.

I liked Lucille immensely and was pleased that she and her husband had bought the house across the street from me and Stefan. But I knew that resentment against her was simmering, and I wondered how it would affect me and my chances for tenure, since we got along so well. I tended to think of everything in terms of my coming consideration for tenure—it was impossible not to.

"Mom and Dad want me to transfer," Angie was saying. "Even though I'm a junior! They think SUM's getting too dangerous."

"But you've been safe, right? Nothing's happened to you?"

Angie shrugged. "They weren't happy that I was doing that investigating with you last year. But I did get extra credit from one of my professors."

I smiled. "Well, I'm glad you helped me out. You were great."

Angie thanked me, then she blushed. "My parents think you're a bad influence, even though I took only one of your courses."

I shrugged. I could see nervous parents feeling that it was dangerous to know me, but the thought of not running into Angie on campus anymore made me sad.

"I understand how they feel. President Littleterry still blames me for those people getting murdered at the conference last year," I said. "Dean Bullerschmidt is pissed off, too, and my chair isn't happy either. The conference was supposed to make SUM look good—instead we got into all the newspapers, *Time*, *Newsweek*, for all the wrong reasons. Alumni donations plummeted."

Angie nodded sympathetically. "You should write a book about it or something," she suggested. "Then you could get rich, and it wouldn't matter if they liked you."

I wondered what kind of book I could write at this point. *How to Ruin Your Academic Career?* Just then someone behind us called, "Hi, Angie!" and we both turned. It was Jesse Benevento, a punked-out religious fanatic with dead-white hair who'd lectured me on sexual morality last year during office hours. His father was chairman of the History Department, which shared decrepit Parker Hall with EAR.

Jesse nodded at me coldly, and he and Angie talked about some assignment they both had due. After registering that he now had a nose ring and pierced eyebrows, I tuned out. I didn't like him. Jesse had criticized me for making a casual reference to sex in one of my classes, and I still felt uncomfortable when I ran into him on campus. I'd often wondered if he'd complained to his father about me, and if his father had mentioned it, even casually, to Coral Greathouse. Though she'd never brought it up, it could have happened, and since I didn't have tenure, any prejudicial information could harm me, no matter how minor.

Even though campus was enormous, I ran into Jesse enough times to wish he would just disappear. I sipped my coffee very thoughtfully, trying to be detached from the conversation without being rude.

"Gotta bail," Jesse finally said. "Meeting a prof." He slowly moved off, heading up the path to the bridge, but his meeting couldn't have been urgent; I saw him stop to chat with a guy in an SUM tracksuit. I turned away.

Angie must have picked up my discomfort. "He's pretty intense," she said apologetically.

"Are you two dating?"

Eyes wide, she seemed too startled to laugh. "He's just a friend. Jesse doesn't date anyone—he's always saying you have to avoid the near occasion of sin. I think that's a quote from some pope."

"Saint Augustine."

She shrugged. "Whatever."

"Get out of here, asshole!" came a shout from the bridge. And the bridge was suddenly twice as crowded, swarming with students. I thought of army ants boiling over prey that couldn't escape the flood of terror.

From where Angie and I sat, I could make out some kind of scuffle. Flung up from the growling little knot at the center of this melee were shouts of "Stop it!" "Devil!" "Asshole!"

I turned to say something to Angie, but she was gone, and when I looked around in surprise, I saw her twenty feet away, hanging up one of SUM's emergency phones on its bright orange pole.

"I called nine-one-one," she said, rejoining me. Angie had told me last year that all 911 calls on campus went directly to the dispatcher for the campus police.

"Has that phone always been there?"

"Oh, yeah. I've taken night classes, and I know where *every* emergency phone is on campus."

Around us, students were on cell phones either calling the police or—more likely—describing the melee to their friends, imagining they were CNN reporters.

Just like a tornado, swiftly, darkly gathering fury into itself, the swirling, roiling mass of students on the bridge grew larger and more violent as people threw punches. Alarmed, I stood up and saw several students knocked down. It was all very confusing—I kept seeing fists fly toward chests, stomachs, and faces, and students being grabbed by their crimson-and-gray SUM sweatshirts or jackets and flung about. But in the reeling, cursing, grunting mob, I couldn't tell how many people were getting hurt—or how badly. Were students falling and being kicked, or was it simply that I couldn't make them out anymore as they whirled or struggled away?

"This is unreal," Angie breathed, standing very close to me as if I could protect her.

It *was* unreal, and hard to fathom. The seething, wild mass was almost bizarrely purposeful—as if enmeshed in some ancient, ugly ritual. I felt as distanced and confused as when I'd gone to SUM football games and had consistently failed, even with binoculars, to follow the ball from the line of scrimmage. Jesse was somehow in the middle of it all now—you couldn't miss that white hair.

"Jesse, no!" Angie shouted, mesmerized, but he couldn't have heard her.

At either end of the bridge, clots of students stood staring, pointing, gaping. Some had rushed into the fray, but now the rest just watched.

And then that cardboard box of blood-red Bibles came hurtling over the side of the bridge into the shallow Michigan river. It landed with a thudding splash, splitting open. Outraged ducks went flapping and flying out of the river and up the grassy banks.

Awash with water, the darkening box started to sink, its red-coated contents drifting into the current as if they'd been hatched and set free.

Everyone near the Administration Building bridge on both sides of the river was standing up now, pointing, staring, amazed. It was one thing to tear down the goalposts at a football game, or get drunk and knock over parking meters in town on a Saturday night and break store windows, but this kind of outburst was beyond the pale.

The preacher boy went berserk, flailing about him with the strength of a hooked shark fighting a deep-sea fisherman. So that's what someone looks like when he's apoplectic, I thought, astonished by the young man's livid, contorted face.

He leapt at the rail, trying to climb over and jump after his Bibles to rescue them. Several burly frat boys yanked him back, but it wasn't easy, because he was so unexpectedly strong, and because other students were pummeling *them* in what was beginning to look like a drunken spring break brawl in Florida. I felt horribly rooted to my spot as the crowd grew thicker and more frenzied on and near the bridge.

"Let him jump!" a girl called out from the crowd.

Around me there was appalling laughter from some students, tongue clucking, and cynical comments about the whole thing just being "a stunt."

Suddenly I heard the yowl of a campus patrol car. Students fled like startled, angry crows as the black-and-white car veered off a road and screeched to a halt on a wide path to the bridge. Its doors flew open, and two campus police emerged with the goofy speed of circus clowns popping out of a Volkswagen Bug.

They waded into the mob with their batons swinging, and I winced each time one of them came down, feeling utterly helpless.

Then there was a shrill, agonized scream, followed by un-earthly silence.

Angie and I raced for the bridge. Had a student been badly injured by a campus cop? Maybe it was more shock than pain. Pushing to the edge of the crowd of what now looked like hundreds, I could make out a small cleared circle in which the two cops were leaning over a prostrate, bloody-faced body.

It was Jesse Benevento. Blood pooled out from underneath his head in a terrible slick halo, and his face was almost as white as his hair. I felt a wave of fear.

"Trampled," I thought. How horrible. A backpack lay open at his side, spilling notebooks, pens, CDs, and paperbacks out onto the unyielding concrete. One of them was a blood-spattered slim Penguin paperback of an old French novel I'd never read, *Adolphe*, by Benjamin Constant. The cover bore the portrait of a dark-haired young man whose enigmatic smile leered up incongruously at me from the midst of carnage.

I closed my eyes to steady myself, feeling a rush of shame as strong as nausea. I'd been musing over how much I disliked Jesse just a few minutes earlier, and now he was hurt. And all I could picture was the terrible scandal about to hit the university. Religious frenzy—riot—department chair's son gravely injured.

"What is it?" Angie cried. "What happened? I can't *see*." I could hear Angie in the crowd struggling to get closer, and she popped up right behind me. I was blocking her view.

In the circle, the young preacher was on his knees near Jesse's body, arms wrapped around himself as tightly as if he was afraid he might burst apart. Head down, sobbing, he rocked back and forth. He was moaning, "Oh my Lord Jesus Oh my Lord Jesus Oh my Lord Jesus."

Angie squeezed around me. "No!" she cried.

"Call an ambulance!" someone shouted. But from the stolid, angry looks on both cops' faces, and the stillness of Jesse Benevento's body, I realized it was too late for that.

Angie stared at the body. "Jesse," she breathed, disbelieving. She turned sharply away from the tableau of death, looking up at me, face frozen with surprise.

What could I say? As I moved woodenly from the scene, with Angie trailing after me, I couldn't help wondering how Stefan would react when I told him that trying to have lunch at the bridge didn't seem to be the best way of helping me deal with my phobia.

Angie and I edged through the crowd back to the bench where I'd dropped my thermos in the confusion. The coffee had spilled out, staining the concrete just as Jesse's blood had darkened the bridge. I was loath to even touch it, but I forced myself to pick up the thermos, screwing the top back on and slipping it into the plastic SUM bookstore bag I'd carried it in.

Angie scooped up her pink knapsack, hugging it to her chest as if it were a teddy bear that could heal the fatigue and outrage of a tearful bedtime. Her face was as stricken as I imagined my own was. "I knew something like this would happen," she said through tears.

I nodded—hadn't we just been talking about violence on campus? But that's not what Angie meant, because with a start of terror, she said, "I knew Jesse was going to get himself killed." And before I could ask what she was talking about, she dashed off up the wide steps away from me, into the crowds that had gathered.

And I couldn't chase after her, because I had to head back to Parker Hall for a meeting with Coral Greathouse about my future at SUM.

2

The Great and Glorious Oz had smoke, flames, and a thundering voice to scare people with. Our chair, Coral Greathouse, was armed with a very different weapon: her composure. Bullies made me defiant, and boors made me crack jokes, but people whose silence left me feeling paranoid and exposed scared me, and Coral was in that dismal pantheon. So I had been definitely uneasy about my required pretenure meeting with her.

Now, though, I was deeply shaken by the riot and Jesse Benevento's death, not to mention Angie's peculiar getaway. I was unsure what to do or say. Before the meeting I'd had a few minutes with Stefan on the phone to tell him what had happened at the bridge. He'd urged me to cancel my meeting, but I didn't think anything less than civil war would be an acceptable excuse for Coral, so I kept my meeting and didn't even mention it to her.

The meeting was crucial for her, too, because SUM was terrified of lawsuits, so administrators rigidly adhered to procedure at all times, and it was officially time for us to get together.

Coral would tell me where I stood and what I needed to do as my application for tenure and promotion to associate professor lurched forward from now into next year. What could she say that I didn't already know? I was in deep shit. And being told so would be a profound humiliation, yet it wasn't one I could avoid.

"Nick," she said flatly, not rising from her chair behind the gunmetal-gray desk. She waved me to a matching chair that stood back from the center of her desk a good five feet. I suppose I was meant to be intimidated by the distance. I was.

As always, Coral looked a bit owlish behind her red-framed Sally Jesse Raphael glasses. She had the flat, neglected, colorless look of an ex-nun, and except for several full bookcases, her office was almost as spartan as a cell. Did she mortify her flesh when the door was closed?

"Nick," she repeated, and I wanted to say, "Yup, that's me, Nick." But I was silent, trying to cross my legs in a dignified fashion and seem respectfully attentive when I was afraid, and images of blood and spilled coffee filled my head.

"I suppose you understand how the tenure process begins. I've appointed a committee of three department members. I've chosen Iris Bell, Carter Savery, and Serena Fisch, who'll be back from sabbatical at the end of spring semester."

So that's why I'd seen Iris and Carter together at the bridge before. They were talking about me. It couldn't be anything good, because neither one of them seemed to like me. And even though Serena was my friend, I didn't think that would be enough to save me.

But what was tenure anyway? At least I was alive, not like poor Jesse. What a vile way to die.

I must have looked inattentive, because Coral raised her voice.

"*Nick.* Your job now is to pull together your portfolio with dispatch. After the committee reviews it, they pass on a recommendation to the department's Policy Committee, of which I'm the chair, and we then do the same, sending the portfolio and our assessment on to Dean Bullerschmidt."

Coral paused, and I knew it was in an effort not to reveal any aspect of the intense rivalry between herself and the dean for the position of provost. Becoming provost would be a triumph for Coral; it would mean not just more power, but tripling her salary and making it possible to leap to the presidency at another school when she was ready to move on.

"The last stop," she continued, "is the provost's office."

Last stop was right, I thought, hoping I could keep looking optimistic. Last stop for me, anyway. Next stop for her. I was praying for tenure; she was probably praying to be in the provost's office this time next year. Maybe we needed a prayer group.

"Your student evaluations are superb," Coral said. "Truly superb. Your students clearly think the world of you."

"Thank you."

She frowned as if I were stepping over a boundary by speaking up. Or maybe it was my teaching evaluations that bothered her. Most professors in our department were washouts in the classroom; I heard the details from my students all the time. Even though teaching was what we were hired to do, you could suffer in your department if students liked you. Somehow this got dismissed by other faculty as "pandering." And given that I enjoyed teaching composition—the faculty's least favorite course—good evaluations were more poisonous; they could be interpreted as implicit criticism of other professors.

"But I think you know that in terms of service and publication—" She held out her hands and looked down at the lines in her doughy palms as if reading my fate there.

Service was outreach to the community, an ideal at SUM because it was a state-funded school.

"Nick, I think you've been somewhat . . . distracted, especially these past two years," she went on, bringing her hands together almost prayerfully.

If only she knew what I'd just come from! And why did I feel like I was back in junior high being talked to by an obnoxious guidance counselor who wanted to know if my poor test scores were connected to "problems at home"?

"You have to buckle down, Nick."

I assumed that "buckle down" meant avoid even the whisper of involvement in anything that could cause more scandal for SUM—but wasn't it already too late for that advice?

Assuring me that her "door was always open" if I had questions about the process, Coral rose, signaling that my audience had come to an end.

I thanked her, and just then her phone rang. She took the call peevishly, but as her face darkened, I bet that someone was informing her about what had happened on the bridge.

I fled upstairs to my office on the third floor, avoiding everyone I met, convinced that they would look away from me in pity or disgust, as if I were a French aristocrat about to be loaded into a tumbrel. Surely everyone in the department, including the secretaries, knew there was no way I'd get tenure. Even if I could somehow write and publish a book in the next year, that wouldn't be my ticket. I'd already done enough to deep-six my chances.

As I stumbled into the cavernous, high-ceilinged men's room to wash my face off with cold water, it hit me that Coral was protecting herself too by urging me to avoid scandal. It would look very bad for her as an administrator if her department was an academic version of the old Devil's Night in Detroit.

I washed my hands as if I were Lady Macbeth, enjoying the rush of cold, and splashed my face with vigor, losing myself in the sensation. Mildly refreshed, I turned from the sink to find myself confronted by Harry Benevento. The History Department's main office was on this floor, but I didn't see him often. Oh, God, I thought, he's heard the news about his son. I stared, wondering how he'd come in without my hearing the door, and wondering what to say. Was he going to the bridge? Or was Jesse's body at a hospital now?

Benevento stared back at me, or just stared is more accurate. Hulking, six feet four, pear-shaped, and bald, he usually appeared a bit clownish in his well-cut suits—like a circus performer dressed up to get a bank loan. But today he looked utterly serious, and utterly drained.

I struggled to say something about his son, but could produce only "I'm sorry."

I wasn't prepared for the vulpine sneer. "Everybody's sorry," he said with weary finality, and I felt like an idiot.

Benevento lumbered into one of the stalls, fell heavily onto the closed seat, slammed the door, and started to wheeze out great gusts of grief. I rushed out into the hall and hurried down to my office, hoping I wouldn't run into any of the bats that occasionally swooped into hallways of Parker Hall, no doubt looking for Dracula.

Once I was safely inside my office, the tenure meeting with Coral crashed back onto me, and I contemplated the icy inevitability of disaster. I would be trampled—administratively—as surely as Jesse had been.

Sinking into my office chair, I closed my eyes, hoping I could fall asleep as I sometimes do when there's nowhere else to escape.

But the phone rang. It was Stefan, wondering how I felt.

I snapped at him. "You sound like one of those reporters interviewing a flood victim."

"That's not how I meant it," he said.

"I know, I know. I'm sorry—it's my fault. This has just been a day from hell."

Stefan gently asked me how my meeting with Coral had gone.

"She ate me alive," I moaned.

"Really?"

"Of course not *really*. You know what Coral's like. She's a bureaucratic ninja—she leaves you flat on your back and you don't know what hit you. She said my student evaluations were great—no surprise there—but that's not enough. It's usually considered good service to the university when you put together a conference, but you don't get any points if it ends with body bags! I'm supposed to buckle down, and not get 'distracted.' That means stay out of trouble and publish my butt off. Well, I can avoid all the messes I want, but even if I published *ten* books this year, they'd still can me."

"Who's on the review committee?"

"Iris Bell, Carter Savery, and Serena."

There was a longish pause, and then Stefan said, "Serena will support you."

"But that's not enough, and you know it. Iris and Carter have never liked me."

"We'll figure something out," Stefan said calmly. All I could think of was Lily Tomlin in *Nine to Five*, snapping, "I just poisoned the boss—you don't think they're going to fire me for that?" But I didn't feel like arguing, so I just told Stefan I'd be home soon. Even the thought of getting ready to go down to Ann Arbor for Shabbat dinner with his father and stepmother later that afternoon didn't cheer me in the slightest, and usually I welcomed Shabbat. It all seemed so pointless suddenly.

BEFORE WE LEFT home, I looked up Angie's number in the SUM student directory we had and called her dorm room, but there was no answer, and unlike most students on campus, she had no answering machine. Stefan insisted what she'd said about Jesse was due to shock, but then he hadn't been there to see her face, so I didn't contradict him.

We had a very subdued fifty-minute ride down to Ann Arbor. We listened to Erykah Badu's jazzy new album, and I drifted off on the drums and her voice, part Billie Holiday, part Eartha Kitt. Stefan considerately kept quiet, but then he was invariably quiet when we visited his father. We always brought a CD for the trip because local radio in Michiganapolis was a wasteland of top-forty and country-western stations and moronic DJs that made NPR—when we did catch it—seem like a visitation by aliens from a highly advanced civilization.

Just before we were about to exit Route 23 and drive into Ann Arbor's pretty downtown, Stefan broke his long silence: "I won't talk about the bridge unless they bring it up." I'd been thinking about the same thing, as often happened between us, and I was thankful for his sensitivity. When he mentioned the bridge, though, the scene rushed back on me, and I saw Jesse's pale face and hair, the spreading blood, that Penguin paperback.

"Which writer was Benjamin Constant?" I asked.

"He was a journalist, mid–nineteenth century, young. George Sand's lover. It was a pretty infamous affair. But all of hers were, I think."

"Hey—did I ever tell you the story of Henry James and Wharton visiting George Sand's country home, and James asked which room she'd slept in, then answered it himself: 'In which room did she *not* sleep?'"

"I think I've only heard that twice."

Usually I'm energized by Ann Arbor's density of culture, bookstores, restaurants, and general sophistication compared to Michiganapolis, but not that night. It all slipped right by me. Stefan's father's small stone house with gabled roof and mullioned windows was up one of Ann Arbor's longer and prettier hills, and I thought it charming and romantic, though I knew Stefan still pictured it as a house out of a nasty fairy tale, full of peril and pain.

He had good reasons. This was where his father, transplanted from New York many years ago, had revealed the crushing family secret when seventeen-year-old Stefan was reluctantly visiting one Christmas. Still bitter about his parents' divorce, almost ten years in the past at that point, Stefan had been convinced to come along from New York with his uncle Sasha only because his father's health was bad.

Terrified that he might die of a heart attack, Max Borowksi had told Stefan that not only was the family actually Jewish, but Stefan's parents and uncle had survived concentration camps. Hoping to protect Stefan, they had razed their past and haphazardly tried bringing Stefan up as a Catholic. A Polish Catholic, since they were from Poland. It was not an entirely successful charade.

For years after the revelation, Stefan told me, he had felt like Frankenstein's monster down from the cruel lightning: grotesque and cobbled together. He was a freak, and he'd been utterly, completely betrayed. It had taken him decades to come to terms with being Jewish, to slough off the romantic identification with Poland.

All of that made his parents' divorce and their remarriages even harder to accept. Yet Stefan knew in his heart that the whole tangled mess of his upbringing was what had fueled his desire to write, to make sense of the world. And this very subject matter was what had made him stand out among a thousand other young novelists when he started getting published a decade ago. He'd had considerable success for a while—but at a terrible price.

"Stefan, Nick," said Mr. Borowski softly when he greeted us

at the door. Short, gray-haired, plump, with precise, vaguely English-sounding speech, Max Borowski was always amiable with me and stiffly distant with Stefan, as if waiting for an attack. Taking the job in Michigan this close to his father in Ann Arbor had been difficult for Stefan. At least with his mother and her second husband, Leo, he had plenty of physical distance since they'd retired to Israel.

Max Borowski looked us both over, nodding, and gave us a very pointed shrug, which I took to mean, "See what kind of school you both teach at? People get *killed* there." But Mr. Borowski was too polite to say it. He, after all, had retired from teaching at the University of Michigan and wasn't going to rub our faces in the U of M's excellence. But I was sure he was thinking with satisfaction of his affiliation with a school that hadn't turned into a house of horrors. Any scandal at SUM was a potent source of entertainment and satisfaction for its rival school, and sometimes it seemed to me that the U of M's very identity was tied up with SUM being inferior.

Maybe I was seeing everything through the filter of what had happened at the bridge. Perhaps Max was simply expressing his discomfort with Shabbat, a weekly refuge and set of observances that had been an inestimable treasure for Jews in their centuries of exile. It was a gift he'd withheld from Stefan, who had come to love its ritual and peace because of me. Could it embrace the two of them together?

Minnie bustled out of the kitchen, grinning and throwing her arms wide. "My boys! You made it!" she cried, as if we had macheted our way across a jungle to reach her. Max's second wife had no children of her own, which explained her joy in being with us. I handed her a bottle of wine, which she took with a grin, dashing off to set it on the dining room table.

Then she trotted back and hugged me. "Good Shabbos!" she

crowed, and I replied in kind, hugging her, but Stefan just let himself be hugged, and his Shabbos greeting was more subdued. I settled into a fat armchair in the cozy, gleaming living room. The entire house was filled with wonderful built-in cabinets, molding, panelwork, and window seats, all in the same gorgeous bird's-eye maple that made it seem intimate to me and, probably, claustrophobic to Stefan.

"Something smells great," I said.

Minnie winked at me. "Doesn't it always?"

Stefan and his father joined us, both silent. That was okay, because Minnie and I could talk up a storm. Given to bright green outfits that complemented her now-retouched wavy blond hair, Minnie looked like an aging Stella Stevens, whom I vaguely re-membered from *Hollywood Squares* and maybe some *Love Boat* episodes as perpetually peppy. I loved Minnie's enthusiasm, her eager smile, her warmth—all of which made her so different from my very correct, very formal European parents. Of course it was easy for me to get along with her, and even Max, since I had no history with either one of them. That grated on Stefan a little, just as his fluency in French with my parents annoyed me, and reminded me of my dismal subjunctive.

"Something to drink?" Minnie asked brightly, and Max rose to the bar cart to get Stefan and me the Pineau des Charentes on the rocks we asked for. They stocked this delicious cross between a sherry and an aperitif wine just for us after we'd discovered it on one of our summer trips to the Shakespeare Festival in Strat-ford, Ontario. Imagine—the best repertory theater in North America, less than a four-hour drive from little Michiganapolis.

I could tell that Max was relieved to have a task, however minor. We'd had Shabbat dinner together only once before, and Max had been distinctly uncomfortable, as if each blessing were an indictment of the way he'd brought up Stefan. I wondered if

I'd ever work up the courage to ask Max what it had been like coming out as a Jew after all those years in hiding.

Minnie said, "I've got a lovely leg of lamb up because I know you boys like your lamb!"

"We do," I said, enjoying being fussed over. Whenever I went back to New York, my parents took us out to dinner.

Stefan tried to smile. Around Minnie, he was often like an insect desperately frozen on a leaf, hoping its camouflage would protect it from a predator. Minnie was a passionate and intelligent reader and had read all of Stefan's books, but her enthusiasm seemed to irritate him. That, and her calling him "darling." She had presumed familiarity with Stefan right from the start, with no sense of boundaries—in his words.

I just thought Minnie was warm and loving, and determined not to get caught in the maelstrom of resentments churning just under the surface between Stefan and his father.

"What's new in your department?" Max asked us.

I grinned as Stefan said, "We have a colorful visiting professor."

"Really? How so?"

Stefan hesitated, and I wasn't sure if it was the subject matter or his general discomfort talking to his father.

So I dived in. "Her name is Juno Dromgoole, and she's Canadian, but not like any Canadian I've ever met." She was replacing Serena Fisch, a friend of hers who was on sabbatical, and I think Serena had championed Juno out of a finely developed sense of mischief, since Serena had a long grudge against EAR.

Max asked, "What sort of name is that?"

"You mean Dromgoole?" I asked. "Irish, I think."

"She's loud," Stefan said. "And rude." Stefan described how Juno disrupted or at least subverted department meetings by muttering "Balls!" or "Bollocks!" when she disagreed. Or worse, "God, I hate America!"

Except for that last remark, her sentiments were hard to disagree with, and I was often on the point of laughing, though I knew other EAR professors not only found her alarming but thought she was disturbed. How could anyone act like that in public? was the complaint. Well, the emperor had no clothes, and our department had no sense—that's how.

Max shook his head. "Strange," he said. "We've never had anyone like her at the U of M. Juno," he said after a pause, as if marveling over parents who could choose such a name for their child.

"It's better than Clytemnestra," I said.

Max sniffed. "Not much."

Minnie leaned forward with her tiny hands on both knees and said, "Isn't it *horrible* what happened at SUM today! Such a young boy. Such a terrible way to die."

Stefan and I exchanged a cautious shrug.

Minnie went on like that for a while about Jesse Benevento, replaying what little she'd caught on TV, shaking her head, sighing with that slightly removed compassionate contemplation we can give to disasters that haven't affected us personally. I didn't feel like telling her then that I'd seen it happen.

I could imagine tomorrow's newspapers. This would certainly push Jack Kevorkian's latest assisted suicide—of an entire bridge club—right off the front page. No doubt every account would exaggerate the chaos. But however the story played, it was sensational: antireligious bigotry, violent teenagers, one dead.

"He was a former student of mine," I told Minnie now, sipping my drink. "Jesse was."

Minnie stared at me, wide-eyed. "Really? What was he like? Did you sense he had a tragic fate ahead of him?"

I smiled, because I could just imagine Stefan thinking, Your fate is *always* ahead of you, but I knew he'd squelch his desire to point that out. If nothing else, around Minnie, Stefan was polite. Hey, he had to be. She'd given us her terrific cottage up north when we got to Michigan. *Given* it to us, because she wanted us to love Michigan as she did, and because her first husband had built it, and it stirred up too many memories for her.

Stefan had insisted we refuse the offer, but once we'd spent a weekend up there I'd been able to convince him to accept her gift. It was easy—we'd both fallen in love with the Traverse City area and the cottage overlooking the Big Lake.

"Minnie, I can't say I sensed much of anything about Jesse Benevento," I said. "He was kind of a typical student—at least the way he looked lately. Tattoos, earrings, nose and eyebrow rings—"

Minnie shuddered and said, "Feh."

"I don't think he had as many rings when he was in my class. But even then he wore black all the time and looked like a punk rocker. He was a capital-*C* Christian, I think. Once he came to my office to complain that I mentioned sex in the classroom, and he explained that sex was God's gift to man, blah, blah, blah— And I shouldn't push my immorality—that's how he put it—on my students."

Minnie slapped her hands together. "That's outrageous! You should sue him! It's harassment!"

"The boy's dead," Max pointed out dryly.

Minnie slumped. "Oh. Yes. Still . . ." She rallied. "I can't believe he would say something like that."

"Believe it," I said. "Minnie, students nowadays will say anything. At least at SUM. They keep hearing this garbage from the administrators about the students being 'consumers' and how the university should be 'service-oriented,' so some of them end up acting like their professors are stupid salesclerks, and *they're* complaining to the management."

Stefan finished his drink, and Max leapt up to make him another. Stefan shook his head, and his father sat down as if defeated.

"Well, in my experience, it's seldom students who harass their professors," Max pointed out. "It's usually the other way around, if it does happen."

"No, Nick is right," Stefan demurred quietly. "Students harass professors all the time. It's passive-aggressive behavior. They turn in assignments late. They don't pay attention when you explain the syllabus. They read newspapers during class, or talk on their cellular phones, or work on papers for other classes on their laptops. The worst harassment is not taking the class seriously."

"Well—" Max began, but Minnie cut him off: "Dinner's almost ready, boys. Nick, won't you help me in the kitchen?" I followed her out. I loved the cozy room they had recently remodeled with granite countertops, mirrored backsplashes, and a skylight. I asked Minnie what I could do, and she said, "First, just sit. So. How do you think it's going?" And she grinned like a conspirator. Shabbos dinners had been her idea of bringing Stefan and his father closer.

"It's too soon to tell. Wait a year."

She grimaced. "A year? We could all be dead by then! Nick—what did I say? You don't look so good all of a sudden."

I made some vague excuse.

Minnie had set a lovely table, with gorgeous Flora Danica dishes and St. Louis crystal, all relics of her first marriage to a wealthy realtor, and a small centerpiece of exquisite pink tea roses, baby's breath, and one Stargazer lily throwing out perfume as if it were battery-powered.

We lit the Shabbos candles, blessed the wine and the challah, and dug in to a feast of spicy hot borscht, the leg of lamb and *pommes Anna,* and asparagus and red peppers vinaigrette. Max and Minnie didn't drink much; Stefan and I had finished the Haut-Médoc we brought.

Max was evidently still struck by my comments about student rudeness. "There should be more respect for teachers," he said, and I knew just what he'd been brooding about.

"I agree completely, Max. But students don't seem to respect much of anything. They think everything's a talk show. And why not? The only TV most of them watch is Jerry Springer, or Geraldo, or Jenny Jones. Hell, that's where most of them get their information, if you can call it that. You can't expect them to catch any references to books or movies or even television, unless it's been on *E.T.* or something like that."

Stefan nodded gloomily—and he taught graduate students!

Though we went on to discuss lots of things—the meal, the weather, Bosnia, with some detours back to the decline of higher education across the country—by the time we were having dessert back in the living room, we had returned to Jesse Benevento. I found myself thinking about what Angie had said before disappearing. Was it a mistake to have told Stefan? Would that endanger Angie somehow? Was she mixed up in something terrible—and was that why she'd fled the scene of Jesse's murder?

I drifted in and out of these speculations, lulled by the wonderful meal and by Minnie's Russian tea cakes and the Russian tea she ordered from Chicago, a rich and slightly fruity mix of Ceylon, Darjeeling, and black currant that she served, Russian style, in glasses set into silver holders with handles.

"I've been wondering something," Minnie said to the room, casually, as if we were all tourists desultorily admiring a view. "This Benevento boy. What was he doing on the bridge?"

Stefan shrugged. "Going to class, probably. Why?"

Minnie pursed her lips, nodding carefully. "What if he was

there for a reason?" Now she had our undivided attention, and we waited. "You said he was religious. Suppose he was there to help stir up some kind of trouble?"

Stefan noisily set down his coffee cup, shaking his head.

Minnie shrugged. "Why not?"

I seized the idea. "You mean that somebody was trying to stage an anti-Christian incident on campus to get sympathy, and it went wrong?"

She nodded. "Exactly."

"Wow," I said. Is that what Angie might have been involved in—or knew about?

Stefan was making noises of disbelief, and I stopped him. "Listen, Stefan, given how crazy people are on campus right now, anything is possible. The place is a snake pit, and it's crawling with fanatics."

Minnie nodded sympathetically.

Ever logical, Max chimed in, "Well, which side was the boy on?"

"He was religious," I said. "Of course he was defending—" I stopped, because I couldn't really tell what Jesse had been doing in that whirligig of struggling students. I said as much, and Max shrugged.

"Wait a minute," Minnie said. "You were there? It sounds like you were there. What happened? What did you see?"

Reluctantly, I laid out my story for her, which she took in goggle-eyed.

"Thank God you're all right, Nick!" Then Minnie seemed to shift gear. "Whatever's going on, it's an amazing story!" she enthused. "You should write about it. Not just this boy, but the other murders that happened to you last year, and the year before."

I asked, "Who says it's murder?"

"But of course it's murder." Minnie frowned. "They announced it on the radio just before you got here. I thought you knew. I assumed—didn't you hear?"

I shook my head. On the way down, we'd played the CD. And when I got home from campus, I was so busy talking about my meeting with Coral and what I'd seen at the bridge while Stefan and I changed for dinner, neither of us had bothered to turn on the radio and check the news—I never did, except when we woke up.

Minnie nodded, savoring the impact of her revelation. "He was *stabbed*."

"Stabbed!" Stefan looked outraged.

"I'm not making it up," Minnie rejoined a bit primly, and she glanced at Max, who said reluctantly, "Yes, there was a knife wound."

Minnie waggled a finger at him. "A knife wound means he was stabbed. He didn't just fall on a knife that happened to be lying around."

Stabbed. Someone in that chaos of angry, out-of-control students on the bridge had stabbed Jesse Benevento. Had stabbed a student I'd taught for a whole semester, a student I had run into on campus, a student who had emerged from the vast, dim, background of SUM to imprint himself on me for years to come. And that was *before* his death. I'd never forget his moralistic superiority and how it had unnerved me.

I sipped more of the hot, fragrant tea.

Even though it rarely happened, I did not enjoy being criticized by my students, though every semester there were always one or two students who disliked the things about me and my classes that the other students praised. I remember my first teacher evaluation by a colleague years ago had said I was a little too eager to please, too much of a performer. Both were true, because I had gone into teaching as a double major in English and theater, and being in the classroom did feel like acting. I had a costume—academic drag—a role to play, lines, the potential for great ad-libs, a captive audience; and even better, I was rarely upstaged. The set may have been dreary and predictable, but the performance never was. I felt as intensely alive and concentrated in the classroom as I had onstage. I enjoyed working with an audience I had great potential to influence, and while I couldn't expect applause, I did expect to be appreciated.

"What kind of knife," Minnie was telling Stefan, "the news said nobody knows because it hasn't been found. Who cares what kind? Stabbed is stabbed. Hoodlums. Trash and hoodlums—that's who's going to school these days."

Max shrugged. "That wasn't my experience at the U of M."

"You were lucky," his wife snapped.

"Murder," I brought out, coming back to the room. I'd been a witness to murder, sort of.

"Or manslaughter," Stefan pointed out. "It could have been an accident."

Minnie and I exchanged a glance as if to say that Stefan wasn't being very imaginative.

"So who d'you think did it?" she asked me. "And why?"

Max was chuckling and stroking his chin. "Minnie, you read too many mysteries."

"Life," she intoned. "Life is a mystery."

"That's Madonna!" I said.

Minnie grinned at me, and nodded. " 'Like a Prayer.' "

"You listen to Madonna?" Stefan asked her, amazed.

"Of course! Don't you? Doesn't everybody? She's today's Rosemary Clooney. But forget her. I think it was jealousy that killed that boy on the bridge. He must have been stealing some-one's girlfriend, and his rival followed him across campus, saw an opportunity, and plunged in the knife!"

Max frowned.

Before anyone could comment on that possibility, Minnie forged ahead. "Or maybe he was secretly gay and someone gay-bashed him."

Max sighed. "Minnie, Minnie. First he's a Romeo, then he's—"

"Homeo?" I suggested.

Even Max and Stefan laughed, but Minnie didn't. She was flushed, narrow-eyed, obviously playing out various scenarios in her head. "How about this. The boy was in a religious cult and trying to escape, and they wouldn't let him. They had to kill him. No, no—he was killed because he knew somebody's secrets. Drugs, maybe. A roommate was selling drugs. That's it!"

Captured a little by her enthusiasm, Stefan asked, "What if it wasn't really murder, but someone wanted to threaten him, or warn him, and it went too far?"

Minnie nodded vigorously. "That's good, that's very good."

"We're playing a parlor game here," Max interjected sharply. "A parlor game with somebody's death."

Minnie took Max's hand, and his face softened. "It's natural to wonder when so much trouble has happened to the boys."

"Well, it didn't happen to us," I said, feeling defensive. "It happened to the people who got killed. Stefan and I were just involved, sort of. And that's even less true this time." I was beginning to worry that somehow, because Jesse had been my student and I'd been at the bridge, I might get drawn into the murder investigation. I couldn't afford any more scandal at SUM.

But what about Angie? She was a former student I cared about, and she had looked so frightened, as if whatever subterranean trouble had struck Jesse down might envelop her next. Had she expected he would be murdered, and did she think she might be too?

Minnie waved her hands dismissively at me. "Yes, fine, whatever you say. So it didn't exactly happen to you. But you have to admit it's just incredible that you've been surrounded by death ever since you started teaching at that school."

What was I supposed to do if Angie was in trouble?

Max shook his head. "That's an exaggeration, Minnie. They haven't been *surrounded* by death."

"Okay, Mr. Thesaurus, how about confronted? Is that accurate enough for you? They've been *confronted* with death and murder—and who'd expect such a thing on a quiet college campus? In the Heartland, yet?"

I laughed. "I don't think SUM's been quiet since the end of Prohibition."

Minnie shook that off. "So. You should write about it."

Stefan smiled wanly. "Me?"

"You, Nick, both of you."

Stefan and I exchanged a bemused glance. We proofread and edited each other's work but had never been interested in collaborating. He was a novelist, I was a bibliographer. I couldn't imagine the kind of literary hybrid we'd produce.

"Boys, boys, boys. What are you making faces for? How can you pass this up? It's a natural. But I have one piece of advice for you, okay? Whatever you do, please, please don't write anything like Patricia Cornwell. I know she's a best-seller and makes millions. But there are just too many corpses in her books!"

Since I'd read Cornwell, I thought it appropriate to point out that her heroine was a medical examiner.

"Even more reason to tone down the gore," Minnie said triumphantly. "She shouldn't wallow in it. Kay Scarpetta, I mean. The girls in my reading group agree. She should develop herself, get a hobby, go shopping."

"Have a fashion makeover?" I asked.

"Don't be fresh, Nicky!"

Minnie was the only person I enjoyed hearing that diminutive from, because it was always affectionate. My full name was Nick, not Nicholas. My parents had named me after Fitzgerald's Nick Carraway.

"Boys, you'd better start thinking about what you're going to wear on Oprah. Your book is a natural! *All* the ladies in my reading group think so. And I came up with the perfect title."

How could I not ask what that was?

"State University of Murder!" she crowed.

3

tefan and I called the young men doing yard work in our neighborhood "lawn avengers"; sometimes they'd pop off a truck with such alacrity they seemed like horticultural warriors: mowing, trimming, sawing, with great speed and accuracy, then sweeping off in quick triumph. Three of them could do an acre lawn in under an hour.

Lawn-care firms sprang up around town as quickly as you could say the words "pickup truck," and faded even faster. Most of the guys in this shirtless, shifting army were current or former horticulture majors at SUM, and they tended to be tanned, skinny, and cute in their uniform of thick socks, work boots, and longish shorts.

The one across the street the Sunday afternoon after the fatal bridge riot wasn't just cute. He was extraordinary, not least because he was alone and mowing very slowly. He was clearly not in a hurry on this wonderfully sunny day, nor was he trudging away as if bored.

Stefan and I watched him from the front window of the living room, gaping, I thought, like little kids at an aquarium tank.

"He looks like Peter Gallagher," I said, and Stefan nodded.

I wasn't exaggerating: There was the dark curly hair, the thick lips and thicker eyebrows adorning a fleshy, sexy face.

"A *buffed* Peter Gallagher," I corrected. Because this guy's shoulders, chest, and biceps were so well defined and large they seemed draped on his slim-hipped body like a woman's thick fur stole.

"And look at that waist," I said. It must have been what *People* magazine had once said was de rigueur for Hollywood hunks: 27 or 28 inches, looking even smaller given that his thighs were so meaty. "How come the aliens on TV shows are always skinny with big ugly eyes and little heads? Why can't they ever be studs like him? Then people would *enjoy* being abducted." After a moment, I answered my own question: "David Duchovny probably wouldn't want to play opposite anyone really humpy."

Stefan nodded, but when he spoke I realized he hadn't been listening to me. "Not a Michigan body," he said. I knew from the gym that a Michigan body meant big on top but "no legs." Supposedly that was because it wasn't warm enough for long enough in Michigan for guys to concentrate on their legs, since they didn't wear shorts as much as people do in California. Stefan did not have a Michigan body either; his legs were strong, though not overdeveloped.

Looking down at Stefan, I could see that this guy was definitely beginning to put the *pen* in Stefan's Lower Peninsula, and I wasn't far behind.

Michigan's a pretty homoerotic state, if you think about it: those two big peninsulas pointing at each other? It's a wonder Jesse Helms hasn't tried to do something about it—like ban all maps.

Just then Lucille's husband Didier came bounding out of the house, bald head gleaming in the sun, his jeans, heavy boots, and white T-shirt making him look like the head of a work crew. He called something indistinguishable to the lawn avenger and went back inside.

I watched the mystery man mow up and down the front lawn opposite our house, wondering where our new neighbors Lucille and Didier had found him. However it happened, I was going to have to see they were commended by the neighborhood association for setting such a high standard for yard workers. Personally, I think anyone paid to work in your yard should be fun to ogle; otherwise what's the point of hiring him? You might as well do the weed whacking and other stuff yourself if the "technician" is overweight and has scraggly hillbilly teeth.

"I feel like I've seen him recently." I tried to remember where. "At the gym? No—it was with his clothes on. Someplace else."

"Of course you've seen him—he's a grad student in American Studies. Don't you recognize him? His name's Delaney Kildare. You've probably run into him in Parker Hall."

"No, I haven't."

"Well, Lucille is his graduate adviser."

I shook my head. "I would remember someone like him, and he hasn't come to the office when I was there. Is he new?"

"Not really. He used to be in History. He transferred, maybe last year—?"

"Jeez—someone like that should be making history, not studying it. But what's he doing in our department? That seems just as bad. Why doesn't he hire out as an artist's model?"

"Are you thinking of taking up a brush?"

"Sure—in my spare time."

Just then, Delaney stopped the mower to pull a blue paisley kerchief from his back pocket to wipe the sweat from his face and neck. He looked up and seemed to be staring right at us.

We jerked back as guiltily as Jimmy Stewart in *Rear Window*. Embarrassed, we quietly headed for the blue-and-gold sunroom at the back of the house to read our Sunday *New York Times* and go back to our Sumatra coffee, which waited for us in a carafe. Settling now into the *News of the Week in Review*, I thought it was true what Robert Plunkett says in *Love Junkie*: gay men can be as boy-crazy as teenage girls.

We'd already read the *Michiganapolis Tribune* that morning, with its banner coverage of Jesse Benevento's murder. Conservative state legislators were talking about cutting SUM's funding. The governor had called for an official panel of inquiry. Pat Robertson had condemned SUM on his TV show for being "a nest of infidels," denying the word of God and abusing his messengers. Even President Clinton had weighed in with some blather about the importance of free speech and the need to keep American education competitive in a global economy.

The article made me try calling Angie, but there was no answer again, and I wished she were home to tell me what she thought had been going on with Jesse and why she'd run off.

My cousin Sharon had phoned me from New York to find out how bad it had actually been, and urged me to be careful.

"Sharon—you live in New York, and you're telling *me* to watch out for myself?"

"Sweetie," she purred. "I've traveled all over the world, and I've never been involved in a riot or a murder." There wasn't much I could say to that.

I told her the entire story of what happened at the bridge, and Angie's disappearance. Sharon, a mystery buff, asked if I wanted her to fly out and do some "consulting."

"Nothing's happened!"

"Not yet," she warned.

Sharon, of course, was right. She's the smartest person in our family, and the most well known because of her former modeling career. Though, given my own brushes with crime, I suppose I could have tried angling to host a talk show.

The *Tribune* article had brought home to me again how close I'd been to death the other day, but it also made me think that there'd been something odd at the scene of Jesse's death, though I couldn't remember what it was.

Stefan, going through the *Times Book Review*, suddenly made a noise back in his throat that would classify as a growl if he had four legs.

"What's wrong?"

"Tiara Duvet," he said. "Her book's on the best-seller list."

I shook my head. Tiara Duvet was the female George Plimpton. She'd done everything, been everything—a supermodel, a junkie, a race car driver, a flight instructor, a bricklayer, a PI, a shoe salesman; she had appeared in movies with each of the Baldwins, and was now an author of a feisty self-help book, *Dare to Be a Diva*, which Oprah had featured on her book club. Sexier than Iman, she was photogenic beyond belief and given to publicizing herself with charity functions, marathons, balloon trips across the Atlantic—anything to see the words "Tiara Duvet" in print. *Dare to Be a Diva* had been sold to Random House for two million dollars, and was going to be a movie starring Whitney Houston, with a script by Joe Eszterhas.

"Stefan, no one's going to read that shit fifty years from now. Hell, twenty. There's nothing more dated than old self-help. Who even touches *I'm Okay, You're Okay* now?"

"I'd rather sell books now than be famous after I'm dead," Stefan grumbled. It was an old complaint, made raw recently because his last novel hadn't gone into paperback and he was waiting longer than usual to hear from his publisher about the new one.

I shrugged.

After a companionable silence in which Stefan continued leafing through the Book Review, he spoke up again. "I feel old," he said.

From the corner of my eyes I could see him sinking into his favorite chair, the one with the best view of the little gazebo in the backyard. He sighed.

I peered up from the magazine crossword over my reading glasses. "Honey, you *are* old." I was suddenly struck by how at that moment I must look very much like my mother, who also did the *Times* puzzles (which had sharpened her English), and had for years been putting on glasses to read her answers and her clues. Yet Stefan was only forty-five.

"No, I'm not!" Stefan snapped, before he met my eyes. Then he smiled, relaxed a little, and shook his head at his own gloom.

"That's right," I said. "You just feel old. Me, I *am* old."

"What do you mean?"

"Haven't you noticed my eyebrows? I'm turning into Brezhnev!"

It was true. In the last year my eyebrows had started to sprout rogue hairs that seemed to want nothing more than to embarrass me. I was constantly having to trim my eyebrows to keep from having people predict the weather based on the caterpillars marching across my face.

Stefan smiled.

Outside, several huge noisy crows swaggered across the lawn in a ragged *V* as if surveying it for a house they intended to build. They seemed powerful and smug, the only birds I ever saw in our neighborhood who didn't fly off as soon as you opened or closed a door, or even walked toward them. They eyed you, speculating their chances, I suppose, if they decided to attack.

"Look at them," I said. "They're as big as chickens. Yuck."

"They're just birds," Stefan said.

"Yeah, well, my folks made the mistake of letting me see *The Birds* by myself when I was a kid, and nobody's going to tell me those vultures out there are just birds. They're evil, and they like it that way."

Stefan studied the crows as if trying to see them as I did.

"Listen, Stefan," I went on. "If you really do feel old, well, instead of teaching at a university where the average age is eighteen and everyone's skin is so tight, why don't we move to Florida, and you'll be young again—*really* young, for a while, anyway. . . . And don't forget driving the freeways with all those Lincoln Towncars going twelve miles an hour! That's guaranteed to make you feel like your metabolism will never slow down."

Stefan laughed. People like me laugh easily and all the time, but with Stefan, who was serious to his core, there was an exciting edge of abandon and surprise to his laughter. Making him laugh always made me feel good.

There are some of our friends—not the closest—who bristle when I tease Stefan, as if love demands the seriousness and decorum of a state dinner, and any lightness, especially when tinged with good-natured poking fun, is vulgar and rude. These, of course, are not our Jewish friends, and generally not anyone we knew from New York, where most people are bilingual in English and Sarcasm.

We had seen some people blush or turn away while we joked with one another, as if shocked and ashamed to see Snow White and her prince suddenly playing *Who's Afraid of Virginia Woolf?* They tried to change the subject or intervene in some soothing way, or just tensed their shoulders, eyes darting between us. This reticence, this incomprehension and even fear, made us feel superior, I confess, and relieved that we had command of more than one or two conversational tones.

Relieved, too, that while we may have called each other "hon," we could just as often call each other "toad"—and that these shifts didn't mean that our decade and a half together was in danger of crumbling like a withered leaf.

I guess the people we made nervous expected the day-to-day, moment-by-moment of love, of life together, to be as bland and unobjectionable as a strip mall.

Lucille and Didier across the street loved to spar good-naturedly with each other, too, which was a good reason for liking them.

Stefan sighed again, and I assumed we were back to his original complaint, though he didn't say anything for a while.

"Do you think my father looked okay at dinner Friday night?"

I tried to picture Max Borowski. "Okay how?"

Stefan shook his head. "I'm not sure. He just seemed quieter than usual."

"He's always quiet around me and Minnie."

"True." He looked down at his paper and then smiled. "She loves him. That's good."

The way he said it made it clear he was done talking about his father for now, so I went back to my puzzle. I didn't want to press him about how he felt seeing his father; Stefan could be very stubborn and tended to open up only when he was ready.

And right then, I was happy to just sit there on this Sunday afternoon in our favorite room of the house. I could see us camped there when we really were old, elderly, ancient.

When we'd moved in four years ago, it was just a ratty screen porch, but we had it enclosed, painted, added large windows and sliding doors, heated and air-conditioned it, had it painted French blue and gold, like the living room, and built on a deck, also painted French blue. It was cool, relaxing, hung with ivy, dotted with ferns on English-looking plant stands. The couch, chairs, and table were very solid and comfortable wicker.

That renovation was the first major change we had made in the house, one we felt comfortable with after we both agreed it would probably be a long time before we left Michigan. Though now with my tenure looking doubtful for next year, maybe that dream was over. . . .

The grinding roar of the lawn mower across the street had faded, so I assumed Delaney had moved to the back of Lucille and Didier's house.

"Wait a minute," I said, putting down my puzzle.

"What?"

"Lucille teaches in EAR, and she has an EAR grad student doing her lawn? Her *advisee*?"

"What's wrong with that? You know how kindhearted she is. Grad students are always broke, and he was probably complaining about it to her, so she wanted to help out a little."

I nodded. That made sense, but there was something about the arrangement that left me a bit uneasy. "That's not inappropriate?"

Stefan shook his head. "Why? It's not like he's a live-in handyman or anything."

I nodded. It stung a little that Stefan knew about Lucille advising Delaney, and I didn't. Lucille Mochtar was my new officemate, but because she and Stefan primarily taught graduate students, they were colleagues in a different way than I was, at least so far, since I had no graduate classes.

Lucille had joined the faculty this past fall and only moved into my office during the semester break, after the ceiling of her office a floor down had collapsed in sodden chunks after a downpour. It was apparently still leaking and unusable.

I liked her because she was completely unpretentious, probably because she'd taken on the academic life late after a career as an editor in her thirties and early forties, and because she had an easy round laugh that was like a gift, especially in our department. The first time we met, I looked up to find her smiling that soft smile in the doorway, shoulder-length dreadlocks framing her honey-colored face like a headdress.

She looked me over and said, "So you're the one nobody wants to share an office with, huh? Well, you don't look scary— and you don't smell bad. You smell good. What's that cologne you're wearing, Paul Sebastian?"

I grinned in reply. "Are you on Dionne Warwick's 'Psychic Friends Network?' "

"Sorry—I can't trust anyone with teeth that big. I'm an independent."

From that moment on, I enjoyed every conversation with her, so it was a double delight that she and her husband Didier were our neighbors. He was a burly, bald Quebecois with the jaunty, rolling, arm-swinging air of a stevedore and no Canadian accent that I could detect, though he was given to exotic-sounding Quebecois curses that Stefan and I had never heard before, and did sometimes end his sentences with "eh?" He and Stefan had taken to working out together at the Club adjoining SUM's eastern border, which meant that there was less pressure for me to accompany Stefan and pretend I enjoyed what I was doing when it was mostly a question of keeping up with him.

Before I could ask Stefan what else he knew about Delaney Kildare, the doorbell rang and we both started laughing.

"It's him!" I joked. "Asking if we need help with our lawn."

Stefan grinned and headed out to see who it really was.

But I cringed when I heard the door open on a bright, reedy, eager voice: "Hi, neighbor!"

It was Polly Flockhart, who lived down the street from us

and felt perfectly free to drop by whenever the spirit—or spirits—moved her. It had started innocently enough when her bichon frise, Spartacus, had wandered into our garden one summer day and dug up a bed of continuous bloom lilies. Stefan calmly rounded up Spartacus, who like all bichons was a real sweetheart, and dealt with Polly's effusive apologies when she tracked her dog down. Polly insisted on buying replacements and planting them herself, and as if having dipped her hands in our soil constituted some kind of bond, she seemed to have adopted us.

Polly bounded into the sun room, grinning and waving as broadly at me as if I were on a cruise ship pulling out to sea and she were on the dock wishing me bon voyage. She was the chairman's secretary in History, and considering that we worked on the same floor of Parker Hall, it was a miracle that we seldom crossed paths there.

She swept up sections of the *Times* from a chair, dumped them onto the floor, and shuddered. "How can you read any of that stuff—it's such a bummer!"

I said, "Hi, Polly," as politely as I could. Stefan sat opposite her with what I called his "Polly smile" on. He looked like an indulgent grandparent fondly watching a toddler wreak havoc he didn't have to clean up.

We disagreed sharply about Polly. I thought she was intrusive and weird, that she was more ridiculous than her name. Conversations with Polly generally started on well-lit streets but invariably veered off into some back alley of astrology, conspiracy theory, extraterrestrials, or past lives. All of which made me gag. But Stefan enjoyed her as much as a travelogue of some exotic, unreachable spot, that you watch grateful for having journeyed there without any effort. I'd accused Stefan, "You're just studying Polly so you can use her as a character in a novel!" And he'd shrugged as if that were obvious.

Polly was nattering on now about how depressing the news was in general and why she avoided it. I watched Stefan drink her in, nodding and "uh-huh"-ing as if he agreed with every word, but he was just stoking her conversational fire.

Fiftyish, slim, sandy-haired, perpetually tanned from golf in good weather and one of Michiganapolis's Tanfastic Studios in bad, Polly dressed like a much younger woman and carried it off very well thanks to her excellent figure and her apparent lack of self-consciousness. She tended to wear camisoles, lacy tops, sheer tunics—much racier apparel than the other secretaries in History wore. Today, she was swathed in filmy, pajama-like cerise pants with a matching violet-and-cerise blouse that looked like a jacket.

"Poor Dr. Benevento. He's devastated. Crushed," Polly was saying, and I woke up.

"Who? What?" With a start, I realized I hadn't been thinking about the riot and murder for a while, eased by the calm of our life and our home.

"Dr. Benevento?" she said, sounding like a teenager going "*Duh!*" She went on. "Just devastated." And her voice was so fond and concerned, I was convinced on the spot that she was a living cliché: the secretary hopelessly in love with her boss. Face tight with emotion, she said, "And still no progress on that horrible murder."

It was truly a puzzling case. With all those people on the bridge, the campus police inquiry hadn't yet produced any witnesses as to exactly how Jesse had died. Because his skull was fractured and his face was bloodied and crushed, it was possible that he'd been stabbed first and then trampled in the rioting crowd after he'd fallen. That made the most sense, but the medical examiner was not releasing much information. A call for witnesses to come forward to the campus police hadn't yielded any clues as far as we knew. I had been wondering if I should call and talk to Detective Valley, whom I knew from previous trouble on campus but wasn't sure if I had anything to tell him.

"First his wife, now his son," Polly said, clucking her tongue.

"What happened to his wife?"

"Don't you remember?" Stefan said. "She killed herself last year."

"Oh, yeah . . . vaguely. Wasn't there a rumor that she was having an affair?"

Polly glared at me. "Absolutely not!" But then she shrugged. "Dr. Benevento is very unlucky. There's some bad energy there."

I froze, expecting her to launch into some wild story about former lives or channeling or something. For Polly, words like "energy" were her own little doorway into the Outer Limits.

I was right to be wary; she nodded sagely and said, "I've had my darkness. But I'm all over that, now."

Hurray, I thought, she's joined the Prozac Generation.

Stefan said, "Really?" to Polly, as quietly as a therapist prompting a jittery patient.

"Oh yes," she assured him. "Oh yes. I was at the mall today, that's why I came over, and that's where I got this outfit."

Polly jumped up and curvetted like a dog angling for a treat, and just as suddenly plopped back down in her chair.

"It was on sale for twenty bucks, can you believe it, I think because it has this stain"—here she crossed her legs and waved one. I could make out what looked like a small flaw in the material. "But outside Hudson's this woman came up to me, real gnarled, you know, like an old apple tree, maybe ninety years old, and she started talking to me in a language I'd never heard, but somehow it was familiar and I felt like I was at home. Finally at home."

Stefan was eating this up, nodding, eyes right on her as if she were a painting at a museum and he was listening to the audio tour, determined to glean every bit of information he could to get his money's worth.

"And she placed her hand right on my forehead and told me I was *healed*."

Polly breathed in deeply as if reliving the moment.

Eyes narrowed, Stefan said, "Did she mean you were healed already? That this was the end of a process? Or did she mean that you were healed right at that moment?"

I gaped at Stefan. How could he humor Polly like this? She was consorting with lunatics at the mall, and he was taking her story as seriously as a news report.

Polly frowned, considering the question. "A little of both, I think. But then she told me she and I were both from another planet."

Now, *that* I believed.

"And that we had always felt lost, out of place, but we would be going home soon."

Please, I thought, real soon.

"Where?" Stefan asked.

"To a planet near the Dog Star, Sirius." She pointed out the window, back toward the mall.

At first I thought she was saying "the Dark Star" and she was "serious," but as it sunk in, I was tempted to howl or bark or scratch for fleas.

"That's where we're from," Polly said. "That's our home. Only, we have work to do here first on this planet. That's why we've been sent. I can't tell you what it felt like to feel so free, finally, to feel like I'm not alone anymore."

Stefan nodded, leaning forward, intent, captured. I wanted to yell at him—this was absurd. How could he indulge her like this? I kept waiting for something, some sign that he knew she was nuts, but he just kept nodding and smiling at Polly. He was reveling in her oddities, and I knew he kept track of her Michigan speech—the way she said "alls" for "all," "grosheries," "pop" for "soda," "heighth" for "height," and "I cracked a window" when we would say "opened."

I tried distracting Polly. "Hey—did you see that hunk across the street? Do you need some yard work done?"

"I saw him," Polly said quietly, completely out of character, and then with a rush started talking about her true planetary home again. What was her problem? Surely this space cowgirl wasn't a prude?

Rather than leave the room—it was my house, wasn't it?— I decided to bring Polly in for a landing. Something she'd said before had intrigued me, so I interrupted. "Your chairman was really close to his son?"

"Oh, no! They hated each other, at least that's what I've heard in the office. One time he even kicked Jesse out of his office after they had some argument. They were screaming at each other, throwing things, and later on Dr. Benevento came out and apologized to us secretaries." Given that Harry Benevento was such a large, bearlike man, I imagined his rage could be pretty scary.

"So they hated each other—why?"

Polly shrugged. "He was an honors student, but he didn't work very hard at all. Some professors might have given him good grades because of his father."

I blushed, because I had felt some of that unspoken pressure myself, though in my class Jesse had completed every requirement and honestly earned his 3.5. "Did you know much about him?" I asked, wondering if Polly had heard anything that might explain his murder.

"I'm not nosy," she said, implying that I was. But then she burst out, "One of the things Dr. Benevento said to Jesse the time they argued, it was pretty awful. He told Jesse he was a disgrace, and he wished he was dead." She blinked so rapidly I feared she was about to go into a trance.

"But you said that he was devastated by Jesse's death."

Polly looked at Stefan quizzically, as if asking was I always this prying and difficult. She drew herself up. "Of course he was devastated—he's not a monster, for God's sake! His *son* died."

I moved on. "How'd Benevento's wife kill herself? I don't remember the story."

Polly blinked a few times. "They tried keeping it quiet. It was a hanging. I mean, she hung herself, in their garage, from a bar her son used for pull-ups. It was very high up because he's so tall, like his father."

"Was there a note?"

Polly shook her head. "Not that I heard. It was a shock because they had a wonderful marriage, everybody said so. They were very happy together. But I do know that she left him pretty valuable real estate in her will. It's land up on the Leelenau that she inherited from her family. On the Lake Michigan side. They had plans to build, but it never happened."

That was one of the prime vacation spots in the state, I knew, with almost no open lots left. A beautiful site could be worth over half a million dollars.

"Hmm. First his wife, now his son," I said slowly, as if trying to match a stranger's face with a name.

Polly cracked her knuckles and said quite sharply, "So?"

"Nick." Stefan swatted my knee with the section of the *Times* he was holding. "Benevento didn't kill his son—he couldn't have. You would have seen him there on the bridge."

"You were there," Polly breathed. I nodded.

"Unless he hired somebody. What if he killed his wife, and then had his son killed because Jesse discovered what happened?"

This is what had happened to me from being around so many murders. All too easily, I'd start testing theories of what had happened. Just as Minnie had at dinner.

Stefan frowned.

"Unless it's somebody taking revenge on Benevento by striking at his family," I said. "Maybe it's some kind of vendetta thing. What if that guy hawking Bibles was actually a hit man?" I knew that couldn't be true; The *Tribune* reported briefly that the young preacher had been questioned and released. My guess was that he had disappeared into the murky Michigan underworld of religious fanatics, Klansmen, and militia members.

"This is sick!" Polly said, looking disgusted. "How can you say things like that!" She barked out a quick good-bye and stormed out to the front door. Stefan followed, shaking his head at me. When he returned, he was frowning.

"You did that on purpose, right? You don't believe any of that. You made it up to get rid of Polly, didn't you?"

His face changed when I said, "No. Not at all. It all seems like too much of a coincidence to me. Don't you think somebody's after Harry Benevento or his family? And that they've been having pretty good luck so far? Harry could be next."

4

onday morning, I was surprised—and a little embarrassed—
to find Delaney Kildare standing outside my office door in
Parker Hall. I spotted him down the hallway as soon as I
opened the door from the landing, and in that sepulchral gloom
his handsomeness gleamed like the gold of an icon in a dusky
shrine.

Dressed in jeans, Doc Martens, and a thin, clinging maroon
turtleneck sweater, Delaney looked like a model posed as a student more than a real student. I wondered if he had seen us at
our living room window ogling him when he was mowing Lucille
and Didier's lawn, even though the light was behind him there.

My father had quietly mocked me as a child when I'd pulled
my shade down during the day to change clothes. "Don't you
understand physics? No one can see you with the light shining
into the room from outside." What my father never understood
was the physics of my discomfort.

As I headed toward my office, Polly Flockhart came dashing
out of the women's rest room down the hall and flitted past me
into the History Department office, a blur of chartreuse and

aqua. I was grateful that though she felt free to drop by our house, she had never once ventured into my office.

"Hi, Professor Hoffman," Delaney called easily as I approached with my key out. He was as effusive as if we were old friends, and that annoyed me. I tried to remember if we'd ever been officially introduced, but I was sure we hadn't.

He held out his hand, saying, "Delaney Kildare," as if he'd read my thoughts. I shook it, briefly. Up close, I thought that there was something excessive or fussy about Delaney, like a cartoon drawn with too much cross-hatching. His eyebrows were too dark and thick, his lips too full.

"I have an appointment with Lucille—Professor Mochtar," he corrected himself, smiling ironically. Graduate students knew they were expected to use titles when talking to faculty members and referring to other faculty. Still, something about his smile bothered me, but what? His teeth seemed too bright, too large, too regular—but there was something else. . . .

"Oh."

Delaney reminded me of the kind of guys I hated in high school: the jocks, the theater majors, the National Honor Society members. Everyone who was attractive, successful, zooming into the future like a high-speed Japanese train. I had never had their unconscious ease in my own body or their true lightness of spirit. Of course, Stefan wouldn't say people like that had a light spirit, he'd say they didn't have a very rich interior life.

"I don't mind waiting out here," he added cheerfully.

Before I could think about it, I blurted, "No. Why don't you wait inside where you can sit down?"

He grinned, and I felt subtly outmaneuvered. He'd wanted me to say just that. I'd been taken in, and it annoyed me that I'd responded with knee-jerk politeness because graduate students were treated so badly in EAR and I often felt the need to make up for that. I really just wanted to be alone in the office as long as possible before he and Lucille started their meeting.

I let us both inside, ruefully hung up my jacket, put my brief-case by my desk, and waved Delaney to the chair near Lucille's desk, but he'd already sat down, plopping his blue knapsack between his feet. His comfort made me feel oddly displaced, a guest in my own office.

People like him unconsciously claimed whatever space they entered. Even my cousin Sharon, very warm and unpretentious despite her successful modeling career, had that same quality. As if the energy of all the staring eyes that had ever studied her, admired her, envied her, formed a penumbra she could never shake.

Jeez—maybe I was really no better than other professors in my department. I might talk about how graduate students should be respected more, but when faced with one who didn't cringe, I was uneasy. Like now, when I subtly positioned my desk chair so that I couldn't see Delaney, even with peripheral vision. I did not want to be distracted, and I did not want him to know I could be. I took out a set of student papers to record the grades.

Delaney brought a copy of SUM's student newspaper out of his knapsack, unfolded it, and whistled. "It's amazing," he said.

I had to look up, and when I saw the enormous upside-down headline, I knew what he was talking about: BRIDGE MYSTERY LINGERS.

"What do you think he was doing there?" Delaney asked. "Did he help throw the box of Bibles over the rail? Or did he try to stop it?"

We'd asked similar questions at Stefan's father's house. They were still good ones. Apparently some students had been arrested for assault, but the full story of what had happened wasn't clear yet, and I doubted it ever would be.

Almost to himself, Delaney said, "I wonder if he had a criminal record?"

"Jesse Benevento?" I asked. Could that be what Angie had meant? But what was her connection with Jesse, and why hadn't I been able to reach her? I'd called several times, but no one answered her phone; she apparently didn't have a roommate. Should I call the director of the residence hall where she lived and say I was a faculty member concerned about her safety? Would anyone take me seriously, or would I be suspected of stalking or harassing a student? An unusual query like that could easily be misinterpreted these days, and I had no natural connection to Angie that would justify a call, since she wasn't in any of my classes.

Delaney said, "Why not? Son of a department chair, maybe he wants to rebel, it makes sense."

"You should be talking to the campus police," I said.

Delaney smiled. "I bet they've thought of all this already. It's the first thing they'd check. But he sure was an exceptional student."

"Jesse? He was your student?"

Delaney nodded. "Forms of Literature."

Exceptional? Bullshit, I thought. Jesse was not an exceptional student, but Delaney would have to say that because of Jesse's father. And then I wondered about Delaney getting to teach such a plum course as a TA. Usually it was the more senior teaching assistants who taught that introduction to fiction, poetry, and drama.

I went back to my papers, but I felt sure that Delaney was staring at me or studying me. After a moment or two, he said, "I truly admire your work."

I whirled around, bristling. "Is that a joke?"

He flushed, the color rising into his face as if draining out of his maroon sweater. "Your bibliography," he said. "I loved reading it."

"My bibliography?"

"Of Edith Wharton." Now he sounded strained, and I confess I was glad to see him off balance.

"I know what bibliography it is. I've only written one. I'm just surprised, because nobody reads a bibliography," I pointed out. "People *consult* it."

Delaney's flush was fading, and he shrugged. "I can't speak for anyone else. But I did read it. I was thinking of working on Wharton and wanted to get a sense of the current scholarship."

"What's your favorite Wharton novel?" I asked, like a grade-school teacher terrorizing kids with multiplication problems.

He didn't falter. "*The Mother's Recompense*," he said. "I think the later novels are underrated."

That was my opinion, too, but I'd never said it in print, so he couldn't be conning me. I relaxed a little.

Delaney nodded. "Everyone told me your bibliography was the place to start if I was interested in Wharton."

"Really?" It was hard to imagine that beautiful face poised over my endless series of paragraph-long descriptions of every article, essay, pamphlet, and book about Wharton ever written in any language. It was as incongruous as an angel in a Fra Angelico fresco reading an AAA Triptik.

"I think you did an amazing job. It was very helpful and clear—especially with the four indexes. That's the kind of work I'd like to do."

There was an odd insistence to his mellow tenor voice, and I had begun to notice that Delaney had a curious tic. He smiled the way a lizard blinks, mechanically, quickly, the corners of his mouth darting up with no clear connection to what he was saying. And his eyes never changed.

"You like indexes?"

Delaney shrugged. "Whatever it takes."

This kid had to be the biggest bullshitter I'd ever met. "You'd like to do scholarly work like that? What the hell for?"

He leaned forward, fixing me with his dark, large eyes as if this conversation was a hunt and I were his prey. But my predisposition to think less of him because he was so good-looking kept me defended.

"Your bibliography is truly important. It's not one of those freaky monographs professors churn out just so they can get tenure, the kind of book someone writes to show how conversant he is with abstruse critical jargon." And he glanced ironically around the office as if expecting a dozen such authors to leap out of hiding, lasso him, and make him submit to the law of the academic jungle. "Those people are so smug you want to throw a bomb into their lives to shake them up," he said. "But your bibliography isn't like that. It's truly useful. It's concrete. The kind of work departments should encourage and reward."

I was charmed by his use of the word "truly." It seemed so awkward and unaffected. And I was surprised by his praise.

"I bet your colleagues don't take you seriously. They don't think that spending a few years in libraries—"

"Not a few. *Five.*"

"Five? Amazing!" He paused, considering that.

Well, it was amazing. Truly. I had plunged into the bibliography with the single-mindedness of someone embarking on a thrilling affair and had emerged as many such people do: tired, cranky, dazed, and guilty for having ignored my partner, wondering if it was worth the effort.

Delaney was still dilating about academics. "They don't think that a solid piece of work like a bibliography is a contribution to the field, and that's what's wrong with the profession.

Being grounded, being steeped in a subject doesn't count for anything. Research doesn't mean anything. Slinging around Lacan and Kristeva and Eve Kosofsky Sedgwick is what matters. The more incomprehensible and self-important your language, the narrower your focus, the better."

I chuckled.

Emboldened, Delaney smirked. "Forget hard to follow. Try boring, try dismal."

"Lugubrious," I said, and he sighed, leaning back into the chair with the gratified smile of a game-show host who's just seen a contestant win big.

We both smiled. To my surprise, I was beginning to like Delaney a bit.

I had said many of these things to myself, to Stefan, alternately mournful or angry, but hearing them from someone young who was still a graduate student struck me as a hopeful sign. Maybe the profession could change and creep out of the corner it had painted itself into. Maybe other academics in the making would see sense, would understand that criticism was only a tool and could never be as important as the literature it analyzed.

Yeah, right. And maybe Bob Dole would appear on *America's Funniest Home Videos*.

"You know, you're bucking the odds," I said to Delaney. "Because you're talking sense. Remember, common sense and the academy don't go well together. Where else in the world can you find so many people who believe that Marxism can improve your life?"

"Good example," he said. And when he smiled that oddly disturbing smile, I felt our roles uncomfortably reversed once again—as if *he* were the professor and I were a graduate student trying to score points in his seminar.

Suddenly I felt someone standing at the open door, and when I turned, it was hard not to moan.

There was Detective Valley of SUM's campus police, eyeing me with a pinched look that made it clear he was not happy to see me. Yet every time I'd seen that look before, it seemed to flicker on and off, so that I assumed the truth was more complicated. He hated having to talk to me, but it gave him a welcome opportunity to torment a faculty member, and a queer, too.

Valley looked like a cross between a freckled, redheaded Ichabod Crane and the Grim Reaper, and he dressed like he worked at a Burlington Coat Factory. He'd been the principal investigator at SUM each time I'd been "confronted" with murder, as Minnie had put it the previous Friday night. Valley had a nasty habit of sneaking up on me that made me feel as guilty as a little kid screaming, "I didn't do it—I didn't do it!" to his mommy before even knowing what he was accused of.

"Professor Hoffman." Valley nodded at me.

"Detective Valley." Jeez, I felt like Jerry Seinfeld saying "Hello, Newman."

"I need to talk to you," Valley said, ignoring Delaney, who seemed intrigued by our exchange. "But not *you*." Valley pointed to Delaney and then out to the hall.

Delaney obediently rose and left the office, slinging his overstuffed backpack onto a shoulder.

I protested. "You shouldn't treat students like that!"

Valley shrugged and came in, closing the door behind him. It occurred to me then that Lucille Mochtar had left Delaney waiting a long time. I didn't know her very well, but I had observed she was very punctual. What if he ran into her out in the hall—Valley surely wouldn't ask Lucille to stay out of her own office, would he?

Valley sat down where Delaney had been perched, lazily crossing his legs as if he were a hired thug paid to intimidate me.

If I hadn't been pissed off about his rudeness, I probably would have quailed.

"That guy was a *graduate* student," I said.

"They're all the same to me. All the students here. Criminals waiting for their chance. Rape in the arboretum, stealing backpacks in the library, lifting wallets at the football games, getting drunk on Friday night and breaking car windows, setting bonfires. Flashers. Vandalism. Graffiti. Peeping Toms. Arson. Drug addicts."

I felt a little overwhelmed by his catalogue. I had heard some of it from my own students, who complained it was impossible to leave your things alone for a minute at the library now—they'd get rifled or stolen for sure. Despite the facts, I rallied. "You see it that way just because you're a cop. That's the only side of students you get to know."

"Right. Tell me that teaching makes you think they're all saints."

"No, not really, but—" He had me there, and he knew it by my hesitation. Teaching freshman composition was like what people in retail often told me: it did not generally instill in you a high regard for your fellow human beings. But neither did associating with my colleagues in EAR, who often made me think that the idea of an asteroid hitting the Earth and starting another Ice Age would not be much of a real tragedy.

"What do you want?" I asked Valley, impatient.

"It's about the incident last Friday on the Administration Building bridge."

"The riot. Why talk to me?"

Valley shook his head. "Because you were there."

"How do you know?"

He frowned. "Are you denying it?"

"No."

"Then cut the crap. You think you can stall by asking dumb

questions? You think this is some stupid mystery novel where everybody's a moron?"

He must read mysteries, I thought, very surprised. I had pictured him reading *Soldier of Fortune* magazine or something like that. And he must like mysteries enough to dislike bad ones. I think I knew exactly the kind of book he meant: the ones where writers obviously desperate to churn out book after book filled them with long stretches of pointless dialogue that ran in circles, and had their characters talk the way no human being ever did, constantly asking for clarification in conversation. It was highly stylized, and highly boring. Like: "Where were you last night?" "Last night?" "Yes, last night, after the party?" "The party?"

I said to Valley now, "I wasn't stalling. It just made me feel nervous to be singled out."

My honesty seemed to surprise him. He cleared his throat behind a fist and said, a little less combatively, "I've been talking to a lot of people—as many as we can find—who were there at the bridge. So tell me what you saw." He took out a small red memo pad from his notebook and a chewed-looking ballpoint.

"I thought you said you had a good memory and didn't need to take notes."

He shrugged. "Getting old." He looked up at me, pen poised.

I took him through the scene from the moment I spotted those blood-red Bibles to when I stood there looking at the cops examine Jesse Benevento's body. Talking about it had become easier, as if I were seeing everything through some kind of protective scrim: Jesse's pallor, the blood, that ironic book cover. Slowly I supplied as much detail as I could, explaining that he could also discuss my story with Angie Sandoval.

Valley shook his head. "I know about her. She's the first one who called nine-one-one—she gave us her name. But she's gone. We're trying to track her down."

"I wonder if her parents *did* make her leave, after what happened."

"What's this with her parents?"

I shrugged. "Before people went nuts on the bridge, Angie was telling me they were pushing her to drop out—her parents, I mean—and transfer because they thought SUM was getting too violent and they were worried about her."

Valley looked pained, as if I were blaming him personally for the deteriorating conditions on campus.

"Nothing ever happened to her personally," I rushed to point out, absurdly trying to make Valley feel better. "But, hey, being that close to a murder, I can see how it would freak people out."

"You think so?" He shook his head. "Just wait. Next year's freshman class will be bigger."

Thinking of the gawkers at the bridge who had loitered there before the riot ever happened, making jokes about Perry Cross's death, I said, "God, that's so sick, but you're probably right."

And we both shared a silent, cynical, "Kids!"

Valley and I sat there for a moment, in full agreement. It seemed amazing after all we'd been through together over the last few years. Stefan would never believe this.

Maybe I'd been too harsh in judging Valley up until now. Maybe he wasn't such a bad guy, just doing his job and a little over his head at a university where there were many difficult people. Hell, my colleagues could drive *me* crazy, and I hadn't ever investigated a crime. Well, not officially. And what if Valley knowing me had actually made him more tolerant? Was that possible?

At any rate, I certainly didn't envy him working on such a high-profile murder case: the death of a department chair's son, national publicity, state legislators sharpening their budgetary fangs.

"Why did you want to talk to Angie?" Valley asked.

I shrugged. And I lied: "To see if she was okay." I didn't want him to suspect her of anything.

He nodded. "Did you see anything suspicious before the riot—or during?"

"Define suspicious."

He waved a hand, clearly wanting me to make the definition. I thought that over. "Not really. I mean, someone suggested to me maybe all that stuff with the Bible box was some kind of setup, but I don't know if that's plausible—"

Valley eagerly interrupted me. "Who told you that?"

Now I regretted having been so relaxed. Grudgingly, I said, "My mother-in-law."

"Your—?" He actually scratched his forehead, but mockingly. "How can you have a mother-in-law if you're not married? You are still gay, aren't you?"

His quiet contempt irked me. "*Stefan's* stepmother," I explained. Valley knew well enough who Stefan was. "It was her idea. She reads a lot of mysteries." I half-expected him to volunteer that he did, too, but Valley wasn't here for a chat.

"Gotcha. Forget that. Did you know Jesse Benevento?"

"Yes. He took one of my classes last year."

"Uh-huh. . . . Did you like him?"

"Wait a minute! Are you trying to—?"

"Easy. We have to put together a picture of this kid, okay? Did you like him?"

I sighed. If I was uncomfortable being criticized by my students, I also didn't enjoy letting people know they'd gotten under my skin. "He was very religious," I said.

"You mean he prayed in class? No? Then what? How did you know? He wore a big cross or something?"

How was I going to answer Valley's question without embarrassing myself? His eyes were narrowed, and he licked his thin upper lip with obvious anticipation. For whatever reasons, he delighted in seeing me on the spot, and I was wrong to assume otherwise.

"He gave me a pamphlet about chastity."

Valley grinned. "What the hell for? Was he trying to save your soul?"

Eyes down, I said, "He objected to a mild, *very* mild, sexual reference I made in class."

"What did you say?"

"Is this necessary?" I snapped. "He was a fanatic. He was intolerant of difference."

"And you're not?" Valley sneered. "It bugged you that he was religious."

"That's not the same. What *I* didn't like was him telling me what to do."

"Because you're the professor and he was the student."

I sighed. "No, because it was mean-spirited. Listen," I said. "It wasn't just me. I found out that Jesse had a reputation for confronting professors he thought were trying to indoctrinate students with 'anti-Christian' ideas. He accused people of forgetting this was a Christian nation. But his father was the chair of the History Department, so it's not like anyone could really put him in his place the way he deserved."

"Did anyone try?"

I thought about it for a moment and suddenly felt very uncomfortable.

"Who?" Valley pressed, picking up on my unease.

"At least two faculty members I know of." And I pictured them together near the bridge the day of the riot. "Iris Bell told him he was anti-intellectual, and Carter Savery said he should start a group: Nazis for Jesus."

Valley frowned, jotting all this down.

"Come on," I said. "Nobody's going to kill a student for disrupting a class—that's ridiculous!" But as wild as it was, if it were true, and they were murderers and convicted—then I'd get someone else on my tenure committee. I tried not to grin at the prospect.

"How about other faculty?" Valley asked.

I shrugged. "Ask around." And then something popped into my mind and I said, "What if he was in a cult or something?"

Valley's face went blank, and I wondered if I'd stumbled onto part of the truth, but he moved in a completely different direction. "How about the rest of the class? He piss anyone off?"

I told Valley I couldn't remember, but if he wanted, I'd find my old class roster book from last year at home and see if going over the names brought anything back to me.

"Sure," he said, sounding disappointed.

I wondered if I should mention anything that Polly Flockhart had told me about Jesse arguing with his father, but decided that I'd said enough for one morning. Besides, I assumed that was hearsay anyway, and useless.

"Do you know what really happened?" I asked. "How he died?"

Valley gave me a sarcastic stare that said he wouldn't tell me the time if he could avoid it. He was about to get up when suddenly loud footsteps sounded in the hall, and the door was flung open. Delaney stood there, pale. "I was just down in the EAR office—something's happened to Dr. Mochtar!"

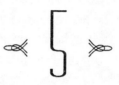

efore either one of us could ask Delaney what exactly had happened to Lucille, he rushed off back down the hallway, heading for the stairs.

Valley and I followed, though Valley stopped to eye me curiously as I closed and carefully locked my office door. I didn't explain my suspicions that last year someone had gone through papers on my desk and used them against me.

On the way to the staircase we bumped into Harry Benevento—at least Valley did. They glared at each other. I assumed Benevento was angry that there'd been no progress on solving his son's murder, but what was Valley pissed off about? I asked him as we headed down the stairs, and he muttered, "Guy doesn't think we're competent. He's talking about lawsuits, private investigators." He shrugged.

When we got to the EAR office a floor below, I was surprised to see Lucille sitting on a battered wooden bench in the hallway, looking very calm. No, she was more than calm; she actually seemed to be enjoying herself, and she certainly didn't appear injured or even shocked in any way. So why had Delaney been alarmed?

Lucille was surrounded by our department chair, Coral Greathouse; Dulcie Halligan, EAR's prissiest secretary; Iris Bell; Carter Savery; Bill and Betty Malatesta; and Delaney. Lucille had the bemused, indulgent air of a cynical dowager after a fainting spell, watching her heirs dance attendance on her.

They made quite a picture, but then Lucille, a woman in her late forties, drew your eyes wherever she was. It was the contrast of those dreadlocks and her oval, high-cheeked face people often assumed was part Korean, or Japanese. Actually, Lucille was half Indonesian, of Chinese descent. Her cool, appraising dark eyes often seemed at odds with her wide, loving smile, and though she was short and rather chunky, she bore herself regally in Laura Ashley dresses that fit her pear-shaped body perfectly.

By regal I don't mean that Lucille brought to mind the distant kind of monarch. It was the friendlier, Scandinavian kind I thought of. You know, the ones out at the flower market, bicycling to work, doing infomercials about their cosmetics line. Shy and reserved person that I am, I had of course once shared this private imagery with Lucille, and she had laughed. "You don't sound like any bibliographer *I* ever met! You've got too much imagination."

That, of course, had always been one of my problems.

"Hi, Nick," she said now, smiling broadly. "Join the circus." She patted the bench, and I sat down by her. I half expected her to thank me for coming and ask if I wanted a drink.

This was very strange, and I peered at Delaney—why had he been so upset? Then I asked her what was up.

Lucille sighed, but Coral Greathouse, wearing another one of her dreary suits, answered my question. "Someone sent Lucille a horrible postcard. An *odious* postcard." She brandished a white rectangle that looked like one of those pre-stamped USPO cards, the kind that Stefan used when replying to fans he didn't want to hear from again (interesting fans always got a card printed with our address).

Coral shuddered as if wishing she could destroy the card. Betty and Bill murmured to each other, and I suddenly recalled that Bill had wanted to talk to me about something, but it was fuzzy, and I couldn't remember how important it had been.

Valley spoke up. "I'm Detective Valley with the campus police. Who's in charge here?" He probably expected to hear that no one was. Valley had a very low opinion of our department, having run across its denizens twice before during murder investigations and interviewed many of us. We're not really any worse than other English departments across the country, but we're certainly no better. In other words, we have all the charm and dignity of snarling terrorists turning on each other in the last ten minutes of a thriller like *Cliffhanger*.

"I'm the chair," Coral said. "Professor Greathouse."

Lines like that always want me to quip, "If you're the chair, then I'm the footstool." Stefan has made me swear to never say that aloud.

If Coral expected some kind of acknowledgment of her status from Valley, she didn't get it. Instead Valley snatched the card from her, and she glared at him. Coral was quiet and controlled and depended on her absolute straightforwardness to keep the department in line, but I could tell by her tight jaw that Valley was pushing her limits.

"How many people have touched this?" Valley asked sharply, holding the card by its edges as if it were a CD he was about to slip into his car stereo. I wondered what could possibly be on the card to have caused this much commotion.

Lucille answered him. "Me, Coral, the secretaries, I guess. Delaney looked at it, too. That's *after* I found it in my box. Who knows who touched it before that."

Valley shook his head, disgusted. Obviously the fingerprints would be a mess. Suddenly he read the card aloud in a stern, wooden voice as if willing the words to reveal their author: "I hate your black ass."

Carter clucked his tongue, and Iris Bell breathed in as if to start one of her tirades, but Carter grabbed her arm to stop it. She shook loose of him but said nothing. I hoped she wasn't going to file sexual harassment charges against him now and embroil the department in more dissension.

There was a general nervous stirring around the bench, part surprise, part embarrassment. It was not as venomous as I had expected, but it was bad enough. So now the ugliness on campus was being aimed at faculty members. Who would be next? Gay faculty? Jews?

I looked at Lucille, but she still didn't seem distraught or even disturbed.

"Not entirely accurate," she muttered. "But I suppose it was meant metaphorically."

Now, if it had been me getting hate mail, I think I would have wanted to snag the first plane out of town before they started burning crosses on my lawn.

Just then there was a sharp clacking of heels all the way down the hall, and we turned to follow Juno Dromgoole's shapely, black-clad figure down to the women's rest room. Her heels echoed wildly in the high dim hallway, as discordant as laughter at a funeral. I half expected someone to call out "Quiet!" but no one did, and I turned back to Valley, who didn't seem to have noticed the distraction.

"Typed," Valley mused in his normal voice, not much of an improvement over his orator's tone. "No signature. Michiganapolis postmark. Who put this in her mailbox?"

Dulcie Halligan raised her hand. Perpetually huffy and put-upon, she looked like a slimmer version of Barbara Bush, down to the pearls and shapeless suits, and was given to snapping at any faculty member who she felt was acting superior. As if she were dropping a neutron bomb, she'd say, "I graduated from SUM cum laude." Behind her back, people called her "Dull Harridan" and "The Graduate."

Her lips twitched. "But I didn't see the message side."

I wondered if she meant she would have thrown the card away if she'd read it. Had there been other cards before this one?

"Okay," Valley said to Dulcie, "I'll want to talk to you. And you," he said to Coral Greathouse. "But later. Don't go any-where."

Coral and Dulcie started protesting that they worked there, and of course— But Valley just shooed them away and told the Malatestas to scram as well, unless they were witnesses. Since it wasn't clear what they would be witnesses to, they left, glaring at Delaney. What was that all about?

Carter Savery and Iris Bell didn't budge, and Valley snapped, "You can go."

"You're very rude," Iris said, chest out like some elfin warrior throwing down the gauntlet to a giant.

"I come from a long line of rude people. You should've met my father."

Iris flounced off, not easy to do when you're so short. Carter followed, shaking his head, though whether at her or Valley, I couldn't tell. But Delaney hadn't stirred. He hovered by the bench and smiled now and then in that odd way of his.

Pointing at Lucille, Valley said brusquely, "First I want to interview her." He frowned at Delaney as if wondering where he'd seen the guy before, and then cocked his head sarcastically as if to say, You still here?

But Delaney held his ground.

"Go back upstairs and wait for me," Lucille said, her voice warm and motherly. Delaney nodded and moved off. "Sweet kid," Lucille said to no one in particular.

Valley slipped the postcard into the breast pocket of his suit and turned to me. "I don't need to talk to you about this."

"Nick is my friend." Lucille patted my hand. "I'd like him to stay," she said firmly, with a wonderful, solicitous, end-of-discussion smile. "Let's go to the faculty lounge."

Lucille rose, and we followed her into the dim lounge down the hall that wasn't much more than a jump up from a coffee room, overfilled with cracked orange and avocado vinyl-covered chairs whose wooden arms looked as if they'd been gouged by people undergoing electroshock therapy or some other kind of torture—like a speech from SUM's half-wit president. Littleterry was the kind of man who thought calling for "customer satisfaction" at SUM was a bold new move, something that would "re-create the university." There were rumors that he was planning some major initiative, and I was surprised he hadn't already proposed merging the university with Kmart and renaming faculty "course associates."

Valley closed the door and waited for Lucille to take a seat before sitting opposite her. I sat on a chair facing them both, and I suppose if you had come upon us accidentally, you might have thought it was a friendly meeting. But having just been interviewed by Valley upstairs, I didn't envy Lucille.

"Maybe it was a joke," Lucille said.

"What?" Valley shook his head as if he hadn't heard her right. "You think it was funny?" He brought out his pad and green Flair pen.

Lucille rolled her eyes. "I didn't say it was a *good* joke. But it could just be a prank, or somebody got dared to do it. A stupid joke." She shrugged and smiled at me as if inviting my agreement, but I was too surprised by her suggestion to say anything. "Some fraternity stunt."

"You don't think it's serious," Valley summed up.

"No. Not really."

"This kind of thing happens to you a lot?"

Lucille got quieter. "What I'm saying"—and here she paused as if he were an especially dim student who needed her to speak slowly—"is that the sentiments... expressed by this anonymous correspondent... aren't very threatening or abusive."

Why phrase it like an administrative report? Was she mocking Valley, or did she think that kind of language had a better chance of penetrating?

"Okay?" she said. "It's really no big deal."

Valley looked even more surprised than I did. Why was she working so hard to downplay the whole situation? He made some notes.

Lucille nodded at Valley. "I bet you were expecting me to go ballistic, right? Get myself on the news, organize a strike or a sit-in, start a lawsuit, send for Jesse Jackson. That's it, isn't it? Blow it completely out of proportion."

That must have been close, because Valley flushed and said stiffly, "What I expect doesn't matter."

Lucille and I exchanged a conspiratorial smile. I was glad she had embarrassed Valley and put him a little on the defensive.

"Maybe you don't think it's a big deal," Valley said, his composure returning. "But I do. It's my job to be concerned about hate incidents like this."

Lucille's eyes widened, and she breathed in slowly as if trying to calm herself down. "It's not an incident. It's only a damned postcard."

"That's where it starts," Valley said ominously. "Tell me if you have any enemies here on campus or in town."

Jeez, I thought, that sounded so melodramatic, and yet I knew how vicious the academic community could be.

"Oh, lots," she said smoothly. "The KGB's been after me for years."

Valley stared her down until she relented. I'd been on the receiving end of that stare too often.

"Well, I suppose you could say that I'm not the most popular faculty member this department has ever had."

Valley checked it out with me, and I nodded. "Why's that?" he asked Lucille.

She didn't hesitate. "I'm a minority hire, and they're usually controversial. You probably know that this department looks a lot like you: white and male. They need diversity. Well, I'm as diverse as they come. I could be my own multicultural studies program. I'm half black, half Chinese Indonesian, and I'm a woman."

Valley frowned, but I wasn't sure if it was confusion about how this information was relevant, or distaste for her being what he might consider a "mongrel."

"Black? Not African American?"

"Hey, I've never been to Africa, and I'm not going. African American doesn't fit me at all."

"And what's Chinese Indonesian?"

"My father's parents were born in China, he was born in Indonesia."

"Okay. So what's the controversy about you?"

I wondered if Valley was playing dumb. Surely he'd been around SUM long enough to know what Lucille meant about minority hirings?

"To start with, I haven't always been an academic. I used to be an editor, in New York, before I quit and went to graduate school. People here resent that I had another life where I was successful. I know they did in graduate school."

That made sense. All older graduate students coming into the department were treated badly, as if they were cocky recruits who had to be beaten into submission. "Then I got hired before I had the degree in hand," Lucille continued. "And my salary's higher than that of most new members of this department."

I knew that was something of an understatement. Lucille was making a good thirty-five thousand more than any of the newer faculty, none of whom were at all reluctant to complain about the difference. The department was full of rumblings, and had been ever since Dean Bullerschmidt let it be known there was money for a new position, but only if it was filled by a "double minority," at the very least.

Bullerschmidt was dying to be provost, and he wanted his record in the College of Arts and Letters to look as good as possible. When Coral ran for chair of EAR, she was his candidate, even though they had never gotten along with each other. Coral was a woman, and that was all that counted for him. But now that she was his rival for the position of provost, I wondered if he regretted helping her.

Valley crossed his legs, nodding like a talk-show host. "People think you just got the job because you're black, or whatever you are?"

Lucille smiled. "Well, I did, didn't I? Lots of universities were competing for me."

"And you picked SUM." It was a statement of fact, but clearly a question.

"SUM offered more than anyone else."

This honesty was what I most admired in Lucille.

"How much?" Valley asked.

"Seventy-five thousand. And I was hired as an associate professor with tenure."

Valley's tongue worked on the inside of his cheeks. Was he

comparing that to his salary? He turned to me as if expecting I would protest the amount, despite being Lucille's friend. Unless he wanted to hear me defend the sum. I did neither.

The money was amazing, but to me what was most enviable was that she had been hired with tenure. She'd never have to jump the biggest academic hurdle. Even if she didn't ever distinguish herself by publishing, it wouldn't matter, since she was utterly safe. That is, unless the university completely abolished the department—then they could fire everybody. It was possible, I suppose: EAR could be declared a toxic waste dump in need of cleanup.

"This is a seller's market," Lucille said plainly. "People like me are in demand, so why shouldn't we take advantage of the way things are? I've never pretended to be a brilliant scholar, and I sure know I'm not much better than hundreds of new Ph.D.s. But I have what people want. Now, anyway. In ten years it could be Hispanics that are really hot, and nobody will want to read about Toni Morrison." To Valley's blank look, she said, "The Nobel Prize winner? She was the subject of my dissertation."

"Okay." It didn't seem to have registered, but Valley eyed her admiringly. I could tell that he too was impressed by Lucille's candor.

But I also knew that there was spreading tension in the EAR department precisely because Lucille publicly made no effort to pretend that she was anything more than a minority hire or that she was more qualified than the competition. Those who had favored her appointment were angry that she was making them look bad by supposedly downplaying her qualifications; those who opposed it were furious that she was—in their words—bragging about her deficits.

In our department, the truth was not something for public consumption. Hell, that was the case at the whole university.

SUM was, after all, admitting record numbers of students who shouldn't have been in college in the first place, under the rubric of "expanding educational opportunity." These subliterate and maladjusted students of all races and ethnicities were causing problems across campus as faculty withered under the assault of their ignorance and arrogance. They were at the university only because SUM wanted their money. Education had long since stopped being a privilege at SUM and the country at large: It was nothing more than a business transaction, and often a rip-off.

"Is there anyone who's been especially—" Valley hunted for the word.

"Vociferous?" I suggested.

"Loudmouthed," he said to Lucille. "About your being hired? Anyone come to mind?"

Lucille closed her eyes as if mentally running through a list of department members. Why was she stalling? She and I both knew of at least one very vocal critic: Juno Dromgoole. Even though she was a guest professor, Dromgoole hadn't made any effort to fit in. She had been abusive and outrageous at faculty parties and meetings from the very beginning. Juno was a total mismatch for our department: brazenly assertive and alarmingly well dressed. Just the sight of her was like an unexpected electric shock.

Maybe because she was a guest, Juno felt free to say whatever popped into her head, and she had been heard in hallways, in her office, and even in her classroom to describe the spectacle of watching SUM and the EAR department trying to be politically correct as "grotesque—like watching a mad dog bite its own ass in the town square."

"I don't see why you're not hiring more cripples," Juno had announced. "You're scraping the barrel for everything else, God knows." That was widely taken as a reference to Lucille, since she was the only new hire in the department.

Valley prompted Lucille again. "Nobody's been bad-mouthing you?"

She grimaced. "Why should someone in the department send me a puerile card like that?"

Valley leaned closer. "I don't think it came from a total stranger. Or maybe you sent it to yourself to get attention?"

Lucille jumped to her feet. "I don't have to listen to this! Don't pull any of that John Bradshaw bullshit psychology on me. I've got all the attention I want."

Unruffled, Valley said, "You'll be getting more before this is over. Sit down."

She did, and grumbled, "Iris Bell. That dwarfish woman who was out in the hallway. The one who called you rude. She's been pretty vocal."

"What's her beef?"

I jumped in. "Iris has been here twenty years, but she's at the low end of the pay scale for full professors. She hasn't written a book in twelve years since her promotion to full professor, but she bitches about her salary anyway."

"You're pretty new here compared to her," Valley said. "How do you know all this?"

I shrugged. "None of it's a secret. The salaries are public information—they have to be, since SUM's a state school."

Valley nodded. Then he said to Lucille, "Is she following you or something?"

Lucille shook her head. "I haven't noticed anything. But she is pretty hard to spot—"

Valley didn't smile. "Who else?" he asked. "What about that guy with her?"

"Carter Savery?" Lucille mused. "I don't know about him. But every time I catch his eye, he's glaring at me."

Valley wrote something down. "And they were together,

those two, when you got the card. Maybe they stuck around to see your reaction."

Even though I didn't like Carter or Iris, thinking of either of them as responsible for Lucille's hate mail was disturbing.

"Is that it?" Valley asked Lucille.

"There's Juno Dromgoole. She's a guest professor, and she's very vocal in taking on what she calls political correctness."

"What do *you* call it?"

Lucille ignored that. "She's said some unpleasant things at department meetings, not directly at me, but about minority hiring in general. I suppose she could have sent the card." Lucille raised her eyebrows at me, seeking my opinion.

"I don't know if Juno's the type to send hate mail. But she is pretty—" Now it was my turn to search for a word.

"She's obnoxious and offensive," Lucille said. "And she does it on purpose."

Valley took that in. "Anyone else? No? You're sure? Okay, if you think of specific people, let me know. I'll talk to this lady to start. And call me right away if there's any other cards, or—" Valley left us alone with the various possibilities hanging over us in that miserable little lounge.

Lucille seemed to deflate with Valley gone, and I moved my chair closer. I could see now that she was starting to sweat.

"You okay?"

"Fine."

I wasn't convinced. Her initial cool response to the card might have been an act, an attempt to stay above such viciousness. And maybe she might not have been completely honest.

"I didn't tell him the best part," Lucille brought out. She smiled at my curious glance. "The hiring committee thought I was Islamic."

"Wait. You're not?"

Now she laughed. "No, that's only the majority of Indonesians—there are lots of Buddhists and Christians. They just assumed I was Islamic, and maybe they were confused because my father's name sounds almost Arabic. You know, Mochtar, Mukhtar. Of course nobody would have *asked*." She shrugged. "So there are some faculty that think I got in under false pretenses."

I didn't know what to say.

"Come on, Nick. I have work to do," she said. "And Delaney's still up there—he probably thinks I was arrested." She chuckled, and we headed back upstairs.

Looking somewhat woebegone, Delaney was sitting cross-legged on the floor right near our office. He rose as soon as he saw us, or Lucille, and rushed forward, full of concern. Lucille hushed him and there was something very motherly in the way she patted his shoulder.

"I was so worried," Delaney said for the third time when we got inside the office and he sat down by Lucille's desk. That's when I noticed he tended to sit with his legs spread wide apart, as if giving himself room. I made myself not look more closely.

"That's very sweet of you," Lucille said. "But there's nothing to worry about. Really."

She was so comfortable with Delaney it suddenly made me *un*comfortable.

I decided to work at home, and left them to their meeting.

STEFAN WAS VERY quiet when I told him about the post-card incident before dinner. We were sitting in the sunroom drinking some tonic water with lime, and it struck me as an incongruous setting for an ugly little story. Decrepit, roach-ridden Parker Hall, now *that* was the perfect place for bad news and misfortune.

Stefan didn't dismiss the postcard as Lucille had. For him, every such act was an echo of the seething hatred that had smashed apart Jewish life in Europe and murdered millions as if sweeping tokens off a game board. Bigotry like that instantly stirred up his parents' and his uncle's past.

I did not try to palliate the story in any way—that would have made him angry. And when he heard how Lucille had shrugged the card off, his response was, "Of course, she'd have to say that." I guess he meant that Lucille would have to say something to calm herself down, to resist succumbing to paranoia and fear, which is what I'd have done if I'd been unable to make that plane reservation out of town after the card came.

We didn't have time to pick the event apart, because the doorbell rang and someone started pounding on the door at the same time as if being pursued by fiends.

"What the—?" I raced out to the entrance hall, and Stefan followed.

I glanced through the small fanlight window. "It's Juno," I said softly, amazed.

"Juno? What's *she* doing here?"

"Let me in, you sonofabitch!" Juno shouted, pounding some more. "I know you're home."

I ripped open the door to shut her up. It worked. Face mottled and red, her Tina Turner–style blond hair a halo of rage, Juno glared at me as if I were Orpheus and she an advance scout for the Maenads, getting ready to tear me limb from limb.

Juno stepped in. I stepped back.

Stefan, puzzled and surprised, closed the door warily behind her. "Why don't we talk in the kitchen?" he said, gesturing down the hall. He sounded composed, but he was clearly at a loss. I could tell by the way his face looked emptied of feeling.

Juno stomped down the hallway, and we followed, Stefan

blank, me wondering what our neighbors were thinking. Then I realized this must have something to do with Lucille and me mentioning Juno to Detective Valley. I felt guilty and exposed.

"Coffee?" I asked inanely in the kitchen. From the look on Juno's face, I knew she really wanted poison—for me.

Juno stalked back and forth across our kitchen in her black spike heels, muttering, and I studied her, enthralled.

Juno's mission in life seemed to be overturning every conception Americans had of Canadians. She was brassy, vulgar, intensely and inappropriately sexual, with whatever she wore showing off her mesmerizing cleavage. Imagine Joan Collins on *Dynasty* as a foulmouthed busty blond, and you've got Juno Dromgoole. She had a smoky, sophisticated voice, and there was something else about her: She had this sheen to her nails, hair, and eyes—to everything, really—as if she'd been dipped in glitter and it had been absorbed by every pore in her body. Today she wore a black suit with a very short skirt that showed off fine legs in black hose. The cuffs and lapels of her jacket were faux leopard skin.

Elegant French-manicured hands on her hips, Juno surveyed me with contempt. "Who the fuck do you think you are reporting me to the police?"

Feeling my face get hot, I sat down and gestured for Stefan to make me some coffee. I certainly needed it if Juno did not. He busied himself with beans and the grinder. Over the noise I said, "I didn't report you to anyone."

"Oh, no? Then why was that scrawny excuse for a policeman harassing me to find out what I think of that Lucille person?" She advanced on me, stood two feet away, her glossy lips quivering. Yet for all her rage, I wasn't afraid. There was something delicious about her, she was so untamed, so naturally rude and confrontational. I deplored what she said, the way she thought, yet I found her entertaining.

"Know what I told him?" Juno said cockily. "I told him he had shit for brains."

"Valley must have loved that," Stefan murmured behind her. I don't think Juno noticed.

"Does anyone in his right mind think that I have to send you a postcard if I think you're a worthless piece of shit? *Me?*" she brayed, smacking her bust and letting out a very operatic "Hah!"

"That's true," I said. "They'd hear about it whether they wanted to or not."

Juno squinted at me and chortled. "Damn right they would. Nobody ever called me a shrinking violet."

"That's probably the only thing you haven't been called."

Now she grinned and looked me up and down as if we'd just met.

"Fuck the coffee," she said as Stefan offered her some. "I need a drink. A real drink. None of your foofy Campari and sodas. I want Jack. Jack on the rocks. Have you got any?"

Stefan didn't miss a beat. "Coming right up," he said. I changed my order, and soon we were all sitting around the table drinking Jack Daniel's on the rocks. But it wasn't a harmonious conclave, more like the Bosnian peace talks.

I believed Juno when she said again that she hadn't sent the card to Lucille. "If you ask me," she said confidently, "it sounds like one of those morons in town who send those bloody awful letters to the editor of that pathetic tripe passing for a newspaper. All about God damning everyone to hell except them. This place is crawling with drooling morons and twits."

"And those are just the administrators at SUM," I said.

Juno laughed. "You're fucking marvelous." Her approval of me was as fiery as her dislike of Detective Valley.

"Lucille doesn't think it's serious," I said. "The postcard, I mean."

Juno reared back, her well-plucked eyebrows waggling in mock astonishment. "No! Really? Christ almighty! That girl might be smarter than she looks."

Stefan was sending me silent distress signals, but we weren't at a party we could leave, and I wasn't about to usher Juno out of our house. She'd go when she was ready.

Juno socked back the last of her drink. She held out her glass for a refill, and Stefan complied. "I didn't intend to come here, actually. I was going to have a nice chat with Lucille across the street, but there wasn't anyone home. And I remembered someone saying you lived on this street in almost identical Colonial houses—is that what they're called?—opposite one another." She smiled companionably, leaning back in her chair and crossing her legs. "Time to go," she said abruptly, draining her glass and setting it down hard. Stefan's eyes closed in relief.

Juno rose, and we trailed her to the door. "Just remember one thing," she said. "I'm a mean bitch. If I want to do someone harm, it's not going to be with any damned postcard."

"I agree. Overnight mail is *much* more intimidating," I said.

Juno grinned. "Marvelous," she said, turning to sashay down the street to her gleaming black Lexus. Those heels, I thought. That's what she'd use—I could see her stabbing one into someone's heart.

Closing the door, Stefan said, "How could you trade lines with her? Didn't you hear what she said? She wasn't kidding about being mean."

I felt guilty for having let my delight in snappy comebacks take me over once again. Would it ever stop? I'd been doomed to this fate since the time my arrogant fifth-grade teacher sneered at a correct but convoluted answer I gave to one of her current events questions and said, "Nick, a little knowledge is a dangerous thing." The class didn't quite follow, but tittered anyway. I got more laughs, though, when I shot back with, "Then you must be deadly."

After that little victory, I also got letters sent home to my parents from my teacher and the principal, as well as an agonizing lecture from my mother and father about showing proper respect to my teachers and not mortifying my parents with such shenanigans. And my father growled out *"Espèce d'idiot!"* which felt like a smack in the face.

"No," I said to Stefan. "You're right. Juno was definitely not kidding."

We sat in the kitchen, nursing our drinks, speculating on who in EAR might dislike Lucille enough to send her hate mail. I insisted that Juno was a very unlikely suspect, since her criticism of minority hirings like Lucille's was so outspoken. Her disapproval was out in the open, while hate mail seemed underhanded, striking out at someone in secrecy.

Stefan demurred. "That woman is out of control. Look at the way she dresses."

"Short skirts and a short temper don't make you a maniac," I said. "I think she's just doing all that to be outrageous. My money's on someone like Iris Bell. She's all twisted up with jealousy, I bet, and here comes Lucille right out of grad school making all that money, even if she is in her forties." But then I had to add, "Well, the whole department's full of bitter people. It could have been a committee sending that card to Lucille. A consortium."

"Here we are again," Stefan said sadly. "Trying to figure out if someone we know might have committed a crime."

"Well," I said, trying to cheer him up. "This is just hate mail, right? It's not murder."

Stefan nodded. "Not yet."

≪ 6 ≫

"till nothing new about the bridge murder," Lucille said in her kitchen, checking the spinach lasagna that she and Didier had put together with homemade pasta and one of the best marinara sauces I'd ever tasted. It was Tuesday night, only four days after the riot, and yet I felt I'd been living with the story forever. Still, after all the wild excitement, there'd been nothing at all in the papers or on the radio except brief reports of no progress.

"You know, I hope you're using organic spinach," I said by way of reply.

Lucille closed the oven light and turned around. "Is there any other kind?"

"And I hope it's imported," I said. "Grown in Northern Italy by a remote order of Midianite nuns, prayed over daily, and brought across the Alps on the back of handpicked mules because truck transit bruises the leaves."

Lucille grinned. "SUM needs more people like you." She was wearing bright blue plastic sandals better suited for a beach, a white T-shirt, and a magenta-and-white, flowered wraparound skirt, looking cool and relaxed.

The warmth in her voice reminded me of my cousin Sharon, and I almost felt in that moment that Lucille and I had known each other for a very long time. Or was that simply a projection into the future, a hope? Now that Lucille was in the EAR department, I felt less isolated and besieged. So I guess I wanted to reach a point where we had shared countless such companionable times in the kitchen. I knew it was possible, because Stefan liked Lucille, too, and she and Didier seemed fond of both of us. And we all liked cooking and eating a good meal.

"That smells wonderful," I said. It was not a low-cal lasagna: she'd made it with milk, cream, butter, sweet Italian sausage and ground sirloin, fresh mozzarella, and Parmesan, with nutmeg giving it that special tang.

Lucille nodded as if all she'd done was slide a frozen entrée into the microwave. Though I'd known her only a few months, I'd learned that Lucille was always offhand about her cooking, which she excelled at—just like Stefan.

When Stefan and I had come over for drinks earlier, the pasta had been hanging near a kitchen window like some sort of sculpted chime. Making pasta was something neither one of us had gotten into, and I'd been half tempted to see what sort of sound it would make, if any, but Stefan had caught my curious look and yanked me away from the drying rack.

"Did you hear from Juno?" I asked.

"Juno Dromgoole? Me? Why would she contact me?"

I told her about our confrontation with Juno the day before, and Lucille seemed as appalled as Stefan had been. "What makes someone like that tick?" she asked.

"A time bomb."

"You're probably right. But if she came to see you only because I wasn't home, why hasn't she stormed the gate here yet?"

"She could have gotten the shouting out of her system," I

suggested. And then a darker possibility hit me. "Unless she never intended to talk to you, and it was me and Stefan she wanted to intimidate. But God knows why. Maybe she's just nuts and thrives on making a scene."

"Did it work? Did she intimidate you?"

"Stefan thinks she's a menace. He doesn't like her."

"And you do."

I tried to explain it. "Juno is like performance art, or a one-woman show. She's so over the top, and that's saying a lot given our department. I can't help enjoying the spectacle a little." I realized as I said it that my reaction to Juno was similar to Stefan's when Polly Flockhart came by—why hadn't I seen that until now?

"You must be starved for entertainment."

"Well, you've figured out by now that Michiganapolis isn't exactly anyone's idea of a cultural mecca. It's a great place to live—"

"—but an even better place to leave?"

"Exactly. Well, sometimes." I hesitated, and then asked Lucille what I'd wanted to since Stefan and I had come over. "Do you really think the postcard you got was a fraternity prank?"

She came to sit by me, hauling herself onto one of the diner stools, which were decorative but very uncomfortable, I thought, unless you had perfect posture.

"No. But I didn't want to say that to Detective Valley."

"Why not?"

Lucille sighed. "Because it might not have come from someone at SUM."

"You mean you have some enemy out there?"

"Nick, *enemy*'s a pretty loaded word." She squeezed her eyes shut as if sorting and shaping what she was going to say, then opened them and looked very sad. "Didier's family is split. Not by divorce, it's by politics. He may be Quebecois, but he moved from Montreal to New York right out of college to live with some cousins, and he never returned. He went into education, taught *English*, then he married an American—half black, too. If my mother was from Benin or some francophone country, that might have been acceptable. But Brooklyn—? His family saw him as a traitor, and his brother took it worse, for some reason. Didier was supposed to stay in Montreal, have children, and fight for Quebec's independence." She shook her head. "It's not as if I don't understand how the French have been beaten down by the English there. Second-class citizens, humiliated for two centuries, and having it shoved in their faces. There's a column celebrating Nelson's victory right in the middle of Old Montreal, right? So how could they ever forget?"

I thought of the Quebec license plate with its slogan, *Je me souviens:* I remember. But connecting all that with what had happened to Lucille, well, it seemed far-fetched.

"If somebody in Didier's family sent the card, how would they get it to Michiganapolis for the postmark? And why now?"

"Well, I just started teaching at SUM this year, right? And his brother's doing a Ph.D. at the University of Michigan, in international relations. It's just an hour away. Maybe he wants to be an ambassador when Quebec becomes independent."

I nodded. "Younger brother? Older?"

"His brother? Oh, much younger. It's a huge family, nine kids." She smiled. "His name's Napoleon, can you believe it? They haven't talked in years, but you know how it is in families, news filters out about the big things: moves, babies."

I nodded. My parents and my cousin Sharon's parents were likewise distant, but they still kept track of each other through me and Sharon, and also more tangentially through neighbors and friends.

"Didier doesn't suspect it might be his brother, at least he hasn't said anything." She went to the fridge, removed a wine-bottle-shaped magnet and a photo from one of the doors. "This is his brother," she said, handing me a crowded family snapshot and pointing to one corner.

Napoleon didn't look at all like Didier, but he looked very French: dark, wiry, with a foxlike face and almost pouty lips. I handed back the picture. I could see why Lucille wouldn't want to share this story with Valley, having lied to him myself before, or at least held things back. Telling Valley could cause more friction between Didier and his brother, but it bothered me. I would have been glad to have Valley's attention turned away from EAR and our campus.

"Wait a minute, Lucille. If Didier and Napoleon are estranged, why can't you talk about your suspicions? It couldn't make the relationship any worse."

"Are you kidding? Didier would drive down to Ann Arbor and beat the shit out of his brother. He's a Taurus, and they don't explode very often, but when they do, it's like Mount St. Helens." She gave me a long, hard look as if warning me never to make Didier angry.

I had no trouble picturing Didier on the rampage. He may have been in his fifties, but he was more fit than most men half his age, and there was a great deal of power in that barrel chest, those enormous arms, and his tight springy walk.

The image of violence triggered another question for me. "Say Napoleon is the one who sent the card, and he sent it from here in town. Doesn't that classify as stalking? Aren't you worried?"

"How about another sidecar?" Lucille asked, her smile a clear "Don't go there."

Lucille made a great version of that Roaring Twenties cocktail, so I said yes, then watched with anticipation as she carefully poured equal parts Cointreau, sweet-and-sour mix, and Courvoisier into a 1930s-style monogrammed silver shaker filled with crushed ice, shook it well, and strained the drink into a large martini glass whose rim she'd sugared. The sweet, strong drink was very potent and knocked me on my ass if I had more than two.

We raised our glasses, and Lucille suggested we toast Didier and Stefan: "To the Writers."

They were off in the living room, bitching about the publishing industry. That was ironic, since publishing had treated Didier very well. Ten years older than Lucille, and an undistinguished poet, Didier had retired from teaching high school English after getting a contract to write a memoir based on an essay he published in the *New Yorker* about his and Lucille's fruitless attempts to—well, bear fruit. They'd tried for ten years to have a child, and nothing had worked. But the decade of frustration had given birth to the makings of a starkly titled book, *Sterility*, which had earned him a half-million-dollar advance.

Stefan, on the other hand, had never made much money from his writing and was growing increasingly anxious about whether his publisher would like his new novel. Every editor these days seemed to want a Big Book, and Stefan wrote literary fiction that had a discerning but small audience that was steadily declining.

"No news," Lucille said again, shaking her head sadly, and I knew she was back to the bridge tragedy. It was disorienting to have been immersed in a story for a few days, and then suddenly be plunged back into normality, knowing all the while that there'd been no resolution.

"I think this is turning into our version of the O. J. trial," I said. "Trials," I corrected.

"How so?"

"It's all anyone can talk about on campus or in town, but there's nothing new to say. It makes me think of when Lady Bracknell complains about the end of the London season in *The Importance of Being Earnest*."

Lucille grinned. "And what's that?"

" 'Everyone has practically said whatever they had to say, which, in most cases, was probably not much.' " It was strange quoting that late-Victorian play in such a contemporary kitchen, which took its tone from the stainless-steel worktable and table and diner stools at its center. The walls were lined with open-backed freestanding stainless-steel shelves, and Lucille and Didier had equipped their kitchen very well, thanks no doubt to that huge advance: Sub Zero fridge, thirty-two-bottle wine refrigerator, chrome deluxe Cuisinart, convection oven, KitchenAid mixer, Dualit toaster, Gaggia espresso machine, Henckel knives, Calphalon cookware.

"You've got a great memory for quotations." Lucille smiled indulgently and raised her martini glass to me. I echoed the gesture with my glass. "Have you always been able to remember what you read?"

"Since I was a kid. Can you stand another quotation? I feel like Anatole Broyard—he said that books were his weather, his environment, his clothing."

"That's great," she murmured. "Not enough professors love books anymore."

"You're right. You know what Iris Bell said to me once?"

"Iris." Lucille almost shuddered. "She's so strident."

"She's a troll. We were chatting about something in the EAR office, and I quoted Updike. Iris glared at me and said that Edith Wharton was my specialty, not Updike, and why didn't I stop showing off? You should have seen her face—she was so angry!"

"Maybe she's never read Updike, and you embarrassed her."

"Academics are either stuck in their narrow little specialties, or jealous, or nuts about criticism, or they're just too burned out to care about anything. Or nursing a grudge against someone in their department, and plotting revenge."

"Like in EAR, I'm sure." She shook her head. "Iris isn't the only colorful faculty member there."

"Colorful? Be honest. Malignant is what you mean. But it's the same everywhere, Lucille, at every school. And it's a mistake when politicians attack higher education and complain about the professors being nuts. Of course—that's the whole point, that's why most of them are where they are. This society should be thankful that colleges and universities are keeping all these faculty members out of circulation. Can you imagine the kind of harm they could do if they were actually out in the world, working? It'd be like the 1970s, when mental hospitals began releasing patients back into the communities they were from."

"I think it'd be more like *The Night of the Living Dead*." She crossed her legs, smoothing down her skirt. "If I'd known it could be this crazy, I might have considered staying in editing."

"So why did you leave?"

"I decided to go into teaching to be like the professors who inspired me in college, the ones who made me feel excited about literature."

I wondered if she'd also switched paths from editing to teaching to somehow shake the misery of not being able to have a baby. A career change would at the very least have made her feel her life wasn't stagnating, and besides, as a minority hire, she was making much more money than she would in publishing—and had summers off! Did not being able to have a baby account for the motherly way in which she'd spoken to Delaney in Parker Hall, and hired him to mow her lawn, taking care of him, really?

"Didn't you feel like that as an editor?" I asked. "Excited

about books. And like Broyard? Didn't you love books when you were in publishing?"

Lucille shook her head. "Never. Well, maybe when I started. But it was a job, I was always behind, and there was never enough time to read for pleasure. I got sick of it. Ten years burned me out. You have no idea how many manuscripts come in every week. Like lemmings jumping off a cliff."

"And publishing's the sea? No wonder Stefan gets nauseous sometimes."

"And you know what the worst part of it is was?" Lucille continued, as if she hadn't been listening. "Writing rejection letters. The worst! Even a bad book takes work, and I always imagined some dazed author at the other end of whatever I wrote, and I'd have to make it short and unemotional to distance myself from that picture." She frowned. "It's an inhuman business."

"Then the card you got at EAR could have been sent by an angry writer."

"You're kidding, aren't you? It wouldn't make sense to do that now, when I haven't been editing for—" She thought. "For seven years."

I shook my head. "Now's the best time—it's when you wouldn't expect it."

She peered at me through half-closed eyes. "Tell me you're joking."

"Not completely. I never used to think of things like this— revenge, murder—until I moved to Michigan. Look at all that time I wasted growing up in New York when I could have been doing survival training and joining the NRA."

Lucille chuckled way back in her throat as if to say she was giving me one more chance to get real. I took it, asking, "Do you edit Didier's work?"

"I read it. As his wife, not his editor. How about you?"

I smiled. "I edit Stefan's stuff when he wants me to. And Stefan helped me proofread the Wharton bib." Lucille frowned, and I explained, "We started calling my bibliography the Bib after the first few months."

"It makes me think of lobsters, or lettuce."

"That's the point—'bib' makes you think of something pleasant. And when your life is filled with photocopying and phone calls and faxes and trips to out-of-the-way libraries to locate rare manuscripts, you need every positive association you can get."

Lucille nodded, but clearly something else was on her mind. "So. You don't think we should talk about the bridge murder anymore?" she asked.

"No, that's not it at all. We can't help talking about it, and chewing over the same facts and opinions. It's not likely to get solved if nobody's gotten anywhere by now. They know he was stabbed, but they haven't found a weapon, there's no known motive, and the trail is cold."

"What trail? You think the murderer headed out of state? I don't. He's probably right here in town. Or on campus." Lucille set her drink down on the counter behind her and crossed her arms as if to warm herself.

"Why say 'he'? It could be a woman," I pointed out.

"I doubt it. A woman stab somebody that big? Jesse was tall, right? Too risky. What if she missed, or just wounded him?"

This speculation actually refuted my comparison to the O. J. trial, since neither one of us had ever puzzled over the murderer's sex before. Then I told her about Minnie's various suggestions for motive, and Lucille laughed: "Jessica Fletcher's turned every elderly woman in America into a detective! Your mother-in-law's a trip."

We took our drinks and headed into the living room, where

Stefan and Didier were huddled over some book, grimacing.

Didier was as improbable a figure as you could imagine for a former high school English teacher and part-time poet, with his enormous biceps, rolling gait, and booming voice. He typically wore chinos, loafers, and white T-shirts, as if he'd never gotten over his teen years in the 1950s amid all those images of Brando and James Dean. Stefan said that Didier's air of complete self-satisfaction was due to his book advance, but I thought it predated that; he didn't strike me as one of the *nouveaux heureux*.

"You liked books when you taught, didn't you?" I asked Didier, sitting opposite him on a pretty but not very user-friendly black leather Le Corbusier chair that matched the couch he and Stefan were on. Lucille sat on the other chair flanking mine, opposite Stefan.

Didier flashed a big-toothed grin. "Hell, yes. Wild about 'em. Reading's as good as sex, hell, better than sex. Nothing to clean up afterward." He grinned at Lucille, who shook her head with the affection of someone long married who was used to a spouse making wisecracks that weren't always funny. It was a look I'd seen on Stefan's face. "Though I tell you, one more year of *Ethan Frome*, and I might have gone round the bend." Didier grinned slyly, as if expecting me to be outraged in the name of all Wharton scholars and fans.

But I stumped him. "That's my least favorite novel of hers. What were you guys reading?" I asked, pointing at the book between them.

Stefan held it up so I could see the cover: *Family Affections*. "It's a novel by some kid, twenty-five, and it's being advertised all over. Listen to this." Stefan found a line and read it to us: " 'Maria's hair was closely cropped to her head.' "

I smiled. "Who edited that?" Then I noticed Lucille was looking down, eyes closed.

"It's one of hers!" Didier crowed, blue eyes gleaming. "Her publisher put it out. Sorry, ex-publisher. And it's pure crap. How can your hair be cropped close to anywhere *but* your head? Don'tcha love it?"

"It gets better," Stefan chimed in, leafing through for another line. " 'Maria was never angry nor sad.' "

"How does something like that get published?" I asked.

Lucille cleared her throat. "I'll tell you. I know a little about this book. The author's twenty-five, right? Just out of graduate school. Youth sells. And even better, he's very good-looking, and it's his first book. All that is great for off-book-page publicity. And it's a thriller, so he might be the next big thing, since it has a good chance of ending up on the best-seller lists. Any house would throw lots of money at the book without hesitation. They'd expect coverage in *Entertainment Weekly, People,* everywhere."

"It's a thriller?" I asked. "With a title like *Family Affections?* Aren't thrillers supposed to sound ominous, like—like *Absolute Evil* or *Jack of All Deaths?*" But even as I said that, I remembered a line from a novel by Liz Benedict: "The living room, the most treacherous country of all."

"Hey, it's a sensitive New Age thriller," Didier said, reading from the blurbs on the back of the dust jacket.

"Okay, fine. But why's it badly edited?" I asked Lucille.

She leaned back in her chair. "Well, it's probably better now than when it started—I'm sure the publisher hired an outside editor to make it at least marginally readable. You should see the stuff that used to come in. But if it's a thriller and a first book, everyone's afraid the author may be hot, so they don't want to get known as the editor who passed on the next John Grisham."

"Here's another great line," Didier chortled. " ' "Dear," ' Elizabetta Van der Velde's booming voice thundered.' "

Lucille grimaced. "Frankly, for a book like that, the story's what counts. The sales reps aren't going to get hyped up about pushing a book because it's well written. People who read for excitement aren't going to pick apart the writing. So you don't waste time on that, you put everything into marketing. The writing only has to be good enough to keep you turning the page."

Stefan and I exchanged a glance. This was the kind of cynicism we'd each expressed about publishing. Hearing it from an editor wasn't quite as thrilling and depressing as discovering that Nixon really was a crook, but close enough.

Lucille's comments also meant something else, something more personal: she must have felt comfortable with us, because up until now she'd been reticent about her editing career before graduate school. And that comfort pleased me.

Lucille held out her hand to Didier for the book, and he rose to pass it to her. She opened the rather bland black-and-red cover to look at the jacket copy and nodded. "See?" she said. "It's an audio book and a Book-of-the-Month Club Featured Alternate. The same with the Doubleday Book Club. They're pushing it hard." She glanced up at Didier. "But why did you buy it?"

He grinned. "Morbid curiosity!"

Stefan was looking glum, and I knew that his original stance of mockery about this book had started to give way to that gnawing despair about his career, a despair that was his own personal El Niño, wreaking emotional devastation on a regular basis. Though he'd been well reviewed originally, and even had his work appear in the *New Yorker*, those days were over. Fellow graduates of his writing program had gone on to earn film deals and get interviewed on network television or at least CNN, but Stefan had never really taken off as a writer after his first splash, had merely chugged along from one increasingly modest success to another.

And here we were, having dinner with Lucille and Didier, becoming their friends, when Didier's first book had not only earned him a $500,000 advance but would surely be more widely advertised, distributed, and reviewed than all of Stefan's books put together.

I glanced up and realized that the room had fallen so quiet that you could hear every nuance from the CD player as Cassandra Wilson moaned out a languid version of "Old Devil Moon."

Didier was looking right at Stefan when he said, "I don't have any illusions about my book either. It'll be well written at least, but hell, there are lots of books out there that'll be more beautiful. I know what my publisher wants: another *Angela's Ashes*, another painful memoir that can sell like crazy. And it's my first book, I'm older than most starting authors, and I taught high school—just like Frank McCourt. Okay, it's not miserable poverty in Ireland, but why not a book about a couple who can't have a kid even after trying everything? The perfect baby boomer topic. The ones with kids will read it and feel sorry for us, the ones who don't have kids, or can't, hell, they'll feel my pain."

"Our pain," Lucille corrected.

"Yes," Didier said, eyes down. "Our pain. Of course."

Now the room was really silent, and I wished there were John Philip Sousa playing. I headed for the guest bath off the living room, which was lined with gorgeously framed reproductions from the Louvre. Their home almost had the look of a very exclusive travel agency, since the gleaming white walls adorned with lovely crown molding were decorated throughout with travel posters, prints, and other souvenirs from their many trips to Greece, Italy, and France. These were the only real source of color or warmth; otherwise the furniture throughout was rather severe: all black leather and chrome, even in the bedrooms. I found it a bit odd being in Lucille's and Didier's house, since it was identical to ours on the outside (except for the color of their shutters), but utterly different inside.

When I emerged, the three of them were arguing about the current state of English.

"I feel assaulted," Stefan said, "every time I turn on the news or read a magazine or newspaper."

"Language always changes," Didier argued.

"This isn't change, it's ignorance. I have to write these things down because they're so unbelievable."

Stefan wasn't joking—he'd taken to keeping a pad in the kitchen where he'd inscribe each new linguistic indignity. He was passionate about it. Like the reporters who had poor subject-verb agreement, or routinely said things like "It's a fundamental core issue" and "Looking back in retrospect" and "The likelihood is pretty unlikely" and "Something imminent is about to happen."

"Okay, so it's ignorance," Didier said. "What if something beautiful emerges, eh?"

"Spoken like a poet," Lucille observed.

Didier nodded. "Yeah, like a poet who doesn't have to teach horny little bastards how to write an essay anymore."

"Well, I don't care what people say," I announced. "I just can't stand how they say it."

Together Lucille and Didier asked, "What do you mean?" and then smiled at each other.

"My hobbyhorse is that nobody seems to know where the stress is supposed to be in a sentence anymore. So you hear the wrong words emphasized, and it's weird." I tried to recall some examples. "Okay, someone's discussing a controversy and saying there's 'divisiveness *over* the issue.' And talking about an upcoming segment and saying 'We'll bring that *to* you.' Three men get arrested, and 'one *of* them' has a criminal record."

Stefan and Didier nodded. Lucille said, "Those are good reasons not to listen to the news."

"But it's not just newscasters," I said. "It's everywhere. I hear my students do it, faculty members, cashiers, you name it. It drives me nuts to listen to it, and then I feel worse because I know I'm turning into a crank."

A kitchen timer rang, and I said, "Okay, time out on tirades."

Lucille smiled, rising to go check the lasagna. At the kitchen door she turned and said, "Don't apologize. What works *my* last nerve is all the call-in programs and programs with live audiences where all the fools in the universe get to show off how little they know." From the kitchen she called, "I heard some girl saying last week—and I don't remember where it was—that if Saddam Hussein was such a bad man, why didn't the Iraqis just elect someone better? All this chat radio and chat bullshit has convinced the average person he has something to say. I know that's not very enlightened, but it's the truth, and it's getting worse."

"Hah!" Didier cried. "That's all drivel. My bête noire is these politicians who talk to the country about honesty but try to fool people into thinking they're not bald by combing some pathetic strands of hair across the top of their pates! Who do they think they're kidding and how can they expect anyone to take them seriously?" He ran a loving hand over his handsome bald head, grinning, and I wasn't sure if he was serious or not.

We were soon seated around the chrome and glass dining room table (I was glad my shoes were polished) feasting on the rich lasagna and a caesar salad with home-baked croutons. The lasagna was succulent—there was no other word to describe it.

Didier fell on his portion with such gusto I thought of Byron's line, "The Assyrian came down like the wolf on the fold."

"I love this!" Didier crowed. "And I'm going to love working it off tomorrow," he said with glee, wondering with Stefan how much time they should spend in the pool versus on the track, and which body parts to work on with weights. They had already developed dozens of different workout routines.

Silkily, Lucille said, "I'm not worried about the weight. At my age, as Kathleen Turner says, a woman can worry about her butt or her face. If she gets too thin, she'll look old and drawn. If she stays plump, the wrinkles just don't show."

I couldn't wait to relay this bit of advice to my cousin Sharon.

Though we moved on to talk about the day's news, we drifted inevitably to Jesse Benevento's murder. Didier voted for a gang slaying as the motive, but that wasn't what interested him. "This is a TV movie dying to get made. Bucolic campus. Brutal crime. No suspects. And Skeet Ulrich as the kid." None of the rest of us were sure who Skeet Ulrich was, and we spent ten very confused minutes mixing up half a dozen actors in their twenties. I was shocked to discover that Dylan McDermott and Dermot Mulroney were different people.

Into our second bottle of a plummy 1994 Canoe Ridge Merlot, we continued idle speculation about the murder and its film potential when Stefan asked Lucille about the hate mail and if she thought it might be Juno Dromgoole, since Juno had been very public in her disapproval of minority hiring in EAR.

"No. She's too active to sit down and send those cards to people." Lucille shook her head quickly, embarrassed. "I mean those kind of cards. *Card.*"

"Cards?" Didier growled. "There were more than one?"

Lucille's eyes were fixed on some point invisible to us, and slowly, reluctantly, she admitted that there'd been several such cards over the previous weeks.

Didier had turned red. "*Calice!* Why didn't you tell me? You have to call the cops—this is ridiculous."

Lucille demurred. "I don't want to get any students in trouble.

What if somebody's mad at me for what I said to one of my undergrads working on a paper about slavery? He was shocked when I told him that it still existed in Africa, and that Arabs had played a leading role in the slave trade. And I've got some un-happy graduate students in my African-American Lit seminar because I dared to say Toni Morrison was a gifted literary writer, Terry McMillan was a popular writer, and E. Lynn Harris wrote trash."

Stefan nodded, clearly aware of the coming complaint.

Didier said, "What's wrong with that? I've read them, and it's all true."

"It's wrong because you're guilty of rhetorical neocolonial-ism," I said, grinning, "by applying outmoded and oppressive, male-identified, Eurocentric, patriarchal standards that ignore black cultural experience—is that close?"

"You're in the ballpark," Lucille said, disgusted. "I'm not going to add anything to the nastiness at SUM," she concluded, mind clearly made up.

"Fuck the students," Didier rumbled.

"What if it was your brother?" I asked, more than a little drunk by now. Lucille glared at me, Stefan said, "What brother?" and Didier remonstrated with Lucille: "You think Napoleon could have done this? *Tabernouche!* When will you stop being so paranoid about my family?"

"Paranoid?" she sneered. "They hate me."

"They hate all Anglos, it's nothing personal. Napoleon would never send a card like that. It's, it's—" He struggled to find the explanation. "It's just not his style!"

This struck me as so French I started laughing, and so did Lucille and Didier. Still confused, Stefan asked, "What brother?"

Then the phone rang, and Lucille rushed into the kitchen, over Didier's insistence that she let the machine take the call.

"Delaney!"

It was just one word, but Lucille's voice from the kitchen was so warm and caressive, I felt embarrassed and could sense Stefan's unease at my side without even looking. But Didier was smiling and shaking his head. "That woman has such a big heart—she loves her students to death."

Before any of us could launch into a conversation to cover up whatever Lucille was saying to Delaney, she was back, looking troubled. "They found the murder weapon, the knife that killed Jesse Benevento, on campus—in the river. One of those butterfly knives, but that's all he knows."

As if the call had ended dinner, we moved back to the living room for espresso and cannoli from Michiganapolis's best Italian bakery, but we were all subdued by the intrusion of reality into our intellectual guessing game about Jesse's murder. Soon after, the evening broke up.

Crossing back to our house, we saw a dark Jeep Cherokee pull out of a driveway down the street, and as it rushed by us faster than the 25 mph limit, I made out Harry Benevento's large figure looming behind the wheel. "That was Polly's driveway," Stefan noted, as we let ourselves in. "Wasn't it?"

"What was he doing down there this time of night? Do you think he's having an affair with Polly? Oh, jeez, maybe that's why his wife killed herself—or maybe Polly killed her!"

Stefan frowned at me, then headed off to his study, while I hung away our jackets and turned on some more lights. That was always his ritual—he needed to check for phone messages, e-mail, or faxes before he could settle down for the night.

I was puttering around in the kitchen, setting up for tomorrow's breakfast, when Stefan walked in, a page in his hand that I could make out as a fax. "This was waiting for me," he said dully, not moving forward. His face was so drained of emotion, of life, that I knew whatever he'd learned was horrible and doubtless connected to his writing. So horrible that I was afraid to ask, but I knew I had to. We'd entered a familiar and terrible household drama in which Stefan would quietly lay out his news as if reading tarot cards that forecast his doom. And I would be the bystander, helpless and trapped.

I moved to the kitchen table and sat down. "Tell me."

"It's from Peter."

Peter was Stefan's perpetually cheerful, but perpetually slow, agent—the kind of person who would see the sinking of the *Titanic* as a chance to make new friends. Or at least try to convince you that was the way to look at it. All that pep could be wearisome, as could the weeks, sometimes months, it would take to hear from him in reply to a phone call or a fax. Once an editor had called Stefan to ask, "Is your agent dead? He hasn't returned my calls."

"Peter tried calling, but we were out, and he didn't want to leave a message. They dropped me. They don't want the new book, or any book, ever. I've got"—he looked down—" 'a pattern of declining sales.' And Peter says it may be difficult to move me elsewhere right now—though he's going to try." Stefan breathed in, and I didn't know if he was going to shout, or cry, or just fall bitterly silent. He shook his head.

I would have shrunk back into the wall behind me and disappeared if that were possible. Stefan had just experienced the most humiliating defeat an author can suffer: being dropped by a publisher as if he were something unclean that had to be quarantined or expelled. It had always loomed in the distance as a vague threat, but more often it had been a kind of mantra: No matter how badly a book of his had done, or how few reviews he got, or what the *New York Times* had said, at least he'd never been dropped. At least he had a publisher who'd brought out five of his books. But that basic security, that promise, was gone now, and he wasn't as fortunate as a free agent looking for a new team—those sales figures made him damaged goods.

"If only I could stop writing," he said acidly. "If I could stop *wanting* to write, wanting it so much. But I can't stop," he almost spat out, eyes darkened by self-loathing. "It's my addiction. I *have* to write. I love to write. I love all the highs, not just from writing, but the feel of a new book, reading a review, getting fan mail, seeing my books in a bookstore, every single fucking little thing. And the more I get, the more I want, so how can I ever stop? It's a blessing. And it's a curse." His voice was cold.

He was so stricken, so numb, I was hesitant to speak or even move in case I somehow made it worse. That was the easiest thing to do. Making it better, well, that was almost impossible. I knew; I'd tried cheering him up before, and he'd either snapped at me or stormed out of the room. This kind of news was not a boo-boo that could be soothed by the emotional equivalent of a kiss and a cookie. Or even mentioning the stirring end of one of my favorite stories by Henry James, "The Middle Years," in which a dying, failed novelist says, "We give what we have—we do what we can—our work is our passion and our passion is our task. The rest is the madness of art."

"I'm going to bed," Stefan brought out, eyes blind, and dragged himself out of the kitchen.

I didn't follow right away. Like me, Stefan could usually force himself to fall asleep when he got bad news. It was only toward midmorning that he'd become restless, fighting to stay asleep as if his consciousness were a stubborn dog being yanked away from a tree by a demanding owner. He'd eventually lose and be dragged awake by whatever was troubling him. I wanted to give him the chance tonight to have at least a few hours of rest, since I assumed we'd both be up later, talking, talking, getting nowhere.

There was a special cruelty in life to watching someone you love suffer and being utterly unable to help.

More and more over the past few years, Stefan's career had seemed to me like an archipelago of success in a sea of failure and disappointment, and those turbid waters had gotten choppier each year, more hazardous. He worked so hard on making his books the best they could be, and we'd spent a lot of our own money over the years on promotion, sending him on the book tours most people thought publishers routinely paid for. And what had it amounted to?

Last summer we'd seen an electrifying production of *Death of a Salesman* at the Stratford Festival in Canada that had left us and most of the audience in tears. When Willy Loman's brother asked Willy, "What are you building? Lay your hand on it. Where is it?" Stefan had turned to me and whispered, "That's me." He was so hungry for success, notoriety, for the kind of attention he'd gotten when he started out, but there seemed little chance it would ever really come back.

Dispirited for him, anxious, I drifted into my study and turned on the light. This room always worked on me like a massage, with its thick maroon drapes, maroon-and-blue Persian rug, and ranks of books that all helped muffle sound from the street, which was why the faint beep of the answering machine—turned way down—startled me.

There was a single message, and when I played it a second time because I was so surprised, I settled down into my overstuffed armchair, wondering how I could possibly break this latest piece of news to Stefan.

Amazingly, I not only slept through the night myself but through Stefan's waking up, getting dressed, and heading off to campus. When I stumbled down to the kitchen that Wednesday morning, belting my robe, I was sorry I had missed being able to talk to him this morning, but I was also relieved.

After we'd had some trouble in our relationship a few years back, Stefan had taken to leaving me little notes on the kitchen table now and then to wish me a good morning if he'd left before I was awake, but there wasn't a note today.

While I made my egg-white omelet, cut up some strawberries and melon, and got coffee brewing, I mulled over last night's message on my answering machine from Van Deegan Jones and our conversation when I'd called him back. One of the most prominent Wharton scholars in the country, Jones had not only quit his teaching job this year but wanted to divest himself of his last ties to academia and Wharton. He had a contract to do a Norton Critical Edition of *Summer*—Wharton's erotic New England novel, which was like a pendant to the chilly *Ethan Frome*—and he wondered if I'd take his advance and take the project over from him. Jones had raised the possibility with the publisher and assured me that it wasn't going to be a problem with them if I said yes. My name would be listed as editor, Jones's as coeditor (it had to be there, since he was well known and I wasn't).

The deadline was a year away, and I knew that this was a job I could not only do but enjoy doing. The bibliographer in me, the cataloger and organizer, had clicked on overnight, and I felt both competent and ready. I'd have to go through the text, annotate any difficult or obscure references, and gather a series of the best articles and book excerpts about *Summer*, along with any related letters of Wharton's, plus contemporary reviews. There'd be lots of correspondence involved—all the letters asking for permission to get reprints—but compared to the years I had spent on the bibliography, it was a Caribbean cruise (without Kathy Lee). Doing this edition of *Summer* would be limited, intensely focused work that could possibly help me get tenure, and there was something better. My bibliography was used by scholars and librarians and graduate students, but a prestigious and far less expensive paperback Norton Critical Edition would be used by many more students and readers, possibly tens of thousands over time.

It wouldn't be an original work of scholarship, but it might influence my tenure and promotion review. Hell, some kind of book was better than none. And I didn't mind the $2,000 and the promise of earning more on the book, though that was always speculative. In publishing, the only sure thing is an advance on royalties. You can't ever completely trust a publisher, but you can always trust cash up front.

When I'd hung up last night after agreeing to take the book on and telling Jones that he was very generous, I'd realized that this great news for me could easily strike Stefan as cruelly ironic.

He'd just been canned by his publisher, while I'd had a book project appear like Venus out of the sea foam. I was almost ashamed to have something wonderful happen after he'd been mauled by the publishing world, and ashamed to feel glad that something so positive had entered my life after seeing Jesse lying there dead on that bridge. Something I could turn to with confidence and joy, that might counter the helplessness and horror I'd been feeling wash over me like an unclean tide.

After breakfast and a shower, I called my cousin Sharon at work at Columbia University, where she was an archivist, to tell her the news.

"Nick," she said softly. "That's fabulous."

Sharon was like a sister, a cheerleader, a patron, and a favorite aunt rolled into one. I could always count on her deeply felt enthusiasm, but today her resonant, actressy voice sounded strained.

Before I could even ask if something was wrong, she said she'd been thinking of going into therapy.

"You know how it's the New York religion, so I do feel left out when people complain about their shrinks at parties. Though—you'll love this!—one of my gay friends said 'Girlfriend, get real! There's nothing wrong with you except that you live in the craziest city in the world plus you're dating a musician. That's asking for trouble.' Maybe he's right. But I hate when somebody tells me to 'get real.' I mean, honestly, Nick, reality and I have never been on the best of terms."

She was right—what could be more unreal than having been a model? Which was probably why she now, as an archivist, lived in the world of the completely verifiable, the concrete.

"I did not like being lectured," Sharon went on. "So I reminded him that straight people have feelings, too!"

We both laughed.

Sharon often complained about the city and her boyfriends and even the possibility of going into therapy, so I moved past all that to ask, "Have you been sick?"

"What?"

I repeated myself. "You sound different."

She said, "Sorry, I had to switch the phone to my left ear. I've had a bad cold and my hearing's not great."

"For how long?"

She hesitated. "Oh, a while. And I've kind of had some dizziness."

"How often?"

"A few times."

"Are you taking anything? No? Then you have to get it checked out."

She sighed. "I know, I know. I'm just so busy, and you know how I hate doctors."

A former cover girl model (a perfect size 8 with "lingerie legs") before she quit and headed to graduate school, Sharon had never been ill, or never admitted she was, working no matter what the hours were, but I couldn't imagine she faced the same pressures at Columbia that she had doing photo shoots years before.

"Sharon, I don't want to worry about you. Please?"

"Okay. I promise to call my doctor. Now, how's Stefan's doing?"

Mollified, I not only told her the story of last night's disastrous fax but took her through Stefan's stuttering career. Each new book had always started off well, with good prepublication reviews in *Booklist*, *Publishers Weekly*, and *Kirkus*. Then there would be enthusiastic reviews in newspapers and magazines, and good crowds at each bookstore where Stefan did a reading, but sales never matched the publisher's or Stefan's expectations. Though in the past I'd shared some of Stefan's disappointments with Sharon, I'd never laid it all out so baldly, and she was surprised.

"That's so strange, Nick. I see his books in store windows, I read the reviews, and I think he must be doing great. I bet this is really hard for you, sweetie. It's bound to change, though," she said wryly, and I smiled. Sharon had always said to me that nothing turned out the way you planned—it was either better or worse, but always different. As advice went, that pretty much covered every crisis you faced.

"And then," I said, "like he needs to be reminded of what he hasn't accomplished, our neighbor across the street's a guy who sold a book about being sterile—for half a million dollars!—and I know it's eating Stefan up—"

"Wait. Didier Charbonneau is your neighbor?"

"How do you know his name?"

"Nick—it's not a name you'd forget. And besides, he's in the new *Vanity Fair*, in Hot Type, the page they do about big forthcoming books. They even had a little picture—he's cute, if you like baldies."

Great. That was definitely a magazine I had to make sure Stefan didn't read this month. But that wouldn't help. Lucille would probably mention it, or someone in town or EAR would. As much as I wanted to, I couldn't filter out everything that might depress Stefan further. He had to bear the shocks, the reminders of his failure, himself, and work through them somehow on his own. I had never been faced with that kind of burden; after all, I was the only living Wharton bibliographer, for whatever that was worth, and so in a very, very small way I was a combination of celebrity and guru for several hundred Wharton scholars and maybe a few hundred more die-hard Wharton fans. The rest of the world, Wharton-wild or not, didn't know I existed and never would.

"Nick?" Sharon was asking. "What's Didier like?"

I was surprised that someone who'd been around the world, met and partied with stars of all kinds, could still be curious about even a very minor celebrity like Didier. Though if the book was made into a film he'd be much more, and even if he only got onto television, Didier could be launched into the media empyrean—for a while. As Robert Hughes acerbically said in his analysis of America, most of us believe that "to be on TV is to be realer than real."

I described him to Sharon as a lot heartier than your average ex–high school English teacher. "And he has a brother named Napoleon who's a fanatic Quebec separatist and who may be sending hate mail to his half-black wife."

"Whose wife? Charbonneau's? Why? Nick, you're making this up."

I assured her I wasn't, giving her as much information about Lucille's hate mail as I had.

"I thought your school started as an agricultural college? What the hell is going on? *Hard Copy* should open up a permanent office there."

She was less obstreperous when I told her that the knife used to kill Jesse Benevento had been found.

"Sweetie, I am really worried about you. I don't think that's such a safe place to be a teacher. You might as well be in the middle of a civil war."

"Well, I'm worried about Angie—you remember the wonderful student who helped me last year?" I explained her disappearance as well as I could, realizing as I did so that I could try talking to Angie's academic adviser, and also Jesse's. His would be easier to track down because he was an EAR major.

Sharon and I chatted some more. But I had papers to grade and didn't want to let more of the morning ooze away.

Grading papers is the hardest challenge of teaching. It's not just staying focused, as some people think, it's continually *refo-cusing*. Each time you pick up a new essay, you're shifting to an intimate dialogue with someone else. Imagine you're at a party speaking intensely to thirty different people in a row, and you not only have to pay absolute attention to what they're saying, afterward you have to make trenchant observations about what they said. And your comments have to be helpful, stimulating, and enlightening, so that the next time you two are "together," the conversation's moved to another level.

That's a lot of work! Yet I loved it, because I knew I was good at it. I was consistently able to keep from crossing the line between constructive criticism and obliterating someone's ego. Sledgehammer comments are the easiest thing in the world to come up with, and even though my students are dedicated to acting cool, no amount of tattoos and piercings could cover up the disappointment and sometimes fury if their writing was being trashed. After all, many of them are still just kids.

I took a short break to call EAR and find out who Jesse's faculty adviser had been, and got the information right away: Carter Savery. But the Criminal Justice secretary I reached refused to help me about Angie because I wasn't a faculty member in that college.

I worked diligently through the morning, with a few breaks to stretch and get some more coffee, and felt a tremendous sense of accomplishment. During one break, I got my lunch ready. I decided to have bruschetta, so I defrosted a loaf of Italian bread and set about making a sun-dried tomato tapenade with capers, fresh basil and oregano, garlic, and red onion that I'd leave to sit out for an hour at room temperature. A perfect reward for hard work, and it was one of Stefan's favorites, so I thought he might like some when he got back from campus. I briefly considered calling him, but if he was away from his office, I didn't want to leave a message with any of the secretaries—today that would feel too impersonal.

When I was done with papers and had eaten my tasty lunch, the doorbell rang. I assumed it was a UPS delivery or the mail carrier bringing up a package that wouldn't fit in the mailbox by the road.

It wasn't either of those. Delaney Kildare stood at the front door, smiling that odd smile of his, looking as lush and shiny as a box of Perugina chocolates.

"I was nearby," he said cheerfully, as if this were news I'd welcome, "and there's something I've been wanting to ask you."

I was too startled to lie and say I was busy, so I waved him inside and followed him into the living room. As soon as I did so, I was furious with myself. I mean, who the hell was I, some royalist British commoner overwhelmed by an expected visit from the Queen Mum?

I asked Delaney if he wanted Perrier, and his yes bought me a little time in the kitchen to settle down. Maybe someday I would stop being unnerved by men who were so handsome and self-assured, but I didn't think it'd be any time soon.

When I brought Delaney his drink, he was standing in the middle of the living room looking as arrogant as those strutting crows I'd seen a few days before, gracefully holding his backpack in one hand. I couldn't help but wonder how my life would have been different if I had his blistering good looks—what doors would have opened for me? What kind of person would I have become?

"Beautiful house," Delaney said quietly as he sat in a chair opposite me, clearly envious. Most graduate students would have made an effort to keep the remark a compliment, an indication that someday they hoped to live like this. But then Delaney Kildare wasn't like any graduate student I'd ever met. His curly dark hair was too well cut, his clothes too expensive. I knew, because Stefan had a lightweight green-and-brown Jhane Barnes sweater and a Kenneth Cole brown suede shirt just like Delaney's, though Stefan never wore them together, or wore such tight black jeans and cowboy boots. I wondered where Delaney's money came from, and why he needed to mow Lucille's lawn.

"Thanks," I said, suddenly alarmed by the suspicion that he might be modeling himself on Stefan. No, that was ridiculous. There weren't that many places in town where you could get good men's clothing, so it wasn't much of a coincidence.

"I heard you might be teaching a course in the mystery novel next year," Delaney said without preamble. "And I'd like to be your TA."

This was surprising—I had hardly mentioned the possibility to anyone. Like all new courses, this one had made its painful pilgrimage from the EAR curriculum committee to departmental approval, passing on and through a host of college- and university-level committees, reaching the goal of all new courses seeking SUM's imprimatur: the Academic Council. That body was supposed to be magisterial and wise but was rumored to be as unstable as the Queen of Hearts shouting, "Off with their heads!" After all this effort, the person who'd originally helped design the course was no longer in the department, which left a hole in next year's schedule and reports of student complaints. I was the only faculty member with any interest in the subject—not to mention some firsthand experience—but of course when Coral Greathouse had raised the possibility with me over the summer, she'd admitted my low status would make it hard to give me a plum. A plum that nobody wanted! That's the kind of place EAR was: bald men arguing over a comb.

But I'd only talked about the possibility of the class with

Coral, Stefan, and— Lucille, I thought. Lucille must have told him.

"It's not definite," I said. "And how did you hear about it?"

Delaney shrugged. "I thought everyone knew."

"And why would I need a teaching assistant? The class won't be that big."

Delaney grinned and leaned forward. "When I talk the class up, you'll be swamped with students." He sounded like an agent assuring his client he could make him a star. Why was he so adamant?

"Okay," I said. "Suppose the class is crowded—there still won't be any money budgeted for a TA."

Delaney leaned back, worldly, confident—all he needed was a glass of eighteen-year-old The Macallan single malt and a fine cigar. "I've already talked to Dean Bullerschmidt about it." I didn't know what to say for a moment, and Delaney went on: "Administrators can always find money if they want to, whatever the budget."

I knew he was right about that, but how had he learned so much about the way SUM functioned? It really bugged me that Delaney presented himself as an insider. And that he'd gone to see the dean before even speaking to me. "Well, whatever you do," I said, producing my trump card, "the dean hates me for creating PR problems for SUM. I don't think he'd give me a dime."

Delaney shook his head. "The dean was favorable. Besides, technically the money would be for the department."

"That's even worse," I said. "He and Coral Greathouse are rivals for the provost's job."

Delaney didn't look at all fazed. Jeez, I thought, how could he be so cocky, so certain? This whole conversation was getting weirder and weirder. But there was more than one piece missing, and I asked Delaney what his interest was in the course.

Sitting there with his meaty thighs spread, he lit up. "I love mysteries!" he said. And if we'd been sitting closer, I'm sure he would have grabbed my shoulders to shake me into understanding the depth of his feeling. "I've been reading them for years. Everything. Agatha Christie—Lawrence Block—Sue Grafton—Martha Grimes—P. D. James. You name a writer. There isn't anyone I haven't read at least one book of."

I wanted to quiz him on something to make sure he wasn't bullshitting me, but couldn't think of a single question. And it seemed churlish to suspect another mystery fan. The reverential way he said those authors' names made it clear how passionate he was about each one.

"Have you thought about how you want to structure the class?" he asked.

I nodded, but the last thing I was going to do was share my indecision with him. I had no idea at all how to organize the class. A survey from Edgar Allan Poe to Georges Simenon, with a few contemporaries thrown in? British vs. American? Focus on sub-genres like locked-room or academic mysteries? Do women and minority detectives so I could work in favorites like Michael Nava, Lucille Kallen, and Walter Mosley?

When I didn't say anything, Delaney sipped his Perrier and nodded as convivially as if I had answered his question. "I'd be happy to prepare a syllabus for you. When I heard about your course, I thought it was something I had to get in on. I was born to teach it."

His brazenness dumbfounded me. "Why?"

"Well, first, I think you'd be great to work for. Work with." He looked down as if a little shy, and I recalled how I'd criticized Detective Valley for being rude to Delaney. I wasn't any better right now. I forced myself to shape up. After all, it was a compliment, wasn't it, that he wanted to be my TA? Even if all this was only about Delaney needing the assistantship and hoping to use it to advance in the department and outpace the other graduate students, it was still flattering, because it would be my course that was his stepping-stone.

"What really attracts you to mysteries?" I asked, trying to be polite, sensing that there was something more going on here and wanting to understand Delaney better.

Delaney's face seemed to flick closed and then open like a camera shutter. "I've never told this to anyone before, but when I was fifteen, though maybe it was earlier than that, I mean it could have been going on a lot earlier—" He stopped and seemed to quiet himself a little. "I noticed that my mother was always a little strange after she'd get certain letters—once a month, less than that. Personal letters, from an address in Florida. I was reading Sherlock Holmes back then, and when she was out shopping one afternoon, I went through her stuff to look for the letters. I really had to dig," he said ruefully, but with admiration for his adolescent self. "She'd folded them up and slipped them inside old pairs of shoes at the back of her closet." Delaney's eyes were staring off to the side somewhere. "I guess I was made to be a detective." He shifted in his chair, spreading his legs wide and resting his hands on his thighs. I tried not to stare at the keystone of his arch.

It was a creepy story, but I was hooked. "What was in the letters?"

"She was actually still married to another man in Florida, not my father, and he had tracked her down and wanted her to come back. He wasn't threatening her or anything. They were very tender letters. Love letters." Delaney fell appropriately silent.

I didn't know if I was shocked by the story itself or by his telling it to me.

"What did you do?"

"I told my father. I had to. We were too close for me to hide it. He freaked out, and she disappeared. I never saw her again. She may even have been married *more* than twice—that's what the letters implied."

"Wow."

Delaney smiled almost demurely, as if not wanting to make any dramatic claims for himself or his past.

"Listen, Delaney, I don't know if I'm going to get permission to do the course, and everything else is up in the air."

Delaney drew his legs together and folded his hands in his lap. "I really need to TA more than one class next year. I've got a lot of debt, and my father can't loan me any more money. Since I'm a new graduate student in EAR, I won't be allowed to teach more than one class a semester unless there's a special arrangement—and you'd have to say yes first. I'm really good in the classroom."

I stood up and headed for the door. Delaney followed reluctantly, slinging his backpack over a suede-draped shoulder. Then he stopped and asked me to show him the rest of the house. "It's so beautiful," he said, grinning rather seductively.

Opening the door, I said, "I can't promise you anything about the class." Frankly, I didn't want a TA, and if I were forced to have one, Delaney would not be my first choice.

Delaney nodded soberly as if he'd picked up what I was thinking. On his way out, he threw off, "I'd work my butt off to help you make the course a success. And it would be a chance for you to shine. It can't be easy always being in Stefan's shadow."

I closed the door very carefully, marveling at the guy's chutzpah, and just as quickly thinking that he knew what he wanted and went right for it. Was that so wrong? Then the last thing he'd said sank in, and I felt insulted and stung. Putting Delaney's glass in the dishwasher, I felt profoundly uncomfortable, as prickly as if I were having some kind of allergic reaction. Who the hell did he think he was, bringing up Stefan that way?

I wandered back into the living room as if searching for traces of Delaney's visit that I could eliminate, but of course there weren't any. And suddenly the warm bright room was very alien and I was as vulnerable as the gladiator in an arena waiting for the emperor's thumb to go up or down.

Stefan's shadow.

Delaney didn't even know me, know us. So how could he have picked up on something I had barely let myself think about over these past years?

I sunk onto the couch, suddenly weighted down by all the times I'd felt eclipsed by Stefan. No, not by him, but by his career, his reputation, such as it was. We'd always supported and encouraged each other, but the differences between us as professionals were enormous. I remembered all the conferences, the writer's meetings, the bookstores, where if people asked who I was and what I did, they seldom paid attention to the answer. It was something Stefan and I often joked about, but was painful nevertheless. And yet I'd buried that pain, ignored it. Because Stefan's suffering over his career—and over his past—was so enormous it had become the chronically sick child we nursed and worried about. It's not that Stefan didn't take my Wharton bibliography or my teaching seriously, and it's not that I myself slighted my own work. But despite my declining status at EAR, despite the murders I'd been involved in, my own life crises had not really dominated our lives the way Stefan's career anxieties had.

Perhaps that was because my status at EAR had been low from the start. Stefan was the writer-in-residence with the good salary, the attention, the large corner office, the easy schedule, the perks—in academia, his sales figures didn't count. And me, I was just a lowly assistant professor teaching the most despised course possible: writing.

I'm not sure how long I sat there mulling all this over, not making any progress, just spinning inside, slowly. Finally, sick of not getting anywhere, I decided this would be a perfect time to work out at the Club—it wouldn't be crowded, so I could get in and out easily, and the exercise would help me unhook and clear my head. I grabbed my always-packed gym bag from the bedroom closet, left Stefan a message on the kitchen table, locked the front door, and drove off.

Situated on an imposing ten-acre tract of land near campus, the Club was like a mall on several levels devoted to health, boasting an enormous weight room stocked with the newest equipment, two basketball courts, two pools, ranks of racquetball and tennis courts, and legions of aerobic exercise machines. It was plush, lavish, imposing, and the owners claimed it was one of the largest health clubs in the country. If you loathed exercise, I guess it was a fair approximation of hell.

I was easily intimidated there by the hard-core lifters and aerobics junkies, but few of them were around midafternoon, and that had become my favorite time to go, alone. Stefan and I had tried working out together, but it wasn't ever a success. Stefan was a great spotter, but he was in so much better shape than I was, and I often felt him holding himself back so as not to embarrass me. That may have been a loving thing to do—and I did appreciate it—but it wasn't very sensible for him or comfortable for me.

Didier and Stefan were well matched and could tear it up together, goading each other on like the cocky teenagers I remembered from gym class in high school. I'd never been a jock, but I'd had some natural ability in the pool that I'd never bothered to develop. All that seemed immeasurably distant to me now, with middle age creeping up and mirrors turning admonitory.

Stefan was different; always handsome, he'd become better looking as he aged and was definitely fitter than he'd ever been, working out with a doggedness that sent off as much heat as his concentration when he was writing. He wasn't arrogant at the gym in his tight little shorts, deep-cut tank tops, and sexy high-top Otomix workout shoes, just supremely comfortable in his body. I admired that, and wanted to feel at least a modicum of his ease. I was possibly en route. Last summer I'd finally crossed some kind of internal Rubicon and found myself working the Club into my schedule two, then three times a week. I ran, did the treadmill or Stairmaster and some weights, or took a spinning class, mostly when the place wasn't crowded and I didn't have to concentrate so hard on shutting everything out.

The gleaming locker room was almost deserted that Wednesday afternoon, as were the halls leading to the vast weight room at the heart of the Club, every dumbbell and Cybex machine offering as magical an entrance to the world of fitness as the cake in *Alice in Wonderland* that read "Eat Me."

I nodded at one or two people working out who I ran into now and then, but didn't have to say anything to them because they had headphones on. I headed upstairs to do my half hour of cardio and was soon back down in the over-brightly lit weight room, moving from the pec deck to a flat bench for some chest presses and then some whole-body shoulder work with light dumbbells. I liked the squatting involved, it made the lifting less boring.

Back at the locker room, pairs and groups of high school students were drifting in, slouching along in the oversize banjee boy clothes that their upper-middle-class parents must have hated. I felt I'd gotten in a decent workout, but as always, I was even gladder to be finished. The large bright shower room of gray and pale blue tiles was completely empty except for a guy five stalls away, on the other side.

His back was to me, and I couldn't help but stare. His broad-shouldered, thin-waisted, muscular body made me think of a satyr. Dark hair just this side of ugly profusion curled from his ankles up his lean thighs and then stopped as if unable to climb his round hard rear, which seemed even more naked topping those hirsute legs. When he shifted position slightly, rinsing shampoo out of his lathered-up hair, I realized that it was Delaney, and I turned my back to him, embarrassed.

But that passed as I soaped up some more and wondered about this. Did Delaney have a membership at the Club? How could he afford it as a grad student? I considered the possibilities: Maybe he'd bought a one-day pass. Maybe he had a guest membership someone else had given him, or maybe he somehow had enough money. But that didn't square with his needing to mow Lucille and Didier's lawn. And hadn't he just told me he needed to TA for me for the extra money?

Then something else occurred to me. What if Delaney was here because I was? What if he'd been following me, was showering for me? I couldn't imagine he was actually trying to seduce me, but it wasn't any less strange than his having come to my house to sell himself as a teaching assistant for a class I wasn't even sure I was going to teach. Was I paranoid, or was it legitimately creepy?

Out of the corner of my eye I saw someone pass on the way back into the locker room, toweling his hair dry. Delaney. I don't know if he saw me and was pretending not to, but I saw a lot more of his lean and amazing body. From listening to Stefan and Didier talk about diet and vascularity, I knew that Delaney's body fat was well below average for even a young man—that explained the sharp definition of his muscles, and how visible his veins were.

And I knew that given his equipment, if graduate school didn't work out, Delaney could always take up a career in erotic films. Unlike Marky Mark in *Boogie Nights*, Delaney didn't need a prosthesis.

There was no sign of him when I was back in the locker room after ten minutes in the sauna.

I MADE A quick run to campus to meet with Jesse's academic adviser, Carter Savery, who didn't like me—not that I found him at all interesting either. He was one of EAR's blandest professors, though I assumed that behind that round, blank face lurked the typical smoldering bitterness of all the ex-Rhetoric faculty. Like them he'd been teaching composition for several decades and resented the trap the university had set for him. Originally, Rhetoric faculty were supposed to get the chance to teach their specialties in other departments, but nobody wanted them, and so they faced a lifetime of explaining comma splices and the passive voice. Savery was an expert in Byron, I think, but had never once taught a class in the Romantics.

His office was stacked high with student folders, and every bookcase was crammed with writing textbooks, which may have been one of the unrecorded plagues God visited on pharaoh. Carter looked up from a pile of papers he was grading and nodded as if I were the last brick in a wall of misery the day had built around him.

"Jesse Benevento," he said flatly when I sat down on a barely padded, stiff-backed chair.

"Was he doing well academically?"

"Well enough. Some 3.5s, mostly 3.0s." At that I smiled, because students at SUM had come to expect a 3.0 just for attendance. It was a meaningless grade now.

Staring at me without blinking, Carter asked, "What's your interest?"

"He was a student of mine last year, and I was there near the bridge when he died."

"And—?"

"Isn't that enough?"

Carter gave a mild snort, and I kept myself from snapping at him. He would be reviewing my tenure folder—it didn't make any sense antagonizing him further, since he clearly thought I had all the significance of a manual typewriter.

"Do you know if he was in any trouble?"

Carter said, "You're investigating again. Like last year. That's not your job. We have people paid to do that at SUM. You're not one of them."

"Will you at least tell me what classes he was taking this semester?"

Sighing, Carter turned to his computer, pulled up a file, and scanned for Jesse's name. "He was catching up. He dropped a few last year, some personal trouble. Oh, it was his mother—she killed herself, didn't she? Anyway, lots of required courses. Shakespeare, Chaucer, Milton, and a Forms of Literature class. Heavy reading load, and lots of papers to write."

Nothing French, I thought.

I thanked Carter and left, wondering if any of this information was important. I was familiar with the standard anthology used in all the Forms of Literature courses, so why had Jesse been reading that French novel if it wasn't on any of his syllabi? If he had spare time, wouldn't he be reading something religious?

Only a few feet down the hall, I saw Detective Valley headed my way, lips tight. "Find what you were looking for?" he asked coolly, sailing on by.

When I got home, there was something wonderful frying in the kitchen, and Bach's triumphant double violin concerto was filling the air. "You're back!" Stefan greeted me with an enormous hug that knocked the breath out of me and made me drop my gym bag. "Class was great—my students are great. I picked up a bottle of the Joubert Julienas and I'm cooking a terrific dinner, so you'd better be hungry. Oh, I found the tapenade—thanks—it was great. What made you decide to make that today?"

I followed Stefan into the kitchen, wondering at his effusiveness. By the stove, a cookbook stood open in a plastic protective stand, and every counter was covered with various ingredients in large and small glass bowls.

I sniffed. "Lamb?"

He turned from the cutting board slung across the sink, where he was carefully dicing something. "Bingo. That deep-dish lamb pie."

I groaned in anticipation. This was an amazing meal done in a quiche pan, with a crust of russet potatoes and celery root simmered in milk. The lamb, browned in olive oil, minced onion, and garlic, was mixed with minced acorn squash, minced apricots, cinnamon, saffron, cumin, chicken broth, mint leaves, coriander, cayenne pepper, ginger, lemon rind, and slivered almonds. It was a superb blend of flavors and textures, but it took a lot of prep time, and we'd always made it together before.

Satisfied, humming, Stefan turned back to his work, expertly wielding the knife, and said, "I decided I don't care if my publishing career's going down in flames. And don't try to make me feel good," he warned. "I know exactly how bad Peter's news is.

Sales figures are never secret, and being dropped is much worse than declining sales. Everyone in publishing will know what happened. Everyone," he repeated, sounding almost buoyant.

He stopped, wiped his hands on the dish towel hanging over his shoulder, and shook his head. "So what the hell, what can I do? I can't make anything happen that hasn't happened already. After all these years. That's Peter's job, he's the agent. I have to cut loose, and—" He paused.

I couldn't resist. "And?"

Now he turned and leaned back against the counter, eyes closed. "I'm not sure." Then he rolled his shoulders as if shrugging off a coat. "But I am sure about dinner—it's going to be fucking amazing! That's all that matters. Now. Tonight."

I thought of how Virginia Woolf's Mrs. Dalloway says it's "dangerous to live for only one day." This almost manic bounciness was very unlike Stefan. Usually he brooded for days after a fax like last night's, and when he did finally dig himself out after a bombing raid of bad news, he was never energetic but always washed out, weary. And if the mood continued longer, he'd find his battered childhood copy of *The Three Musketeers* and plunge into seventeenth-century derring-do. He read it with the voluptuous satisfaction other people might feel gorging themselves with Twinkies when they're depressed, and the book always worked to cheer him up, or at least take his mind off what had made him miserable.

"How about some wine?" I asked, since he'd already started. And why shouldn't he? What was so wrong about getting bombed after such awful news? It was certainly better and more refreshing than lurking around the house like a one-man Eugene O'Neill play.

Stefan poured me a glass of the 1996 Domaine Joubert Julienas, currently our favorite Beaujolais, an intense wine with good body and depth. "I have another bottle," he said, moving to the stove. "And if this is denial, I want more." He stirred the lamb, checking the timer, then rejoined me at the table, and once we'd mixed and passed the potatoes and celery root through a food mill, and ladled that across the top so it could bake, we proceeded to get drunk and very silly.

Which I suppose is how we slipped back to recalling the time we visited Vaughan Michael, a writer friend of Stefan's who lived in Los Angeles. Vaughan was a clammy-handed, anonymous-looking little novelist who spoke in a weighty undertone that gave authority to even casual remarks, the kind of man that women could project anything onto because he was so unrevealing. And apparently they did, since he'd been through four divorces. The last time we were in L.A., he was living with a porno star named Carynne who had come to one of his readings and moved in that same night. I couldn't imagine a porno star reading one of his long, complex novels—like Dostoevsky without the fun parts—but Vaughan was so proud of Carynne that porn magazines in which she was featured sprouted like baskets of orchids everywhere you looked in his sepulchral black-and-gold living room: garish, hypnotic.

From the kitchen where he was making us drinks before we went out to dinner, Vaughan had recommended we "take a look," and like dutiful guests leafing through pictures from a baby shower where we didn't know a single person, we did.

"I was dying to say something!" I roared, remembering my shock, amazement, and of course, fascination. "Like: Carynne's very limber. Or: She must have a way with animals."

"Thank God you didn't—he would have put us in his next book—he has a bad habit of doing that, and with no real disguise. I would have been Steven, probably, and you would have been Dick."

"Dick?"

We both laughed. Dinner with Vaughan afterward had been uncomfortable for me because I couldn't stop imagining him as some lost traveler in a Shangri-la of extravagantly bountiful flesh. He was black-and-white, and Carynne was so Technicolor.

When the lamb pie was done, and we'd finished it under the broiler, Stefan and I feasted on it at the kitchen table, completely abandoned to the taste and aroma, as if we'd been smoking dope and every sensation was sublimely intense.

After dinner, we stumbled into the living room and dug out the cassette of that quintessential 1930s romantic comedy: *Midnight* with Claudette Colbert, Don Ameche, John Barrymore, Mary Astor, Francis Lederer, Hedda Hopper, and Rex O'Malley. It was a sentimental hit with us in part because it was set in Paris, but also for the witty script cowritten by Billy Wilder, with one of the best throwaway lines ever. After diffident Rex O'Malley remarks that he was always swallowing things as a child, he says offhandedly, "My parents were afraid to leave me alone in a room with an armchair."

Stefan had to stop the VCR because when he heard that line again he was bent over with helpless laughter, but I laughed with some wariness, sobered a little by watching him abandon himself like some 1929 stockbroker flinging himself out a window. God knows he needed to laugh, to forget himself, but I couldn't help thinking of everything we weren't talking about: his future, my good news, the peculiar conversation with Delaney, Sharon's dizzy spells, and of course yet another murder in our otherwise idyllic world.

But all that dissipated when we put the movie away and Stefan turned to me, quoting Sigourney Weaver's immortal line from *Ghostbusters*: "Take me now, subcreature."

How could I say no?

When I arrived at the EAR office late that next morning, Thursday, there was a notice in my mailbox, on that hideous "goldenrod" paper, announcing that Coral Greathouse had called an emergency meeting for the afternoon to deal with the crisis over Jesse Benevento's death. Had something new been discovered? I hoped so. I didn't like the thought of his murder going unsolved, or feeling that there was nothing I could do about it.

People around me groused about the meeting, perusing the memo with distaste. EAR was made up of neurotics and misfits who did not take well to meetings. These were all people who had minimal supervision in how they ran their classes or interacted with colleagues, and calling a meeting was like asking resentful ranchers and miners out west to submit to federal efforts at environmental protection. And like some of those westerners, they read such attempts as a conspiracy to take away their rights.

But then I'd also blame that distaste for meetings at least in part on the horrible room we had available for the purpose. Of course, *horrible* is a relative term in a moldy, bat-infested, sepulchral-halled building with cracked walls and sagging floors covered in cracked and peeling linoleum. Built of sandstone almost 150 years ago, Parker Hall looked perpetually on the verge of collapse, a kind of reminder of the architectural ooze the campus sprang from.

Our conference room had been updated in the 1960s perhaps, so there was no dusty high ceiling, just crumbling ceiling tiles, rat-in-a-maze lighting, and tiny bolted-down chairs with barely functional attached desks that forced you to face forward. Turning around or even sideways, you risked performing ritual suicide.

The prospect of being trapped in that room with my griping colleagues weighed me down even though I taught my classes well and the students seemed to be having fun. We were working in small groups that day, with me circulating among them as students critiqued each other's papers, and each class went smoothly. But as I got ready for the departmental meeting, everything I'd held at bay came rushing back, and I felt even more reluctant to head downstairs to the conference room. Walking to the stairs, I passed Harry Benevento and was surprised when he smiled and nodded at me. He didn't look nearly as crushed and emptied out as he had just a week ago.

Downstairs on the second floor, I could hear a devilish buzz emanating from the conference room, and as I headed across the gloomy hall, Juno Dromgoole swooped down on me, shoving her arm in mine. "Sit with me!" she said. "Do!" Had I been adopted?

"Where else?" I asked.

Juno grinned. Today she was in black Manolo Blahniks, a tight black leather mini, black fishnet stockings, black silk blouse, leopard-print scarf flowing down her bosom, and an even denser cloud of perfume than usual.

"Opium?" I asked.

138 | LEV RAPHAEL

"Albert Sung, darling." With a moue she said, "Opium's hopelessly outdated. You should spend some more time around the right sort of woman."

The room was packed, and crackled with grumbling and hostility, as if Coral's summons had pulled everyone away from work on stunning, life-changing manuscripts. The words drifting my way were "waste of time" and "What crisis?" Juno and I found seats close to the back and by the door, where she somehow crossed her elegant legs and managed to look comfortable in her confining seat.

I'd chatted with Stefan during the day, briefly, and he was skipping the meeting. As the writer-in-residence he got away with doing that, and I was envious. He was mildly hungover, and headed home for a nap before dinner. A nap struck me as a wonderful idea.

"Isn't this thrilling?" Juno said spitefully, rolling her *r*.

People around us glanced sidelong at her as if she were talking in a movie theater and they wanted to shush her but felt intimidated.

"That's all you do here is have one ridiculous meeting after another. What a bunch of wankers."

Whether she meant EAR or SUM as a whole, I couldn't help but agree, though I tried not to smile. We seemed addicted to meetings at SUM, addicted to the appearance of "meaningful deliberation" about something. And it had reached monstrous proportions in the college housing EAR. Our sullen Dean Bullerschmidt was fond of breakfast meetings and had imposed this tyranny on his staff. I couldn't imagine anything drearier than haggling over administrative policy at seven in the morning—at Denny's! At least Coral Greathouse had set a decent time for us to meet, and we didn't have to cope with half-cooked home fries.

Coral swept in just then, her expressionless face even blanker than usual, as if she were fighting to extirpate even the smallest hint of emotion. After her came a tall, thin man and a small woman so round that, standing side by side off behind Coral, they made a number 10. In contrast to her impassiveness, they were beaming so heartily they seemed clownish.

The faculty members settled into a hostile silence before Coral even cleared her throat. Backed by the mystery couple, she nodded her appreciation.

"Thank you for being here. We've all been shocked by the death of one of our students. Because Jesse Benevento was an English major, I know that what happened to him is affecting students and faculty alike. That's why I've invited Douglas and Anka Nelson from the Counseling Center to talk to us today about grief and loss."

There was an unpleasant stirring in the room, like when the sand ripples in a horror movie just before some creature lunges up and attacks the hero. I didn't have much faith in anyone at the Counseling Center, whose budget had been cut year after year, sending the better staffers into private practice, or so the gossip went.

Coral sat in a chair at the front, and the Nelsons took center stage with what I thought was an incongruous delight, as if they were amateur lounge singers finally getting their chance to show us their stuff. But I guess any expression of theirs would be strange, since they were so badly matched even though they both seemed in their late fifties: hulking Douglas over six feet, stoop-shouldered, and crepe-faced, Anka round and red and tiny-eyed.

He began. "I'm Douglas—this is Anka, and we are so genuinely pleased to be here."

His wife beamed and nodded. "That's so very true. We can't

commend your chair enough for her foresight." Together they faced Coral and quietly clapped their hands in a smarmy little ovation.

"Christ almighty," Juno sighed. Lucille Mochtar slipped into the room just then and took a spot standing at the back. She nodded at me.

"Because—" Douglas said, his voice rising, "because as professionals we know all about grief and loss after a trauma—"

"How about the grief of listening to a turd?" Juno rumbled, making no attempt at all to keep her voice down.

"—and understand that you all may feel utterly out of your depth faced with such a situation, since none of you would be professionally equipped to handle it."

"I wish I were equipped with a fucking Uzi," Juno rumbled, and I think the Nelsons may have heard her, because their expression changed just briefly before settling back into inanity. Around us, people were stretching and shifting in their miserable little chair-desks, or trying to.

"And before we get under way, we both want to assure you that we will come to any class of yours or any office whenever we're needed, day or night."

"Great," Juno grumbled. "Counselors on Wheels."

Then, as if they were circus jugglers tossing pins back and forth, they went through several provisos, each starting up at the exact moment when the other stopped.

"So, before we begin, some words of wisdom. Remember," Douglas said. "Be right here every moment."

"—and listen with your heart," Anka picked up.

"Don't blast people with blame—"

"—and be open to change—"

"What you say here is just about you, so keep other people's stories confidential."

"No consequences!" Anka cried out, with her hands locked in sincerity. "No getting even for what someone says!"

Douglas smiled. "Forgive, and give love."

They both sighed together at that, obviously pleased with the sentiment and with their timing. I would not have been surprised if they'd launched into "Getting to Know You."

"Now, studies show—" Anka began, and I confess I tuned out, since nothing makes me sleepier than quotations from social science research—for me it's the intellectual equivalent of curling. I did hear her talking about copycat suicides on university campuses, but I don't know why she brought it up. Jesse's death was a murder—was she saying people would kill themselves in grief?

"What is he *on* about?" Juno muttered, when Douglas took over and started juggling "signs of stress and depression." He looked her way, but clearly wasn't ready to quell or question her. Perhaps he hadn't quite heard what she said.

But Lucille was closer, and from behind us she interrupted: "Juno, could you be quiet, please?" And in the now-silent room, everyone turned. Lucille was looking right at Juno with no hostility on her face, just neutral inquiry. "You're very distracting, and I'd like to hear what the experts have to say about all this so that I can help my students."

I'm not sure what people expected. Maybe for Juno to get livid, leap from her chair-desk, and attack Lucille, but she did none of those. Sweetly, she said, "Coddle them, you mean."

Anka spoke up. "I see there are some very strong feelings in the room."

Juno rolled her eyes, and with all that extravagant hair, it was as dramatic as some colorful bird's mating ritual.

Lucille moved forward. "I don't think we're taking this seriously enough."

Coral Greathouse sighed, clearly relieved to be publicly supported.

"It's an emergency," Lucille pressed. "And we should do everything possible. Why not expand our office hours to make ourselves more available to students to help them through their anxiety?"

That produced moderate pandemonium. Les Peterman, the rangy Americanist who seemed more interested in hoops than teaching, said, "Nonsense! Waste of time!" Martin Wardell shouted, "Not in a million years!" I knew that he never returned student papers promptly, so more office hours would expose him to added student hassling.

Little Iris Bell banged her fist down. "Absolutely not!" she cried. "What about us? We're overworked and stressed out, who's concerned with our needs?" Around the room, she was seconded by moaned complaints—like whiny middle schoolers shocked by a pop quiz.

"More office hours?" Carter Savery shot. "Nobody comes to my office as it is."

"Good, good," Douglas said, nodded enthusiastically, as if this was group therapy. "Feel your feelings." But our chair didn't look at all pleased—in fact, she was turning red.

Juno extricated herself from her chair, thrust her chin and bosom up, and said, "Life is tough, life can be horrible. But I for one refuse to become a touchy-feely bleeding heart. I'm a professor, not Oprah Winfrey, and I don't intend to counsel any student, expand my office hours, or go on a departmental retreat, bang drums, and cry about my childhood so that everyone else will think they know me! I'm not interested in making friends and being close. That's not what I was hired to do!"

Calls of "Bravo" filled the air amid outraged questions: "What retreat? Who's going on a retreat? Where?"

Juno stalked from the room, heels tattooing the linoleum floor. Of course, she could say whatever was on her mind without fear of consequences. She was only a visiting professor and leaving at the semester's end. But her remarks had kindled the easily ignitable spirit of EAR, and her exit was like a cannon shot signaling a rebellion. With almost everyone up and jabbering and the Nelsons vainly trying to hold the floor and promote mutual understanding and tolerance, Coral suddenly shouted, "Okay— enough—this meeting is over!" She hustled the Nelsons from the room as if she were a Secret Service agent protecting her president.

I half expected dancing and a rousing chorus of "Ding dong, the witch is dead!" Instead, my suddenly deflated colleagues drained out of the room, while I wondered how this contretemps would play in the campus newspaper. EAR had a bad enough reputation for contentiousness as it was—this would make us even more of a joke. And would Coral Greathouse blame me somehow for sitting next to Juno and not keeping her quiet? Could she possibly believe that anyone could silence Juno?

But hadn't she been right to call in counselors? Wasn't the simmering hostility a form of denial? One of our students had been killed, and here we were bitching and moaning instead of facing what it could mean to us as professors, and maybe more intimately, as human beings.

Lost in all this dismal speculation, I didn't notice Iris Bell and Carter Savery creep up on me, but there they were, as large as life—in Oscar Wilde's pungent phrase—and not half as natural. "What did you think of the meeting?" Iris asked, eyes pinning me to my seat.

Like *Mad about You*'s Paul facing Jamie, I knew my answer wouldn't even come close, but I popped out with, "It was short?"

Iris and Carter exchanged a look I couldn't interpret, then

nodded and left me alone there. If the question was a test, it seemed clear that I'd failed it. Just as I realized—now that the tumult was over—that I'd failed Lucille. I should have said something to defend her, even though I wasn't convinced adding office hours was necessary. The meeting had quickly turned into a sort of referendum on her, or at least it felt that way—and what had I done?

I hurried up to our office to apologize to Lucille, passing through empty halls and empty stairs. Like schoolchildren let out at the end of the day, the professors of E, of A, and of R had scattered as quickly as possible.

I was disappointed in myself. After only a few years in this department, I'd already been ground down by the cynicism and smoldering rage usually masked as boredom. My first year, if Lucille were my friend, I'd have been conscious of the need to support her from the very beginning, not hashing out afterward what I *should* have done.

But some of that was also due to the rushing events of the last few days, which had left me much less capable of focusing— and hell, after teaching all day, what I needed most was a chance to unwind, not a barrel plunge over the falls of academic discord.

She was gone when I got there. Of course. Embarrassed, attacked, who would stay around? I closed the door and sat at my battered old desk feeling drained, even beginning to wonder if I'd been too cocky taking on the Norton Critical Edition. Well, once that bleak question tumbled out into the open, others followed, and I sat there giving myself the third degree. Who'd I think I was, imagining I could pick up a project originally given to a senior Wharton scholar? And even if I could do it, I'd probably miss the due date on the contract, and the whole thing would be a waste of time—I'd never get tenure based on it anyway.

I had not only checked into Heartbreak Hotel, I'd taken the Misery Suite. I was soon musing over Stefan's disastrous news and worrying again about Sharon's dizzy spells, and even poor Angie. What had happened to her? Should I find out if anyone had filed a missing persons report on her?

Hell, even my office seemed proof of what a pathetic trap my life had become. No amount of well-framed Matisse posters could camouflage the grotesquely high ceiling, flaking gray-green paint, and ominous exposed pipes. It was a cold, decrepit, abandoned kind of room—evidence of how little SUM cared about our department.

When someone knocked on the door, I recalled Dorothy Parker's bleak question at such times: "What fresh hell is this?" But I didn't say it.

"Professor Hoffman? It's Bill Malatesta?"

"Door's open," I called, and Bill entered, looking unusually irate, though stylish as ever in black.

"Can I sit down?" he said, halfway into the comfortable chair I have for my students. I nodded. Lanky, handsome, athletic, Bill was generally cool and communicative, so I was startled to see that he actually seemed to be struggling with himself to frame whatever it is he had to say to me. When he'd knocked, I'd felt aggrieved to be interrupted, but now I felt sorry for him, and thankful, as always, that I was no longer that young, whatever the problem. So what if he was big and lean and had a fairly promising future as EAR's star grad student? He was still only a grad student, a degree-driven serf.

"I'm really pissed off," Bill said, face uncharacteristically taut, and that's when I remembered he'd mentioned wanting to talk to me about another graduate student. God—how long ago was that? "It's Delaney Kildare." He said the name venomously, the way you'd pronounce a curse, and I wouldn't have been surprised if he'd bitten his thumb or performed some other small ritual of disgust.

"Delaney's been nominated for a Distinguished Teacher Award in the college."

"What's wrong with that?" I asked, though the news surprised me.

"How'd that happen if he just got into the department?"

I shrugged and suggested that maybe Delaney was a good teacher—wasn't that the obvious reason faculty and graduate assistants got nominated for the university-wide honor?

"No way. There are rumors he has pull—everybody says so. He's tight with the dean."

I didn't say that Stefan had told me the yearly award, which went to one professor and one graduate student in every college, was highly political and the subject of endless intrigue. Delaney had practically bragged about being able to get Dean Bullerschmidt to do what he wanted, so I figured the rumors about the award had been started by Delaney, whether there was anything to them or not. But if it was more than just braggadocio, and if the dean became provost, then Delaney would have an extremely powerful friend at SUM.

"Bill—what's the problem? So Delaney's nominated—and so he even gets the award, though that's not likely, given that he's a first-year TA for us. The competition from other departments in the college is bound to be more experienced. And why do you care? You've already won Best Teacher. And you're finishing up your degree this year." I knew that Bill had garnered seven interviews at MLA and was currently working through a set of callbacks, which made his job prospects look very good.

"Because he's a fraud," Bill blurted out. "He's a plagiarist!"

Like a gunshot, that word seemed to impose a profound silence on the room and both of us. Despite all the problems and blind spots, the rampant grade inflation and lack of real concern for students' educational and personal welfare, EAR and the university took plagiarism as seriously as a charge of witchcraft in old Salem, and if proven, it was almost as damning. Undergraduates would automatically flunk the course in which they'd plagiarized, with no hope of appeal, and graduates were kicked out of their degree programs.

I waited for Bill to present his evidence, and somewhat belligerently, he dished out some farrago about Delaney stealing an idea for part of a paper in their critical theory seminar. The longer and more angrily he spoke, the more he convinced me that he didn't have any real proof, and I began to speculate whether this series of grievances and charges had some personal core.

Bill's tirade wound down, and suddenly shamefaced, spent, he said, "I don't like the way Delaney acts with my wife. The way he looks at Betty, and talks to her. It's too intimate."

It sounded oddly childish—"Mom, make Suzie stop staring at me!"—and I didn't have the faintest idea how to respond. Besides, I knew from experience that Bill and Betty didn't always get along, and that Bill himself wasn't exactly the most truthful person. I thought of asking him if he'd seen *Chasing Amy*, where the lead tried to work out a conflict by proposing he, his bisexual girlfriend, and his best friend sleep together.

"It's not just her," Bill muttered. "We share an office downstairs." TAs were jammed five, six, or more to an office in the hot, airless, stinking basement that was definitely steerage class in our departmental *Titanic*. "And I see what he does with the girls in his classes."

"Are you saying he's sexually harassing his students? With witnesses?"

"Gimme a break. He's not that stupid. He just sits there and grins, his legs spread out like he's some fucking Antonio Sabato advertising Calvin Klein." He was right about that. I'd certainly seen Delaney spread his legs as if laying out a buffet; but then Bill was not averse to showing off his body either. Bill had been sounding peevish. But there was no mistaking his outrage when he growled, "He better not try anything, or he's dead meat."

"Bill, come on—" I tried to think of something calming to say but felt utterly out of my depth.

He shook his head and shoulders like someone in a bar furiously twisting away from friends who were trying to hold him back from a fight. Then he rose without saying anything and strode out of my office, leaving the door open as if afraid that he might slam it so hard it'd crack.

Wow. Bill—handsome, accomplished, successful—was jealous of Delaney. It struck me as sad and funny that our department's star graduate student was so unnerved. But then graduate students lived in such a strange world; could anything seem certain to them? After all, most of the professors privately called graduate assistants "grad asses," which said it all: They were seen as fools and beasts of burden. And trying to finish a dissertation was an exercise in sadomasochism. Most professors seemed to be unconsciously repeating a pattern. In hassling their advisees, they weren't just enjoying their power; they seemed to be deliberately punishing innocence, creativity, and enthusiasm that hadn't been blunted yet. Like old whores in a Victorian porn novel maliciously disabusing a kidnapped young girl of her illusions. Occasionally professors fought against this exploitation and harassment, but these were in the minority, and they could never change departments and a university that drowned them in a tide of bitterness and scorn.

I sighed. Some days campus was a toxic place to be, and I found myself wishing for the clarity and clear skies of northern New Mexico, anyplace untouched by all this ugliness. We'd vacationed in Santa Fe a few times, and I badly missed that dreamy ocher-and-gold town with its looming hills and secret-looking homes. I always felt so calm there. Stefan would of course remind me that New Mexico might look peaceful to me, but I was romanticizing it. There was plenty of hostility to go around, he'd note, ever the accurate historian, what with Mexican Americans still resenting the war of 1848 that had chopped Mexico in half, and descendants of Spanish colonists feeling cheated out of the land they'd been granted by the Spanish crown; not to mention the native peoples who were there before everyone else. And all of them suspicious of the wealthy Californians who were turning the place into a high-priced curio.

I headed home, making a quick stop at Borders to buy a copy of that Benjamin Constant novel, curious to see what had interested Jesse, and tossed it into my briefcase in the car. When I pulled into the driveway, someone opposite in front of Lucille's house darted down the block, not running but walking quickly away. By the time I got out of my car, he was gone. He hadn't looked like any of our neighbors' adult children (most of our neighbors were retired), and he certainly didn't seem to have been strolling—so why the sudden rush?

Shrugging it off, I crossed the street to Lucille's and Didier's house, I wanted to touch base with her and apologize for not defending her. And maybe ask if she had told Delaney about my Mystery course. Because I didn't know if I could pull it off even if I did get to teach it; I felt very protective of the course and didn't want it discussed.

Didier yanked opened the door. Dressed in his regulation white T-shirt and chinos, he grinned and clapped me on the back. "Come on in! I'm done for the day. Man, have I been ripping up the keyboard! How about a Scotch?"

After the baroque EAR meeting, Scotch sounded great,

though a dip in Didier's and Lucille's hot tub out back would have been better, followed by massage therapy and a three-day coma. I followed Didier into the living room, where he waved me to a seat on one of the cold black couches and fussed at a glass bar cart that looked new. So did the glasses—Baccarat, no doubt—that he filled with two fingers of russet-orange Scotch and several splashes of water.

"You'll love this," he chortled, handing me my glass. "Fifty percent alcohol, so it needs more water. Auchentoshan. Thirty-one years old. Smooth as hell." He hovered in front of me, waiting, as proud as if he'd aged the stuff himself in its casks.

I tasted. Oh, yes, it was incredibly smooth. It should be: I'd read somewhere that it cost over $150 a bottle and was very hard to get because there was so little of it made.

Didier plunked down opposite me. Looking at him smack his lips over the Scotch, I thought of Mel Brooks's line, "It's good to be king." And once again I found myself helplessly wishing for Stefan to have even half the success that had rained down on Didier's life all at once. Publicity, money, and a chance to earn much more of both.

"If you're looking for Lucille," he said, "she's out. She and Delaney went to the mall to catch a movie." He nodded cheerfully. "They love movies. Delaney wants to be a screenwriter someday."

"Oh." Was that what Delaney had said, or had Lucille told that to Didier? And in either case, why, and was it true?

Didier breathed in over his glass. "Smell that," he commanded. "Vanilla, honey, butterscotch, lilies. And violets. Definitely violets."

I tried to make my nose as sensitive as possible, but I responded much better to wines than to Scotch, and more important, all I could think of right then was Lucille and Delaney sitting next to each other in a darkened theater. Particularly after what Bill Malatesta had just told me. As if aware of my discomfort, Didier said, "I'm so busy working on revising my book right now, I'm glad she has someone to do things with. They go down to Ann Arbor for concerts, they drive to Lake Michigan. It's great!" He chuckled, as pleased as a young parent reporting his child had friends at play group.

Though I was trying to hide my surprise, I must have looked dubious, because Didier leaned back companionably as if he were about to tell me a travel anecdote. "You know, Nick, Lucille and I are very different. She's quieter, and I make more noise, but she's the one who needs the excitement. She always has. And she's always had her own life—that's how things work around here."

He gave me a long, steady, blue-eyed look over the rim of his glass. Did it mean anything? Was I supposed to be filling in some blank? Was he actually telling me that Lucille and Delaney were having an affair—and that was okay with him?

Or was he just garrulous after a good day of work, and merely letting go, getting a little high, a little loose and careless with what he said? Maybe I was making too much of this—after all, I thought, as we sipped our Scotch, he hadn't seemed to be confiding in me with the expectation that I'd share something private about me and Stefan. I certainly didn't want to—I didn't think I knew either Lucille or Didier that well, which might have accounted for my surprise and mild discomfort.

"Marriage is tricky," Didier mused. "You do what you have to do, eh?"

I nodded dimly, uncertain where he was going, and trying to think of a way to head off any further palaver about his or anyone else's intimacies. Right now, I wanted to unwind. I wasn't ready to talk about relationships, real or theoretical.

Didier gave me another one of his wolfish grins, and I realized that he wasn't making excuses; he was proud of himself, of Lucille, of whatever sort of private life they had built for themselves, and he wanted me to know it. I raised my glass in a silent toast, and he chortled. Clearly I had read him right, and he took my gesture as approval.

"It's pretty remarkable that I'm writing a book after all these years," he said. "Lucille was the one in publishing, I just taught English. But sometimes she'd show me a manuscript, and I'd think, Shit, I could do that a hell of a lot better. And when we started going to that fertility clinic—" Eyes slightly unfocused, he paused a moment. "Well, I used to think I was pretty romantic, but there's nothing romantic about trying to rush crosstown in New York traffic with a bottle of your own sperm when you've got your schedules all messed up."

"You could have put a ribbon around it," I said. Didier laughed and rose to pour himself more Scotch. I signaled that I could use a refill, and Didier complied. My face was comfortably flushed, and every hard edge in my body, every knot, felt like it had been smoothed away.

"When you finish this book, will you—?"

"Write another? Hell no! I want to milk this book for everything I can. I want to spend the rest of my life doing interviews and talk shows and panels and speeches and columns. Who needs another book if this one's a hit?" He closed his eyes. "The only other thing would be to run for office."

I told him a little about the horror-show EAR meeting, and he urged me to write a roman à clef about the department. "Make it really nasty—kill 'em all."

"Didier, I'm a bibliographer. I describe, I don't invent."

"Then get Stefan to write it."

I frowned, and Didier asked if Stefan was having trouble with his writing.

"No, it's his publisher." I refused to say anything more.

"They're all fuckers," Didier said. "And boy, am I glad Lucille isn't in that cesspool anymore, though I tell you, she sure helped my agent negotiate a great deal."

I suppose if I had sold a book for a half a million dollars, I'd be dropping leaflets from the Goodyear blimp, but since I hadn't, I found Didier's blatant self-promotion a little hard to bear at times. "It's time for dinner," I said, getting up and heading somewhat unsteadily for the door.

"No!" Didier protested. "More Scotch!" But he couldn't persuade me, so he said he'd have Lucille call me when she got back.

Making my way across the street, I wondered if he was really untroubled by Lucille's friendship with Delaney, or if he'd raised it to see what I felt. And was he drinking tonight because he was pleased about his book, or trying to blur any speculations about Lucille?

When Stefan opened the door, he said, "You're smashed."

I admitted that he might be right, then sailed right past him to the kitchen for a large glass of water. Michiganapolis has some of the purest tap water in the country, though I only know the claim and not the reasons behind it. Stefan followed me.

I guzzled down a glass or two, realizing I'd left my briefcase in the car, but as I sunk into a chair, I decided it didn't matter. Damned if I'd get any work done tonight.

"How was the meeting?" Stefan asked, his soft tone indicating he was sorry he'd been less than welcoming just before. I had never figured out why, but Stefan didn't like the rare times I smoked something by myself or got drunk without him; he acted hurt, as if it were somehow directed against him. But it never was. From time to time I liked withdrawing from the world, and as an extrovert, I couldn't just retreat within myself the way Stefan did so readily. I needed help.

Thirty-one-year-old Scotch was certainly quite efficacious.

"How was the meeting?" I echoed. "Indescribable. No—wait! That's a cop-out. It was a cross between"—I fumbled for the right choice—"the *Oresteia* and *Scream 2*, only not as heart-warming. What smells so good?"

Stefan smiled. "I ordered pizza—I didn't feel like cooking tonight."

Well, the pizza was soon out of the oven, where he'd been keeping it warm, and onto the table, where I didn't even bother with a plate. I gobbled as if I were stoned and had the munchies. Stefan looked on, alternately disapproving and amused, though whether it was my lack of table manners or my recounting between bites of what went on at the meeting, I couldn't tell.

Then I told him about my talk with Didier, and the Scotch, but Auchentoshan didn't interest Stefan at all. "Lucille went to a movie with her graduate advisee?"

His shock triggered instant opposition in me. "Okay, Cotton Mather, what's so bad about that? It's a movie, not Las Vegas."

"He mows her lawn, he takes her on dates—"

"Who said it was a date?" I dropped a piece of crust into the box. "You're exaggerating."

"It's one thing to be friendly, but—"

"But what?" I shot. And I could tell he knew I was thinking about our recent and painful past.

Stefan looked away. "You got a message before. From Delaney. I heard your machine. The dean's approved money for him to TA the mystery course." Now he rounded on me, looking hurt. "You never even said you'd decided you wanted to go ahead."

"I didn't! I told Delaney not to do anything—not to talk to Bullerschmidt." But even as I said it, I marveled at the speed with which Delaney had gotten funding approved. What was his secret?

"When did all this happen?"

"There isn't any all this. He came over yesterday to ask if he—"

Stefan was glaring at me now. "Delaney came over here? Why didn't you tell me?"

I was beginning to feel cross-examined, and I shoved the pizza box away, hating myself for having enjoyed something he ordered. "Because there wasn't time, and because you're not a fucking independent counsel."

"I don't like Delaney, and I don't want you working with him. Ever."

"You can't say that!" I pounded a fist on the table. It hurt, but the noise was very satisfying and spurred me to raise my voice. "You're nuts!"

Stefan didn't reply, but the superior, parental look on his face infuriated me. I sprang up from my chair and, banging against the table, accidentally knocked the box upside down onto the floor, splattering sauce and cheese from the remaining pieces.

Ignoring the mess, I said, "This course could be a chance to create my own identity in the department, to branch out, and you can't stand that any graduate students would find me interesting enough to work with. You can't always be the one getting attention!"

The shock and anger sweeping across his face pleased me, and I headed for my study, slammed the door, and dialed Sharon's number. She was in, and I quietly raved at her for a while. When I finished my outpouring, she said, "Was the pizza any good?"

I cracked up. "No, not around here."

"I'll have to bring you a CARE package next time I come west." She made it sound like it was hard to get a reservation on a Conestoga wagon.

"That would be great, even without the pizza. Michigan

really isn't dangerous anymore—they have the mountain lions under control." We chatted about the possibility of her visiting, about work, and about New York's Mayor Giuliani (who she'd just met at a charity function), and Sharon brought up having made a doctor's appointment, without my nagging her. I felt relieved by that news, and by her assurance that she hadn't had any more dizzy spells. Now she wondered if she had simply not eaten enough those days, a holdover from her years as a model when she never ate well and had skated close to anorexia.

"Sweetie, do you think it's the shock of seeing Jesse's body that's getting to you, eating at you, and maybe that's why you exploded? You have to shout at somebody, and it might as well be Stefan, since it's safe. The best thing about marriage is it gives you someone to get mad at."

I was silent for a while, thinking it over, and then I agreed. "That's not everything, but it's a lot. I feel like I should be finding out what happened, but I don't know what to do. Angie's the only student I know who was friendly with Jesse, and she's gone. I'm down the hall from his father—he's chair of the History Department—but I don't think he's going to want to talk to me right now about who might have wanted to kill his son."

"Why not?"

I explained Jesse's behavior in my class last year, and that I thought it might have prejudiced Benevento against me, if Jesse had told him.

"If," she said.

"Sure—but all he has to do is say something terrible to Coral Greathouse, if he hasn't already. I'm sure the department chairs all talk to each other."

"When they go bowling?" she asked wryly. "Or on a trip to the local outlet mall to buy new overalls?"

I laughed. "It's not that bad, Sharon. We do have indoor plumbing!"

"You know, Nick, I wonder if wanting to look for an answer might not just be a distraction now, something to keep you from feeling bad about the murder, and Stefan's career trouble, and even tenure."

How could I disagree when she was so sensible?

"And, sweetie," Sharon continued. "What if the murder was a mistake? The bridge was total chaos, you said, so what if the wrong person got stabbed?"

"Wow. Or a thrill killing, or some kind of crazy initiation," I said slowly, finding myself in tune with her doubts.

"Most murders don't get solved anyway," Sharon pointed out.

"But this isn't Dallas or L. A. or Chicago—this is a quiet college town. At least it's supposed to be."

We gradually worked back to my argument with Stefan. Sharon gently urged me to apologize, and not go to bed angry— "Sweetie, you'll hate it!"—but I felt too proud to let go of my indignation. "He was so bossy," I griped. "What's the matter with him?" My unspoken complaint was, "*He* should apologize," but that was too pouty and juvenile to say.

"I think it's cute. You said this student is handsome, sexy, right? So Stefan's jealous—that's really a tribute to you."

"I thought tributes were supposed to feel better. And come with a banquet and speeches."

"Nick, you'll really feel better if you apologize."

Sharon knew me very well, and she was, as always, sensible and right, like a salesgirl gently warning a customer away from a completely unsuitable dress. Outrage and grousing would not fit me as well as conciliation. Yet I resisted her advice, and I could tell she was sad when I hung up.

I stayed in my study, checking e-mail, reading, waiting to

hear Stefan go up to bed. As always when he was mad, he played Poulenc CDs for some strange reason, and from the living room I heard the *Aubade*, the Concerto for Two Pianos, the *Valse Musette*, and more, until I was sick of all that inexhaustible French wit. It jarred me, seemed as obnoxious as the charm someone in *Brideshead Revisited* decries as "the great English blight."

When the music stopped and I heard Stefan go upstairs to bed, I slipped from my study to check the kitchen. The kitchen floor was spotless, of course. Leaving any kind of mess was beyond Stefan, who had trouble settling down to a meal without making a stab at cleaning up a little. I often joked about his neatness, treasuring it as a lovable quirk, and I felt a sudden access of affection. If Stefan had been standing there, I would have grinned and held out my arms to him. As Ian McEwan wrote, "Love generates its own reserves."

But Stefan was sound asleep when I got to bed, and it felt very awkward slipping under the covers next to him, just as Sharon had predicted.

THE FIRST FEW moments Friday morning, now a full week after Jesse was killed, were even more uncomfortable. When I staggered, squinting, toward the bathroom, Stefan was emerging, and we avoided each other's eyes, abashed by the unusual hostility that had broken out between us the night before. But each moment that prolonged the tension worried me. How long would this estrangement last? Would we have to do couples counseling?

In the kitchen we set out plates, bowls, and glasses, filled everything just like on a normal day of breakfasting together, but silently, as if in parody of some monastic order. We ate without talking, but read separate sections of the *New York Times*, having moved about the kitchen careful to avoid bumping into each other, as if even the slightest physical contact would reignite last night's brawl.

When the doorbell unaccountably rang, I said, "I'll get it," though not right at Stefan, and it was a relief for me to leave the table.

Lucille was there, her face pained and drawn. I was about to apologize to her for not having been supportive at the EAR meeting when she put a finger to my lips and pointed across the street to her house. I saw to my amazement that her living room window bore a jagged slashing hole, which seemed even larger when someone driving by slowed down, clearly startled, to stare at it.

"There's been an escalation," she said. "I guess whoever it was got tired of the Post Office. This time the message was a brick."

9

I grabbed Lucille and dragged her inside, slamming the door as if we were being pursued. That might not be how she felt, but I did. I was the one in sudden flight from the unwelcome rush of images that broken window had triggered. I was flooded with TV visions from my childhood of water hoses turned on civil rights marchers, firebombed churches, maddened German shepherds let loose on demonstrators. It all blurred together as Lucille and I hugged and I felt enveloped by the warmth of her thick arms and the patchouli in her dreadlocks.

"Hey," she said quietly, and I don't know what it meant, but it seemed right for the moment.

When I opened my eyes, Stefan was there, gazing at the two of us with such compassion—even though he couldn't know what exactly had happened—that I said, "I'm sorry." I meant for last night, and I'm sure he understood, because he nodded and said, "Me, too. We'll talk later."

Catching some of this, Lucille broke away, though keeping her hands firmly at my waist. Looking from me to Stefan, she asked, "What's going on?"

Stefan shook his head. "That's my line."

I pointed across the street and explained a little to Stefan while leading Lucille into the living room, happy to be able to shelter her at a time like this. "Coffee? Ginseng tea?" I didn't know what else to say at that moment, and I almost felt as if I were in an English mystery where every crisis was greeted with a nice cuppa.

Stefan was at the living room window, looking out. Wasn't it just a few days ago we'd been staring at Delaney's boldly displayed body in the sunshine? And now there was this.

"Tea," Lucille murmured, settling into the chair closest to the fireplace, even though the doors were closed. Maybe the idea of a fire was all she needed. "Thanks," she said. Stefan nodded and headed for the kitchen.

"Where's Didier?" I asked her.

"Sleeping."

"You didn't wake him up?"

Lucille smiled a little. "He was soused last night—I didn't have the heart to wake him up. He could sleep till noon." Her smile broadened with affection.

"But you called the police, didn't you? Aren't they on the way?"

She looked away. "Not yet."

I realized that, like victims of any kind of assault, she was ashamed, unwilling to call more attention to herself, dreading the exposure. I didn't press her, because I knew how vulnerable she must be feeling.

"I didn't hear anything. I must have been asleep when it happened," she said, almost as if speaking to herself. "At least that's what I assume. It was there in the morning when I came downstairs to make myself breakfast. In the living room." She pursed her lips, breathed in. "Not a big mess. The brick didn't hit anything. It was just lying there in a halo of broken glass. It was scratched with a message: 'Don't forget.' I have no idea what that means." She smiled a little. "The brick's pretty clear, I guess. Who needs more? Nothing like this has ever happened to me—not in New York, not in California. I've been lucky."

Of course, since our house's layout was identical to Lucille and Didier's, it wasn't just easy for me to imagine the same violence done on our home; it was hard to feel it hadn't happened to us, too.

And there was more. I hate it when people say, "I know how you feel," but once in graduate school someone ripped the mezuzah off the doorpost of my dorm room. I'd been stunned, angry, frightened, wondering for days who had done it, and why, and what was next. Was I being followed, studied for a personal assault? I did not report the incident at school or tell my parents. I hadn't wanted to upset them, and I was afraid that any notoriety in the campus newspaper would strip me of privacy and make me more of a target. Haltingly, I told Lucille about that time, and she nodded firmly all the way through my recital.

Stefan brought Lucille her tea and a coaster and handed me a fresh cup of coffee, ruffling my hair. That one gesture was enough to make me feel the connection between us was truly open again. We sat side by side on the couch, witnessing Lucille's pain as she described for us her shock and surprise. I knew it was a moment that she'd relive as many times as she described it to others, and this telling was just the first.

At one point Stefan interrupted. "When I was in first grade, I heard two girls in the playground talking about Jewish babies being thrown up into the air and bayoneted by Germans. They must have gotten that from their parents or TV—it was around the time of the Eichmann trial, I think. And when I asked my parents about it, they were devastated." He paused, and I wondered if he would go on and tell Lucille everything. This was something we hadn't discussed with her or Didier yet. "My parents were Holocaust survivors, but they tried to protect me."

"What did they do?" Lucille asked so quietly I almost missed what she said. But Stefan heard, or heard a question.

"They bulldozed their past and pretended they weren't Jewish. They used coming to America as a chance to start over, completely. And this was like a bomb."

Lucille shook her head. "I hear you," she said.

"It got worse," Stefan went on, eyes half shut. "Some kids in my class had a club. It was called the No-Jew Club. When my parents found out—"

He fell silent, too moved to speak. I took his hand but he pulled it away, not harshly, but as if he felt too bruised suddenly to bear anyone touching him. I understood. Lucille and I said nothing, and I'm not sure how long the silence went on, but Stefan was the one to break it.

"Have you called the police?" he asked Lucille, and I winced at his unintentional blunder and his strange choice of transition.

Eyes down, Lucille just shook her head. I whispered in his ear, "Don't push her."

Stefan went on, gathering steam. "It looks bad, and you're assuming it's connected to the postcards, right? But it might not be about you, Lucille. It could be drunken frat boys wandering through town." Was he trying to make her feel better? "Thursday night's as big a party night as Friday now. Or middle schoolers on a sleepover—you always hear about them sneaking out in the middle of the night. You know how they can toilet-paper trees or egg cars? It's happened before around here."

I wasn't sure if Stefan really believed any of those possibilities, or felt he had to at least mention them so we could move beyond. But he was right. The major crime in Michiganapolis neighborhoods near SUM was vandalism, and the closer your house to the bars downtown, the more likely it was to be a target. We'd been lucky on our street until now.

"What about Napoleon, Didier's brother?" I asked. "Is Didier right that you're paranoid, or is Napoleon really a radical separatist?"

"Maybe some of both," Lucille said.

"And even if Napoleon wanted to go to war with the Canadian government, why would he target you?"

Lucille rolled her eyes. "Why not? The only time we ever talked about the issue, he had to be dragged away from the table, screaming. '*Pitoune*' and '*christ d'épais*' were some of the nicer things he said. I won't translate, but trust me, they're nasty."

"What happened?"

"I got his goat by telling him I was in favor of an independent Quebec as long as it granted independence to its native peoples in the north." She shrugged.

"I saw someone walk by your house yesterday."

Lucille nodded. "Okay, and?"

"He was walking, until I drove up and parked, and then he sped up." Stefan and Lucille were both staring at me, confused. I couldn't blame them. "Now I think that he looked like the picture you showed me of Napoleon, in your kitchen."

Lucille considered that. "Are you sure?"

"I didn't see him clearly," I confessed. "But it could have been. Maybe he was casing your house."

"Maybe it was just somebody taking a walk," Stefan said reasonably.

"But I'd never seen him before."

"Come on, you don't know all our neighbors." He was right. Our lives were so centered on our jobs at the university that we really hadn't made an effort to get to know people on our street or neighboring streets. Sometimes I regretted that; sometimes I thought that if Polly was a presage, we were better off not making anyone else's acquaintance around here.

Smiling, Lucille said, "You know the best ones, anyway."

I laughed and took advantage of her good mood to apologize for my cowardice at the EAR meeting, but I'd hardly said more than a few words when she cut me off, unaccountably energetic. "Nick! It was a free-for-all. Who'd have the presence of mind to defend anyone? I don't blame you, not a bit." She was even smiling now. "I just feel sorry for those poor counselors. They meant well."

I recalled Samuel Butler's withering comment in *The Way of All Flesh:* "If it were not such a terrible thing to say about a person, I should say that she meant well." I didn't share it with her.

"I'm not very popular in EAR," Lucille brought out, evidently musing about the meeting's hostility. "Not that I thought I would be. Individual people smile at me in the hallways, they chat in the coffee room, but boy, when you get them all together for a meeting—"

"—it's a lynch mob?" I asked.

Lucille frowned. "I'm no Clarence Thomas."

"You know," Stefan said carefully, "if it's not kids or rowdy students who broke your window, and given what happened yesterday, I still think Juno Dromgoole may be out to get you, Lucille. She's volatile."

"Volatile, yes," I agreed. "Projectile, no. Cowards do things like throw bricks through windows and send hate mail. Cowards, and people who are chronically miserable and pent up. Juno is anything but pent up. Carter Savery or Iris Bell is more likely to boil over like this, to do something sneaky and vicious. Then Lucille gets hired at a great salary—it all adds up."

Stefan wasn't convinced.

"And they were hanging around when Lucille got her mail at the department—I bet they've been following her," I said.

"I'm right here," Lucille said. "No need for third person."

"Following *you*," I corrected. "Sorry."

"Or even Coral Greathouse," I said. "She was there, too, and who'd suspect the department chair of sending hate mail to her own faculty member?"

Lucille and Stefan both stared at me. "She's the chair, right, and she was strongly behind hiring you when she thought you were Islamic, right? And now you're not, and she must feel like an idiot. She's probably been getting flak from the faculty—you can bet on that. Nobody ever talks to a chairman except to complain."

"Coral?" Stefan asked. "*Coral?*"

I replied, "Why not? What do we know about her? She's grim and quiet most of the time, and she's dying to be provost, and here we have a screwed-up hiring in the department, which she probably got the blame for. What if that's killed her chances of being povost?"

"Coral's been very nice to me," Lucille said. "She had me and Didier over to dinner."

"Perfect cover," I said. "I know it's perverse, but that's the way things operate at this university. It's what Wharton called 'taking life without the effusion of blood.' That way you avoid scandal."

"A good reason not to go public," Lucille pointed out. "It'll get twisted somehow and turned against me."

"I don't believe any of that about Coral," Stefan said to me. "What about your students?" he asked Lucille, and I remembered our having talked about students who might hold a grudge against her. "They're becoming more polemical all the time—I can see how it might get out of hand."

Lucille put her mug down. "Hold on," she said angrily. "I may not be a great role model, but I'm not doing anything reckless that could get anyone in trouble. Students always mouth off inappropriately about something. It's not me or the course material or even what they think they believe. At their age, when they cause trouble in class it's family-of-origin crap. I'm an authority figure, a perfect stand-in for Mom or Dad. They're just college students, they can't help it. Look at that stupid pamphlet that comes out every year on campus, the one where they get to grade professors anonymously. Most of it's garbage."

I winced, since the student-funded report "Does Your Prof Make the Grade?" had consistently given me and Stefan high marks as teachers.

Lucille leaned forward, seized by an insight. "That pamphlet is exactly the same. It's hate mail—anonymous and nasty and just stupid."

"Then you *know* it's a student who's tormenting you?"

Lucille acted as if I hadn't said anything. "Students hassling faculty—it's a psychodrama," she insisted. "You can't take it seriously."

"What if there's more psycho than drama?" I asked. "Remember Jesse Benevento? Somebody *killed* him. It started for you with letters—then a brick. What if it's a firebomb next time?"

Impatient, Lucille waved the possibility away. "You're being overdramatic."

"No, overdramatic is saying I was abducted by aliens who injected me with hormones that are turning me into Newt Gingrich. That's overdramatic. I'm just being reasonable, and the police will see it the same way."

"They won't see anything," Lucille said a bit smugly.

Stefan asked her what she meant.

Lucille glared at us defiantly, chin raised. "I haven't called the police, and I'm not going to. There's nothing to show them."

"What about the window?" I asked.

"What about it? A broken window doesn't mean anything. I cleaned up the broken glass, I threw out the brick, and I called a glazier."

"That's destroying evidence!"

Stefan shushed me. "Lucille's not a criminal."

"Thank you," she said, sounding as prim as I'd ever heard her.

I couldn't believe that Stefan was siding with her. "You think it's right to hide what happened?"

"It's not your decision," Stefan chided me, gently.

"But what if this is connected to Jesse Benevento?" I asked. "What if there's a killer after you, Lucille?"

"Please! Did Jesse get hate mail?" Lucille sipped her tea, looking disdainful, but her expression changed after a moment, and I guessed that she was opening to the unlikely possibility that what had happened to her was connected to Jesse's murder.

"We don't know," Stefan brought out. "But—" He hesitated. "I can't see how even if he did get hate mail, this would be the same, really. A stabbing's different from a hate crime—"

"Are you serious?" I shot. "Stabbing sounds like hatred to me."

"Well, Jesse wasn't in any of my classes," Lucille said. "He had nothing to do with me. In fact, the only connection I can see between us is you, Nick."

"What!"

"You're my officemate, and Jesse was your student."

"That's just coincidence," I protested.

"It's enough connection for that psycho you were talking about before." Now Lucille looked almost cocky. Whether she was serious or not, she had a point.

"I wish we knew more about Jesse's death," Stefan said.

I offered to call the county medical examiner, Margaret Case. "She might tell me something that's not in the papers." I explained to Lucille that Case's son had taken one of my classes and raved about it, so his mother had in the past been willing to talk to me where otherwise she'd probably just say "no comment."

Lucille and Stefan followed me into the kitchen, and they sat at the table while I called Case. Her secretary remembered my name from last year's trouble and put me right through.

"Dr. Hoffman?" Margaret Case asked with a chuckle, and I pictured her in the office filled with Michigan memorabilia, smiling ironically. She was a dark blond version of Janet Reno, just as large and imposing, but not at all dowdily dressed and definitely not plain. "Murder at SUM, and it took you a week to call? I'm surprised."

I was ashamed at not having called her earlier. "He was a student of mine. Last year. Can you tell me anything about his death?"

"You know, Angie Sandoval called me with the same question."

"What? Angie called you? Where was she? When did she call?"

Angie had dated Case's son and was still close to the ME. Dr. Case paused, perhaps surprised by my emotion. "I don't know. I assumed she was on campus. Why?"

"Angie disappeared right after Jesse was killed, she fled the scene, but she told me she'd been thinking he was in trouble."

"He's not in trouble anymore," the ME said dryly. "Are you sure Angie's disappeared? Have you tried her parents in Houghton?"

I was embarrassed to admit that I hadn't. Margaret Case

asked me to hold a moment while she looked for the number. When she came back on the line, she apologized. "It's at home. I'll have to get it to you." Then she said that there had been no defense wounds on Jesse's body, which meant that he'd probably been stabbed unawares. The fatal wound was to his heart—the head wound was minor, from the fall. "His killer was shorter than he was, since he or she struck up at Jesse rather than straight in or down. The angle was pretty sharp. Aren't you glad you called? Now you know that the murderer wasn't tall. That should narrow it down a lot for you, right? Was he a favorite student?"

"No, I was just nearby when the riot broke out and he was killed," I explained.

Dr. Case sighed. "Have you ever considered a quieter career—like skydiving?"

When I hung up and passed on what little information I'd gotten from Dr. Case, Stefan and Lucille both looked as disappointed as I felt. Nothing I'd learned made much of a difference, did it?

Lucille thanked us with a grin "for the tea and sympathy," and we both saw her out.

With the door closed, it was Stefan's turn to do the hugging. I wondered how it was possible to be so angry at someone you loved and say such cruel half-truths, the anger shooting out like a flashlight's beam in the dark, distorting whatever it lit up. Clumsily, arm in arm, we headed back to the kitchen to clean up the breakfast dishes and talk our way back home. I told him how sorry I was for what I'd said yesterday, and that I'd barely believed it, convinced by the heat of my own frustration and rage.

"I guess I was jealous," Stefan admitted slowly.

I nodded, making a grave show of listening when I wanted to whoop. I had been so painfully jealous of one of Stefan's ex-lovers a couple of years back that this moment felt like a weird vindication, a wonderful triumph. He was admitting that he was human, as flawed as I was.

"Not jealous of you getting noticed," he explained. "I supported your work on the bibliography completely, didn't I? You know that—even though it was endless."

I nodded. Working on a bibliography is like one of those long medieval sieges that starts with triumphal marches, flapping banners, and deceptive predictions of victory but devolves into boredom, misery, and disease. Ultimately, the city may surrender—but what a price has been paid.

"What I don't like is the idea of Delaney hanging around you, helping you teach a course."

Of course I knew exactly where he'd been headed, and I had to laugh. "Oh, yeah, all that grading of student papers is guaranteed to work just like in Dante when that couple reads poetry together. Can you think of anything less romantic than grading papers?" And yet even as I said it, I felt a certain tingling in my face at the picture of sitting side by side with Delaney in my office, peering down at someone's term paper, aware of each other's heat.

Stefan frowned. "I'm serious, Nick. I don't trust him. He's coming on too strong, from what you've told me—showing up here, badgering you about the course, arranging things for you."

"You make him sound like a stalker."

Stefan relaxed. "Well, maybe I'm exaggerating." He struggled a little, either uncertain of what he had to say, or uncomfortable saying it. "Nick, he's just so young."

I felt suddenly as old as a doddering reprobate in a Balzac novel. Was that what was going on? Was it as simple and timeless a story as that? Beautiful young man using his looks to get ahead? I flushed, remembering Delaney's perfect body in the showers and his earlier request for a home tour.

"So young," Stefan repeated. "And so—"

"Yup," I agreed. "Delaney is very *so*. But how could you worry about me sleeping with anyone? You know how disorganized I can be about anything but my classes and Edith Wharton. I could never pull off an affair."

Stefan crumpled up his dish towel and pitched it at my head. I caught it, holding it with mock tenderness. "I'll always treasure this as a memento of our talk. Now, if you want to hear about studying someone, let me tell you what Delaney was wearing when he came by." I described the outfit.

Stefan looked as if he'd just stepped into something horrid. "I hope it's just a coincidence."

"I don't know. He might have been trying to work on me subconsciously by dressing like you."

"Whose subconscious are you talking about? Because you picked it up right away, didn't you?" He thought a moment. "If he's got money for nice clothes, why does he need to teach an extra class?"

We puzzled that one over and got nowhere, so I told Stefan to sit down. "I have good news. Van Deegan Jones wants me to do his Norton Critical Edition of *Summer*."

Stefan looked stunned. "When? He called you?"

I explained all the details.

"It's a book," he said, navigating slowly through his surprise as if he were a fogbound ship. "It's a book you can do before they make the tenure decision. It's relatively fast, it's prestigious, and you get some money. Unbelievable! When do you start?"

"I already have, in my head." Once again I felt glad to have a deeply involving project that could help blur the recurring image of that bridge and that blood. And this was something I had control over, something that was in no way mysterious and made me feel anything but helpless.

He understood—every book worked away inside you once you'd opened yourself up to it: That was the true beginning. You didn't have to touch a keyboard, open a file, or pick up a pen to be writing. I knew that from watching Stefan.

"We have to celebrate!" Stefan announced, glowing.

I demurred. "Let's wait till it's done."

"The world could end before that."

"That's a cheerful thought."

Stefan cocked his head at me. "Nick—when have you ever not wanted to celebrate some good news?"

"When people are being murdered, when our friend and neighbor's getting hate mail and bricks through her window. Life seems too uncertain right now."

"All the more reason to celebrate. Remember what they say in *The Purple Rose of Cairo*? 'Life's too short to be worrying about life.' "

"Okay, okay, okay. What do you want to do to celebrate?"

Stefan rose and stood looming over me. "I have some long-range plans, and something more immediate in mind."

I grinned. "You are talking my language."

We adjourned to the bedroom, and like Tina Turner singing "Proud Mary," we did the first part nice and the second part rough, rolling on the river.

AFTER A SECOND shower of the morning, during which I lazily soaped his back, Stefan headed for campus, and I headed downstairs to my study to comb through my extensive Wharton library to help myself get more focused on the Norton book. Working on *Summer* would be fun, because this little-known novel of Wharton's was so sensuous and beautifully written, a study of shame and social conventions in rural New England. It pleased me to think that my edition of this book would make it more accessible and enjoyable.

I put on my favorite music-to-concentrate-by on the portable CD player, Mendelssohn's Octet, and took out my Wharton bibliography. As usual, I marveled at how so many years of work and so much money on photocopying, phone calls, and faxing could have produced only this heavy but otherwise unremarkable-looking volume. As my mother had helpfully pointed out, it didn't even have any photographs of Wharton. It was altogether too plain a book for her. After all, my father was the publisher of elite art volumes like the kind Rizzoli does, and so even though my book, since it was destined for libraries, was quite expensive it was to them the bibliographic equivalent of Mission-style furniture compared to the Louis Seize furniture they preferred. Sometimes I wondered if my very chic parents even read the bibliography's plainness, its sturdy dull binding and unimaginative marshaling of facts, as some kind of indictment of their taste, a rebellion in print.

"Well," my mother had concluded in her fluent but formal English, "I'm sure it will be very helpful." She could have been talking about a new kind of plunger, but despite her dim endorsement, my bibliography *had* proven quite useful. Even Stefan was surprised by the fine reviews that drifted in from academic journals during the two years after it was published, and more impressively, the fulsome fan mail from Wharton scholars and students.

Seated in my favorite chair in the study, I let the bibliography slip to the floor, unwinding for the first time in days, glad to feel so deeply connected to Stefan again, sated, hopeful. And curious. I couldn't help thinking about what Margaret Case had said. Someone stabbed up into Jesse's heart—a small wound.

I knew from my students that knives were nothing out of the ordinary on campus, and not just pocketknives or Swiss army knives, but switchblades, butterfly knives, hunting knives. My students had told me lots of stories about friends or roommates who collected knives, showed them off, and occasionally threatened to use them.

The killer wasn't tall, Dr. Case had surmised. Or as tall as Jesse. Well, that fit lots of people I knew, including Stefan, Lucille, Didier—

I wondered if the assault on Lucille and Didier's house was perhaps something quite different from anything Stefan or I had suggested. Maybe it was a warning. Maybe Lucille didn't realize that she knew something about Jesse Benevento's death—but someone else did.

And that made the situation more dangerous for her, especially if she wasn't getting the message. Which is why I wanted to reach for the phone and the phone book to call Detective Valley. I told myself that even though he apparently hadn't done anything about Lucille's hate mail, he should know about this latest incident on the chance that it might be connected. Stefan had told me it wasn't any of my business to intervene now, but how can you let a friend be threatened and not try to help?

I hesitated. Was I really trying to help Lucille, or was I just trying to make up for my own unwillingness years before to go public with what had happened to me in grad school? I didn't know the answer, so I couldn't make the call. Still, I felt guilty doing nothing. Determined to unhook from all this, I took up my bibliography and a notepad and slipped off into a very familiar land, making notes with ease and excitement. I worked for about an hour, and then the doorbell rang.

Going to answer it, I hoped it wasn't more bad news about Lucille, or even Detective Valley and some Michiganapolis policeman come to interrogate. I got my wish, sort of. Delaney stood at our door, asking, "Can I come in?"

I was so flummoxed by his showing up two days in a row that I couldn't think up an excuse to say no, so I let him in. We may have been enjoying an early spring, with crocuses up by our door and the forsythia out back budding out, but right then I wished we were having a late-winter storm. One of those blinding, cruel ones that makes everyone stay home. That way people wouldn't even think of dropping by anywhere.

I did not offer him water today, and he sat down without invitation, wearing the same clothes as yesterday and looking, I realized now, kind of rattled.

"Are you okay?"

"Not a great night last night. Someone stole my backpack in the library," he said. "Can you believe it?" He glanced around the room almost as if it might be stashed there. This was the first time I'd truly seen Delaney at a loss, the smooth surface more than ruffled. "My wallet wasn't in it, but everything else important was. I feel incomplete without it."

"Like when a woman loses her purse?"

He peered at me to see if I was joking, but I wasn't, and he nodded. "Like that, yeah. Then I went to this EAR grad student party, and somebody got really drunk and took a swing at me."

"Why?"

"It was Bill Malatesta. Does he need a reason? He thinks he's king of the grad students, but I won't kowtow to him." Somehow I felt I wasn't getting the whole story from him, but before I could probe any further or ask why he was here, Delaney said, "Have you decided about the mystery class yet?"

This felt so incredibly pushy I wanted to snap at him, but I held back; it would have been inappropriate, and I didn't want to treat a graduate student as the other professors in EAR did.

Matter-of-factly, Delaney said, "Stefan probably doesn't want you to teach it."

I was stung by his insight and burst out with, "How do you know?" almost as if he had been spying on our previous conversation. It gave me the creeps.

He shrugged, and the movement of those powerful shoulders was a strange mix of intimidating and attractive. "Stefan is a wonderful literary writer, but writers like that don't tend to think much of mysteries as a genre."

This was so on-target I couldn't disagree, yet not doing so seemed vaguely disloyal to Stefan, especially after our various reunions of the morning. And the way Delaney had dropped in and what he was saying seemed intrusive and peculiar. How had I gotten myself into this situation? Maybe I needed to hire a doorman.

"You know, Delaney, I'm flattered that you want to TA the mystery course for me, and that's great that you were able to get Dean Bullerschmidt to say yes to funding it, but—"

"I know you're up for tenure next year," he interrupted. "You're worried, aren't you?"

This was obvious enough, but so personal that I couldn't respond.

"And I bet Stefan's not in the best frame of mind either."

That shocked me into speech. "What are you talking about?"

He gave me a smooth shrug. "His sales figures can't be great when trade book sales keep going down, and the audience for literary fiction is disappearing."

He'd been studying us, I thought, feeling chilled.

"Actually," I lied, "Stefan has gotten some offers from other schools, and—" I gave my version of a Gallic shrug, implying we could be gone next year. I was inventing this, but I felt agitated enough about tenure and Delaney's pushiness to make it sound real, and I exulted inside to see that Delaney was completely taken in.

His shoulders slumped, and he said, "Oh. I didn't know that." Even if he did have influence with the dean, there wasn't anything he could do—

Oh shit, I thought. What had I gotten myself into? If the dean heard about this and decided he would try to preempt Stefan's move, I'd have a lot of red-faced explaining to do. But it was too late to take it back, and as Delaney dejectedly got to his feet and I followed him to the door and saw him out with a very dishonest "Thanks," I didn't care how shortsighted my lie was. After Stefan and I had argued about Delaney, I just didn't want to have anything more to do with him.

But as he headed off down the block, I saw Harry Benevento drive by in the other direction toward Polly Flockhart's house—for some afternoon delight, no doubt. The picture of Polly taking a "late lunch" and her chair sneaking off to join her wasn't titillating. Embarrassed at their obliviousness to appearances and gossip, I shut the door.

10

After a haphazard late lunch and enough research and browsing through my Wharton library to satisfy myself that I'd sufficiently laid out the first stages of my work on *Summer*, I decided to drive to campus and check my mail. I left Stefan a note on the kitchen table in case he got back before me.

By the time I reached Parker it would be after 5:00 P.M. and the EAR office would be closed, so I'd be less likely to run into other faculty. I realized that this wasn't the most positive attitude, but after that ugly departmental meeting I wasn't eager to pretend to schmooze or even smile and nod at anyone. Not that I was very popular at the best of times, since so many faculty assumed I had no real qualifications other than being Stefan's partner, given that he was the one SUM had wanted.

In my first year I'd also probably been perceived as too buoyant and cheerful. I'm a gregarious guy, and it hurt me to feel that my enthusiasm was looked at suspiciously—as if I were some prophet of technology offering free time on AOL to Luddites.

Honestly, while I loved Michigan and loved getting to know it better, and SUM's campus was a haven, this wasn't the best department for me. But then I wondered if a good match would ever be possible. Whenever I'm chatting at conferences with faculty members from other universities, the truth comes out after a drink or two: Hardly any academics are happy where they are, no matter how apt the students, how generous the salary or perks, how beautiful the setting, how light the teaching load, how lavish the research budget. I don't know if it's academia itself that attracts misfits and malcontents, or if the overwhelming hypocrisy of that world would have turned even the Van Trapp family sullen. On days like this one I puzzled over whether I'd really want to be teaching at SUM or any place like it until retirement.

Maybe my thoughts had moved in this direction because both Didier and Lucille had changed their lives radically in middle age. It wasn't comfortable for me to be speculating like that on the edge of my own personal version of Here Be Dragons.

But what were my choices? And if I tried anything else, I'd have to face my parents' knowing smiles. They had encouraged me to do graduate work years ago but had always assumed—without saying it—that I'd take some position in my father's small publishing house, which is no doubt why they'd paid my way through master's and Ph.D. work. But that was the last thing I wanted. It was bad enough I had never measured up to my father's European polish and style, that even in a tux I didn't quite shape up. Working under him would have been unbearable. My father wasn't a cruel man in any way, but he had the painful habit of small stinging criticisms, introduced in the same way every time by a soft, disappointed "Oh." I'd be reading a book about the lesser-known impressionist Gustave Caillebotte and he'd say, "Oh. You find him worthwhile?"

My mother laughed off these questions when they were directed at her. And of course Stefan never bristled; he would reply with a forthright and disarming, "Absolutely," or even

worse, hit my father with French slang and call the book "*chou-
ette*" or "*sensas.*"

Teaching was what I loved, what I was good at, so it didn't
seem I'd be making any changes soon unless they were forced on
me.

Late Friday afternoons were lovely on campus. Staff and
faculty had cleared out or were on their way off campus, students
were gone for the weekend or certainly not crowding the bridges
and paths. Today the air was cooler than it had been; still, the
promise of a terrific spring was obvious in the glowing redbud
trees and the burgeoning magnolias.

But if I'd expected not to run into anyone at Parker Hall at
the end of a Friday afternoon, I was wrong. Just as I was pulling
in, Lucille drove past, stopping to roll down her window and ask
if Stefan and I wanted to see a movie with them that weekend.
"Call me," she said, and headed out into Friday traffic.

Getting out of my car behind the building, I saw Dean
Bullerschmidt and Harry Benevento chatting directly in my path
to the closest back door of Parker. Benevento walked off to his
car, but Bullerschmidt saw me. With the florid bulbous-nosed
face of an alcoholic and dead piggy eyes, he reminded me of
Sydney Greenstreet in *The Maltese Falcon*, but without a scintilla
of charm, even the fake variety.

As always, he was dressed like a fashion plate, today in an
expensive-looking pin-striped suit, oxblood wing tips, blue shirt
with white collar, and a gleamingly beautiful tie and matching
pocket square, in burgundy and black vertical stripes. But the
elegant clothes did nothing to disguise his bulk except to give him
a kind of regal looniness: King Farouk for a Day.

The dean didn't move a muscle, just waited for me to approach as if I were a courtier crossing an intimidatingly long
audience chamber to bow to my liege lord. I thought of the sev-

enteenth century Banqueting Hall in London as I approached.

"Professor Hoffman," he said in his colorless deep voice. "I would shake your hand, but I've just washed mine and they're still damp." His lips twitched in a half-smile.

I shrugged.

"I have heard good things about the mystery course you're planning to teach."

The dean had barely ever nodded to me before, and this unexpected compliment left me puzzled. Was he mocking me, and how could I tell?

Bullerschmidt stared blankly at me, waiting for a reply. "Thank you," was what I managed, keenly aware that this was the man who had ultimate say over whether I got tenure or not. Technically, the provost made those decisions, but the current provost was only in the position temporarily, which meant the dean had more power than usual.

Bullerschmidt blinked a few times and may have said, "Well," before turning to lumber off to Crepe Hall, I assumed, where his office and car were. What had he been doing in Parker, if that's where he'd been? And why was my course suddenly so interesting to people? Coral Greathouse hadn't officially offered me the course yet, and already it was "my" course. This didn't make sense. I glanced after him and thought, as always, that he didn't seem like the kind of person who was fat because he couldn't stop eating; rather, there was something deliberate and menacing in his weight. It was a weapon.

I got out my key to open the door, which was locked at five on Fridays since the night classes in Parker ran only Monday through Thursday. I'm surprised there were any night classes at Parker; it had to be the gloomiest, most decrepit building on campus, a perfect nest for vampires. Just as I was stepping through the door, someone shouted, "Could you hold it!" and

Bill Malatesta came loping up, thanking me profusely. "Forgot my key," he said, several times, apologizing as if I were his supervisor or something. He descended the stairs to the basement where TAs had their cramped and smelly offices, and I climbed to the third floor, aware that Bill hadn't hit me with any of his perpetual lightbulb jokes.

Carter Savery and Iris Bell stomped down the stairs past me, barely saying hello. Damn, those two were inseparable. On the second-floor landing Juno Dromgoole barreled through the stairwell door, hurrying past and barking out, "Sorry! Late!" the stabbing of her heels and the fog of her perfume filling the air.

Was she following Iris and Carter? Why?

I let myself into the mercifully deserted EAR office, emptied my surprisingly full mailbox, and made my way upstairs to my office to sort through it. There was a light on in the History Department office, whose door was half glass just like the door to the EAR office. I assumed Polly Flockhart was working late as usual; perhaps she felt guilty about her affair with Benevento? Unless she was channeling some distant workaholic. . . .

The grim hallway wasn't as dark as it would later become after sunset, but it was creepy enough, and I moved quickly down to my office, unlocking the door as swiftly as I could and turning on the lights. I settled down to sorting my mail, separating out requests from Wharton scholars, announcements of conferences, invitations to write essays for anthologies or submit papers to panels. As I did so, I was aware of how lucky I was that I never pored through my mail with the intensity Stefan did combing through his. Even in his forties, he still had the stirrings of hope that one letter would be there to change his life: the offer of a film deal on one of his books, maybe.

I could still remember the time back in Massachusetts when the long drought was broken and he placed a story with a more than respectable literary journal; his excitement as he ran up the driveway from the mailbox, his wild stare and hollering. These days, good news was likely to come through his agent if at all, and so Stefan often was deflated after sorting his mail even if there was no bad news.

I put some letters in a pile to take home with me, filed others, and turned on my computer to write a few quick replies before I forgot about them. After about an hour of work, I thought I heard a crow somewhere near the building, its strident war cry echoing through the silence. God, those cocky large birds unnerved me. The way they swarmed across campus and town, sometimes you'd think you were watching a new species flex its muscles. What was most off-putting about them for me was their fearlessness. They barely moved out of your way even if you were driving right toward them, whether they were transfixed by some juicy roadkill or simply lurking with intent to commit some raucous bird mayhem.

It was warm enough for some windows to be open, so I figured maybe the cawing was drifting in from a tree near Parker, or even a window ledge. Though bats got into the building all the time and even swooped down on people, crows hadn't been sighted indoors yet. Nevertheless, I confess I waited until I couldn't hear any more cawing to head down the hall to the men's room. But when I opened the heavy dark old door, there was a strange rustling or flapping.

As I stepped nervously inside, the first thing I saw was a huge black crow glaring at me. It was planted on the forehead of a man who lay faceup near the urinals, his arms and legs at weird angles as if he'd been dropped like I Ching sticks. His face was covered in blood, and he was surely dead.

After a soulless glance at me, the crow went back to picking at one of the man's open staring eyes. It was Delaney Kildare—

I could tell from his clothes and the once-powerful shoulders. I staggered back against the closed door, and the impact sent the crow flapping out the wide-open window. I made out lashings of blood on the wall right opposite me.

Stunned, disgusted, I hauled open the door and stumbled back into the hallway. I stood there, commanding myself to think, to think clearly. Police. Call the campus police. But like a dreamer whose feet stick to a floor that's turned hostile and muddy, I walked heavily back to my office, flashing on the blood, the crow, the eye. The blood, the crow, the eye. That horrible flapping. His arms and legs, so twisted and unnatural.

The nightmare continued as I fumbled with the lock, somehow unable to make the key work. On the point of tears I said, "Please, please let it open." It finally did, and in a daze I dialed 911, which connected me to campus police. I gave the operator my name and said there was a dead man in Parker Hall. Third floor. Even as I said it I thought, Unreal. A joke. A prank. It couldn't have happened.

Hanging up the phone, I kept my hand on it, staring at both of them as if I were casually thumbing through a catalog, noting the interesting details. Push buttons. Numbers and letters. Fingers.

When the phone rang, my hand flew off the receiver as if it'd been burned. It rang several times before I picked it up gingerly.

"Hey, Nick—you're still there!" It was Stefan, and he rattled on about having started preparing for Shabbat, which was coming later as the days grew longer.

"Delaney's dead," I told him, and saying it made the fact of his death more palpable. Yet I felt unreal, both involved with something gruesome and distant from it.

"No! Where? How? Are you okay?"

When I said I was fine and it was down the hall, Stefan yelled at me to close and lock my door and shove a chair under the knob. I followed his urgent instructions without question. Back on the phone, I asked him why.

"God, Nick! First Jesse Benevento, now Delaney right there in Parker Hall—you could be next! I'm coming right over." He hung up.

I registered Stefan's fear for me but felt oddly untouched by it. In lots of contemporary books, especially mysteries, it seems that when characters are shocked or horrified they throw up or somehow experience the distress in their guts. I felt nothing like that. What I did feel was cold all over, and I wished I'd brought a warmer sweater with me, though how could I have known I'd need it? For a moment I pictured my closet at home, wondering idly which sweater would have been just right. . . .

I must have fallen asleep somehow, because the pounding at the door startled me so much that I almost fell off my chair.

"Professor Hoffman? It's Detective Valley."

I rose unsteadily, pulled the chair away, and opened the door. The lights were on in the hallway behind him, and I could see other campus police at work. From where I stood I could see the men's room being sealed or marked off with yellow crime scene tape.

"We've closed the building. Nobody gets in or out until everyone's been questioned. You're first."

Surprised I hadn't heard any sirens, I backed up, bumping into the chair, which I shoved aside. I sat at my desk, and Valley looked around. "Do you have any booze?"

I was so startled I almost laughed. "You want a drink?"

"No—it's for you—you look like hell."

I guess that counted as consideration, so I thanked him, but said I didn't have anything.

"Don't all you profs keep Scotch around?"

"On my salary it would be Diet Coke." The idea of a drink was so wonderful, though, that I was tempted to check Lucille's desk. While Valley sat in the comfortable chair my students used, I got up and opened Lucille's large file drawer. Sure enough, she had a bottle of Harvey's Shooting Sherry. Reaching for it, I dislodged a bunch of letters that had been folded in half. I made out the signature on the top one: "Love, Delaney."

I grabbed the bottle and slammed the drawer shut, convinced now that Delaney and Lucille had been lovers.

Valley nodded, obviously taking my haste for relief. "I thought you needed a drink." He shook his head when I offered to pour some for him into a paper cup. I sipped from my own and felt myself calm down instantly. Was it the alcohol itself or simply the feeling that I was tending to myself?

"He's dead, right?" I asked. "And it *was* Delaney Kildare? His face was—it was horribly messed up. You checked his ID?"

Valley nodded uncomfortably, clearly unhappy with being questioned.

"I mean, I figured he was from the way he was lying there, and the crow—"

"The crow," he repeated flatly.

I started to explain, but Valley cut me off. "Tell me everything you saw from the beginning," he said, taking out his notebook. Slowly, woodenly, I started with arriving at Parker, and took him through everything that had happened, everyone I ran into, shuddering when I came to the point of describing the body and the crow.

"The call came in at six-ten. How long were you in Parker Hall before that?"

I looked at my watch. "The building was locked when I got here, so it was at least five. I worked for about an hour."

"Doing what?"

"I told you already. Going through my mail." I poured myself some more sherry.

"You do that every Friday at this time?"

"No. Sometimes I don't come in until Monday."

"Then why today?"

I shrugged. "I was done at home and thought I'd stop by."

"When did you last see the deceased before you found his body?"

"The last time I saw him?" I coughed, damning myself for sounding nervous.

"Take your time," he said, head down, writing.

"Earlier this afternoon."

Valley's head snapped up, his eyes suspicious. "Today? Where?"

"At my house. He wanted to talk about a course I may teach next year."

His face registered that he thought it was unusual. "Couldn't he have called you?"

"Delaney's—He wanted to be my TA for a course—teaching assistant. He's been pursuing me about it."

Now Valley was leaning forward. "He was stalking you?"

"No, not at all. I mean—" God, everything sounded wrong when someone was dead.

Leaning back, Valley said softly, "Did you two have an argument?"

Maybe I'd had too much sherry too quickly, but I shouted at him. "You're crazy! You think *I* killed Delaney and then waltzed down to my office to report it? I didn't hate him, he didn't hate me. He wanted to teach a course with me!"

Unperturbed by my outburst, and jotting something down, Detective Valley moved on. "I met him here a few days ago, when there was that hate incident with the postcard. He was acting . . . protective toward your officemate."

I nodded and said, "Lucille Mochtar," but of course Valley knew her name, since he'd questioned her.

"What kind of relationship did she have with the deceased?"

"He was her advisee," I said, determined not to say more.

"Anything else?" Valley wondered, with a leering tone of voice.

I shook my head, thinking of the letters just across the office in her desk. "I won't speculate about a friend."

Something in my demeanor must have given me away; he said, "Is there a husband? How's the husband feel about all this?"

"I want to go home. Why don't you question me there?"

"No way. I want to know everyone who might have had a reason to kill Delaney Kildare, if he was killed."

Incredulous, I said, "*If* he was killed? What do you think happened to him? He couldn't get the paper towel dispenser to work, yanked on it too hard, and gave himself a fatal concussion?"

With no irony, Valley noted, "You've got a lively imagination. But you're not an ME, and the body hasn't been examined yet."

Suddenly it hit me. "Jeez. It's Friday again," I breathed, making the connection with last Friday's riot and Jesse's death. "There's a serial killer on campus, killing people on Fridays."

Valley put his pad down. "Listen to me," he snapped. "Delaney Kildare could have had a stroke, a heart attack, whatever. Last year an SUM cheerleader died running to catch a bus, remember? She was an athlete, in perfect condition. So don't spread rumors about what could or could not be going on."

I don't know why I felt so calm then, unless it was my typical pleasure seeing Valley at any sort of disadvantage. "You know it's too late. This is going to be all over campus, it probably is right now, and all over the media soon, even if I don't say a word to anybody."

A stocky campus cop knocked, leaned in, and said, "There's a professor downstairs says he wants to see this guy." He pointed at me.

"That's Stefan," I said. "I want to go home."

Valley held up a finger and told the cop to wait: "I'll let you go after two more questions. Who else did you see in Parker or nearby before you picked up your mail?"

I rattled off the names while Valley copied them down: Iris Bell, Carter Savery, Juno Dromgoole, Harry Benevento, Bill Malatesta, Dean Bullerschmidt.

"Who would have a reason to kill Delaney Kildare?"

Exhausted, stunned, I said, "Ask them. I have to go home." Valley relented and told the cop to escort me outside. Did he think I would go anywhere else? Valley shut his pad and stepped into the hallway, waiting. I replaced the sherry bottle without opening Lucille's desk drawer all the way, closed the lights, and locked the door. Then I trailed downstairs after the cop, determined to ignore the activity at the other end of the hallway. For some reason, he tried to make conversation. "Dangerous place, SUM. I thought this would be easy work after being a state trooper." I don't know if I even acknowledged him by anything more than a grunt or two. Staggering outside into the welcoming night, breathing freely, I fell into Stefan's arms.

"I'm so sorry," he kept saying as he led me to my car. "Are you okay to drive? Because we could go in my car and pick yours up tomorrow."

Through half-shut eyes I made out an ambulance, several campus police cars, and a growing crowd of gawkers. I suppose I got into my car, fastened the seat belt, and followed Stefan's Volvo home, because a few minutes later we were in our driveway, and Stefan was opening the front door for me. I looked around as if expecting everything in the hallway to be shattered, ruined. But the Regency-style console table and mirror gleamed their typical bright welcome. I drifted into the living room, sank onto the couch, and curled up.

"What do you need?" Stefan asked. "Tylenol? A drink? Hot bath? Valium?"

As if I were reading tea leaves, a line from *Play It as It Lays* floated up through my consciousness: "In the whole world there was not as much sedation as there was instantaneous peril."

"What's wrong with me?" I asked, as Stefan sat by my side. "Why does this keep happening to me? Am I being punished for something? What did I do to keep running into death? It used to be something I only saw in movies or on the news. I grew up in New York City and never even saw a car accident, but I come to Michigan and it's a Stephen King novel. I thought life was quiet in the Midwest."

Stefan said, "This doesn't have anything to do with you, Nick."

"No? Then who? My officemate is killed, people die when I organize a conference; hell, I'd be criminally irresponsible to teach a mystery class—the students would probably all be wiped out by a mass murderer! And I can't believe I just saw Delaney a few hours ago."

"What are you talking about, Nick?"

"He showed up before I had lunch to talk about the mystery course again. I wanted to shut him up, so I told him you might be leaving next year. We might. So talking about him as TA was moot."

Stefan frowned, eyeing me as if he thought I was delirious. Then he surprised me by grinning. "At least you didn't tell him we were both getting sex changes and moving to Northampton. But sometimes, Nick, you are a very silly person."

I bristled. "George Bush, he was silly. Innately silly. I'm— I'm picturesque."

Stefan rose, and I watched him put on the sound track CD from *How to Make an American Quilt*. As the dreamy, cool music flowed out into the room, it was like a soothing flow of water, and I shut my eyes and leaned back. Just then, the doorbell rang. Cursing to myself, I hoped it wasn't Valley again or a reporter.

Stefan went to the door, and I heard Lucille's and Didier's anxious overlapping questions about me.

"I'm okay," I called as they surged into the living room. "I'm okay."

Lucille and Didier sat down protectively on either arm of the couch.

Didier said, "We heard your name on the news, that there was an accident at Parker, someone was dead, and you're a witness."

"I hope it was Juno Dromgoole," Lucille said viciously, and when Didier hushed her, she retorted, "That woman works my last nerve." Lucille peered down at me hopefully.

"Not Juno," I said. "Delaney."

Lucille looked utterly blank, as if the name meant nothing to her, and then slid from her perch to stand over by the fireplace, facing away from us all, shoulders hunched. "Can't you turn that damn music off?" she said bitterly. Stefan hurriedly complied, but the abrupt silence was so uneasy that he turned the radio to a classical station, which was playing something painlessly Baroque.

Didier had also switched places, easing himself into a chair, where he crossed his legs and brought his tented hands to his mouth as if stilling the desire to talk—or making plans. Underneath his habitual self-possession, he seemed agitated and trying to control it.

Stefan rejoined me on the couch and slid an arm around me. I launched into what I knew Lucille and Didier wanted to hear, making my description short and vague enough to keep myself from wincing, though Lucille, still with her back to us, shuddered once or twice. "Lucille. Valley's going to be asking you questions," I said, painfully aware of the letters I'd seen in her desk drawer.

She whirled around. "What for?"

"You were his adviser," Didier said equably, as if he were a lawyer rehearsing her in a narrative she had to tell in court. But the effort to calm her down didn't work, and looking quite fed up and angry, she said, "Let's go, they don't need us around."

After they left, Stefan asked me if I'd followed what was up with them, but I could only tell him I was going up to bed.

"For the night?" he asked.

I shrugged.

It was only two hours later when I woke up, but instead of feeling logy or sick, I was remarkably relaxed—and hungry. Perhaps because something smelled wonderful downstairs. I slipped on sweats and followed the scent. In the fragrant kitchen, Stefan had set the table and lit the Shabbat candles. Their gentle flickering was amazingly soothing, and it touched me that Stefan had lit them by himself.

"I turned the ringer off on your phone. You got some calls from reporters. Minnie and my father called me. I told them you were all right, and not to worry."

I breathed in. "Not the most peaceful Shabbat, huh?"

"They're all different," Stefan replied, ruffling my hair. "Sit. Are you hungry? I made dinner just in case."

I was ready to dig into the gnocchi with broccoli, sun-dried tomatoes, lots of garlic—and shrimp—the last a rebellion against my parents' kosher home.

"We can skip the blessings tonight," I said.

"No, I don't want to."

Surprised, I looked to him for an explanation, but all he said was, "I need the peace. Tonight more than ever."

So we stood, blessed the wine and drank it, then blessed the challah, holding the braided bread together while I felt tremendously thankful that Stefan had come so far from his alienation and ambivalence about being Jewish. Stefan dipped the small piece he'd broken off into salt—a reminder of incense in the Temple—and handed me half. We wished each other good Shabbos. I was moved beyond words by these simple ceremonies that brought peace and order into our lives each week. This was very personal *tikkun olam*: repairing the world.

He had chilled a crisp Muscadet that went perfectly with our meal. Had anything ever tasted this good? Or was it the comfort and security of sitting there with Stefan? Safe. Alive. We didn't talk much and ate too quickly, but that was okay.

Finishing the after-meal prayers, we settled down even more with some freshly brewed Kona decaf, and I let Stefan tell me about all the calls he'd fielded while I was asleep. Reporters, faculty members. As he laid it all out calmly, I found myself flooded with relief that he was such an unflappable man. While sometimes I wished he were more demonstrative, I knew that in this household, if he were more outgoing not only wouldn't I get to talk as much, life would also seem too bruising because there wouldn't be his deep inner calm to shelter us both.

"And Minnie warned us to get out of town," Stefan finished. "She says we can hide out at their place if we need to."

"From what? Cameramen?"

Stefan grinned. "From the Grim Reaper, I think." But then his expression changed and he said, "She was really worried about us. And so was my father." Wonderingly, Stefan said, "He sounded emotional."

"You were surprised."

"Very."

"How much did you tell them?"

Stefan stirred more cream into his mug. "Not everything. But enough."

"That Delaney was the victim of a serial killer?"

"Nick, maybe you're being an alarmist—"

"You didn't see all that blood! It was spattered on the wall like a Rorschach. And that gruesome crow sitting on his head, pecking at his eye. I can't stop thinking about it."

"Okay, okay. But a serial killer?"

"But you practically said that on the phone!"

"Practically. I was scared for you."

I shrugged and finished my coffee. When I got up to pour myself some more, Stefan waved me back and poured it for me. "Well, somebody killed him, Stefan. And Didier looks like the best possibility. He's probably been seething underneath all that composure—that could be why he was so defensive about his brother. What if they're both explosive? Didn't you see him tonight? He looked like he was hiding something."

"Seething? About what?"

I described the letters in Lucille's desk drawer.

"What were you going through her desk for?"

"I wasn't snooping, Stefan. Valley asked if I had anything to drink, and I didn't, so I looked in her file drawer."

"You were drinking with Valley?"

"No!" I grimaced. "He wanted me to have a drink, to calm down, I guess. Or perk up. I probably looked like Death eating a sandwich."

"You did look terrible when you came out of Parker. But the letters—lots of people sign their letters 'love.' It doesn't have to mean anything."

"True. But put it together with the way they've been acting

around each other. Remember when Delaney called her at their house the other night when we were having dinner? How strange was that?"

"So Didier couldn't take it anymore," Stefan said slowly, the words like an advertising slogan flying behind a biplane. "And even though he got half a million dollars for a book that could be a best-seller, he threw that all away to kill some kid?"

"I know it sounds stupid, but—"

"It doesn't just sound stupid, it *is* stupid. No writer would give up success just because he suspects his wife's having an affair. Trust me."

"You make writers sound pretty superficial."

He nodded. "In some ways we are. Like actors without the glamour. And you don't really know they were sleeping together. She cared about him, and probably he had some feelings for her, too."

"Had some feelings? You make it sound like having gas."

"Did Delaney strike you as somebody thoughtful and deep? It was all on the outside. He was a human Potemkin Village."

"If you get any nastier, I'll start thinking you killed him to keep him from TA'ing for me."

Stefan shook his head. "Let's clean up." We loaded the dishwasher and took our coffee into my study.

"I guess you might be right about Didier. But Bill Malatesta was much more jealous of Delaney, and not just because of Betty, remember? He couldn't stand Delaney's success. And the way he had pull with the dean."

"Did you say Bullerschmidt was right near Parker Hall tonight?" Stefan frowned. "I wouldn't put anything past him. He's a monster."

"What if Delaney was blackmailing him? And he decided to end it." It was easy to picture Bullerschmidt's massive bulk turned deadly, bearing down on the well-built but smaller man. I would have quailed at 350 pounds of vengeful dean determined to wipe me out.

"We don't know how he was killed, what the weapon was," Stefan brought out regretfully. "And you didn't hear anything in your office? I guess not," he answered for himself. "That hallway's pretty long, and all those old doors are thick. So Delaney might have been dead by the time you hit your office, but maybe not. . . ." Then he shook himself. "We're talking about a murder again." He looked down, embarrassed or distressed. "Unbelievable." Now he must have been feeling something similar to what I'd been talking about before. The sheer improbability of it all.

"Well," I quipped, "look at the alternatives. What do most academics talk about? How nobody appreciates them enough and how other academics don't deserve whatever they have. Or boring new research in their field that isn't really new. Or they gossip—"

"Aren't we gossiping?"

"We're detecting. It's not the same thing at all."

"There's no turning back," he said quietly, eyes closed, and after a moment he began to quote what I instantly recognized as *Moby Dick*, though I'd never been able to wade all the way through that soggy masterpiece. " 'In the soul of man there lies one insular Tahiti,' " he said, his voice as rich and round as an actor's, " 'full of peace and joy, but encompassed by all the horrors of the half known life. God keep thee! Push not off from that isle, thou canst never return!' "

I was going to tell him that Melville seemed just a bit melodramatic for tonight, but then as I let the words sink in, I realized that nothing could be more appropriate than that terrible dark vision. We sat there letting the silence fold in upon itself.

It was Stefan himself who broke us out of the mood. "Okay, Sherlock," he said at last. " What about Carter and Iris?"

"The gruesome twosome? I know they were leaving the building when I showed up, but what would they have against Delaney? That he was young and attractive and had his life ahead of him and they're miserable middle-aged failures?" I stopped talking for a moment. "Hey—that's possible, that's really possible."

"There's always Juno Dromgoole."

"God, you must hate her."

"No, I just think she's dangerous. And you did say she tore out of Parker like a harpy, didn't you?"

"Yes, but—" I finished my coffee and set the mug down on my blotter. "It looked like she was chasing after Iris and Carter. Maybe they pissed her off somehow, or the three of them are plotting a coup. Juno would never kill anyone, no matter what kind of line she spins. She'd never risk ruining her manicure."

Stefan vigorously disagreed. "Nick, if Juno had been the one fighting Evander Holyfield instead of Tyson, she would have won, and she would have bit off more than a piece of his ear."

"Well, I know what I need to do tomorrow. I'm going across the street to have a good long talk with Didier and find out the truth. I can't live with them as neighbors and friends unless I know."

Stefan cut his eyes at me and asked if I thought Didier would wither under my cunning barrage of questions and confess. "That is, if he did kill Delaney, which I still think is impossible. Why can't you leave the whole thing to Valley, to the campus police? Stay out of it."

"No. I found his body, remember? And Delaney was trying to hook up with me somehow. I feel obligated."

"To Delaney?"

"To myself."

"Nick, we can talk about who might have killed Delaney, but

your looking for the killer isn't sensible. Coral won't like it. She told you to stay out of trouble. Besides, you have to do *Summer*."

I told Stefan that tenure didn't seem very important right now, and he didn't challenge me.

We closed up shop and headed to bed. I took some melatonin and two Benadryl to make sure I slept and wasn't kept awake by the image of that casually brutal crow picking at Delaney's bloody, battered face.

Even though Stefan had been trying to discourage me from looking more deeply into Delaney's death, I could tell that he was as captured by events as I was. How could it be any other way when I'd found Delaney the way I had? Lying there in bed trying to fall asleep, I ran through everyone I'd seen on my way into Parker: Lucille, Bullerschmidt, Harry Benevento, Bill Malatesta. Then inside, Iris Bell, Carter Savery, Juno Dromgoole. If Delaney was already dead by the time I got there, it could have been any one of those people.

"So what exactly did you tell Delaney about next year—what was your story?"

"That you got offers from other schools you were considering. Why? Are you worried he might've told someone? There wasn't much time," I said, wincing at how crude it seemed to talk about Delaney's death that way.

"If he did, and it gets around, we'll have a lot to explain."

"I'm sorry, Stefan."

"Well—there are worse things to worry about."

Like his writing career, I thought.

The last thing I remember Stefan saying before drifting off was, "We've been thinking about who killed Delaney, but the real question is whether Delaney and Jesse's murders are connected, isn't it?"

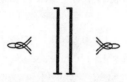

aturday morning I woke up feeling somehow dazed and emptied out, perhaps like someone in Florida after a tornado has crushed neighboring houses and left his standing: unaccountably saved, but desolate just the same. Once again, our lives had been raked by devastation.

Stefan had woken up before me, put *Chant* on downstairs, and left me the *New York Times,* the *Detroit Free Press,* and the *Michiganapolis Tribune* on his side of the bed. When I started sorting through them, he appeared in the doorway with a bed tray.

"*Omelette aux fines herbes* with chevre," he said. "Peppered bacon, grapefruit juice, and green tea."

"That's it? No choices?"

He carefully settled the tray down on the bed over my outstretched legs, ignoring the joke. Or maybe he didn't hear it. With an introvert, you can't always be sure that something you said gets through the first time you say it. So much of his attention is focused inward. Even though Stefan is a writer and a keen observer of people, he can often just mentally slip away. It's a gift

I wish I had, because even when he does go to department meetings, they don't fray his nerves like a yappy little dog.

"I'm not sick," I said, pointing to the tray. "You didn't have to."

"How about just enjoying it?"

Chastened, I thanked him and settled back into my pillows after a bite of omelette and some juice. Stefan held up the *Tribune* for me with its enormous headline: SERIAL KILLER STALKS SUM. As bad as I'd expected.

While I appreciatively consumed the omelette, making sure he heard each and every yummy sound, Stefan read the garbled article out loud to me, interrupting with sarcastic comments about the writing. "At least they spelled your name correctly," he said. "But this is stupid. Serial killers have a pattern. There's no pattern here."

"Friday," I said. "Two stabbings on the same day, a week apart."

"You don't know if Delaney was stabbed." And when I glanced at the phone, he added, "Margaret Case won't talk to you this soon. We'll have to wait for the official report."

I decided I would call the ME later. Sipping my tea, I countered Stefan's assessment. "What do we know about serial killers? We've watched a few gross movies like *Seven* and read a couple of Patricia Cornwells, that's all. What if this murderer is canny and disguising what he's done? And what if there's stuff at the scene we don't know about, or the pattern he's leaving won't show up right away?"

"Or she."

"Right. Or she." I thought about Lucille's reaction to the news last night. What could be better cover than hurrying over and pretending she didn't know who was dead? But I felt uncomfortable suspecting my new friend of murder. "You know, Stefan, we're turning into conspiracy freaks. Paranoids. Not that we think somebody's trying to take over the country, or that Clinton slept with Vince Foster and that's why Foster had to die. I mean—"

"—that we can imagine people we know committing murder?"

"Exactly. Because it's happened—too often. It's not far-fetched anymore."

"Then we're not paranoid, just smart. Better to think every-one's guilty than to think that no one is."

I suppose he was right, but I didn't like it, and I didn't like how our lives had changed in the last few years. "Doesn't it bother you?"

"Of course it does, but . . ."

"But what?"

He shrugged. "Doesn't it bother *you* that the world watched ethnic cleansing in Bosnia, and no one really did anything? All that talk about 'Never Again' after the Holocaust, and it hap-pened right there on the nightly news. You couldn't say you didn't know, or it was only a rumor. It was incontrovertible." Stefan sighed. "And compared to all that, SUM's *Bambi*. The world is crazy—that's reality."

It was a grim conversation to have with the calm, echoing Gregorian chant drifting up from downstairs as background. Stefan cleared the tray, and I headed for the shower, glad that we had spent the money over the summer to redo the master bath so that we now had a two-person tiled shower with jets on both sides. It felt more refreshing than ever.

When I was dressed, I called the ME, but she was unavailable and I didn't feel like leaving my name. I found Stefan in the sunroom, gazing out at the backyard with a contented, dreamy look. "I'm going to see Didier," I said. He nodded, and I went across the street, enjoying another day of sunshine, which you can never take for granted in mid-Michigan.

Didier opened the door in only a thin white towel. Because of his baldness, he seemed more than naked.

"Nick, hi! Lucille's out, and I was just about to get in the hot tub—want to come?" Warily, I followed him out back. Unlike our house, theirs was built on a slight hill that dropped behind the house to an unplanted yard surrounded by a six-foot cedar fence, which made the four-person hot tub on the two-level deck very private. The deck was lavishly appointed with a wrought-iron mosaic-topped table and matching chairs and a mammoth Frontgate cooking island and professional grill, which was perfect in case a wild boar should stumble into their yard and croak.

Didier dropped the towel, pressed some buttons, and slipped into the bubbling tub. Even with my eyes averted, I caught a glimpse of his brawny body.

"You look great," I said as he groaned, arms flung wide on the edge of the tub.

"For fifty-five?" He laughed.

"For any age."

"That's what my agent says. Big biceps and good teeth will do wonders on the talk shows. Join me."

"Thanks, but I just showered."

"That's perfect."

Though I tend to be physically shy, I wagered that it would be a lot harder for him to be deceptive with both of us in the nude, so I changed my mind, drew off my clothes, and gingerly stepped into the tub. The water was just on the edge of being too hot for me.

"Good quads," he said, shaking his head because he knew I didn't work out as intensely as he and Stefan did. He said it in that matter-of-fact way that guys at the gym talk about each other's muscles, but that would have sounded phony if I'd tried it. "Genetics," Didier said with disgust. "I'd need steroids to get my legs that big."

I almost blushed. My large thighs had always made fitting pants more difficult, and even though Stefan had praised my legs before, this assessment was from a relative stranger. Besides, I'd had too many years of being made fun of at school for the praise to get all the way inside.

I sat opposite Didier, legs drawn up so that I wouldn't accidentally brush against his.

"You can relax," he said with a toothy grin. "I'm not worried you'll try to seduce me. If I was, I wouldn't have invited you in, eh?"

I stretched out a little more.

"Okay, what's on your mind? You look like a man with a mission." He sounded as jovial as men in the hot tub at the Club who boomed at each other to create, I thought, a wall of sound to hide behind. They did it because they weren't as nonchalant about sharing a confined space with other naked men as they thought they should be.

"How's Lucille?"

He frowned. "About what you'd expect. Distraught. She was very close to Delaney. He was a good kid." It seemed such an inadequate label for Delaney that I must have made a face, because Didier said, "You don't think he was a good kid?"

"I don't know what he was. But he wasn't a kid."

"Well, he helped me out. I've been so consumed by the revisions on my book, I'm glad he paid so much attention to Lucille. It was good for her. I mean, I'm not the man I was when we got married, and she's hit her prime in bed." He said this as matter-of-factly as a narrator describing a caterpillar's camouflage on an after-school special. "Not that I know for sure they were sleeping together," he added. "If they weren't, I think they were going to, eventually."

I tried to act cool, but I was shocked by how casually he said it, as if Lucille were contemplating a hobby or a new hairstyle. "Didn't you ask her?"

He smiled. "We don't spy on each other. No interrogations. You see, I don't need anyone else but Lucille. Never have. But she gets restless, she needs adventure, variety. So if Delaney was giving her pleasure of any kind, great. That department isn't the friendliest place to work. Whatever helps make it easier for her there is fine with me."

He made an affair sound like air-conditioning or an ergonomic desk chair, and I felt as prudish as a monk talking to Casanova. "Delaney was her graduate student," I pointed out.

Unfazed, Didier said, "I've never interfered, never criticized. Lucille promised me she would always be safe, and so I'm satisfied." It was almost as if he'd delivered this rap before. Closing his eyes, he leaned his gleaming bald head back, rolled his neck and shoulders, and I heard some muscles crack. "That's what matters."

If this equanimity of his was an act, it deserved applause. "It really doesn't bother you?"

"Well, aren't you and Stefan in an open relationship?" he asked, head up.

"*No!*"

"I just assumed—"

"Because we're two men together?"

He nodded, unabashed. "Plus you're both from New York. And Lucille did mention the way you look at Delaney."

"Jeez, so what? Everyone looks. Stefan and I have no problem with looking, but that's all we do. I know the stereotype is that gay men are as hot for random sex as Republicans are for constitutional amendments, but that's not true for us. I mean, we love sex, just not with other people, okay? And in case you're wondering, we don't do drag, don't wear leather, and have no intention of getting pierced or tattooed."

"Sure," he said equably, luxuriating in the hot water.

I was amazed at what he had told me about himself. Lucille and Didier seemed so ordinary in some ways, a happy couple, but despite his hints a few days ago, I hadn't imagined their private life was so colorful.

"You've been trying to figure out if I killed Delaney," Didier brought out with a wicked smile. "Eh? But I had no reason to. Not that I have an alibi. I was working at home all afternoon yesterday. On my book. That's what I told Detective Beanpole last night."

"Valley was here? Does he know about—whatever there is to know?"

"I gave him an edited version of what I told you."

"What did Lucille say?"

"I don't know—Valley interviewed us separately. Like I said, I don't spy on her."

"You're not that upset Delaney's dead."

"Should I be?" Tongue working in his cheek, he considered that. "I am sorry that I won't ever get to work out with him. The guy had killer lats—back work would have been something." He drifted off for a moment, obviously hearing the clank of barbells. "In general," he continued, "when someone young like that dies, it's sad. But I was more broken up about Princess Di, frankly, and me a Quebecois! I just didn't know Delaney well enough."

Either I was right that Didier couldn't hide the truth in the hot tub, or the hot water and jets were diminishing my capacity to weed truth from fiction. He seemed honestly at peace with himself, with Lucille, and not at all deeply troubled by Delaney's death. But couldn't he have killed Delaney and be satisfied and quiet inside?

That's what I asked Stefan a little while later when I was back home. "Or would you have to be a psychopath to be that calm?"

Stefan couldn't say, but he asked me to sit with him in the sunroom and reflect on walking into Parker Hall yesterday, and what everyone looked like—the dean, Bill Malatesta, Iris and Carter, Juno—to see if I'd missed something. Clearly he was as hooked by what had happened as I was, and unwilling to let the puzzle go.

He'd brewed some vanilla hazelnut coffee, and it was just what I needed. I tried remembering, but nothing came to mind.

"I've been wondering," Stefan said. "You told me there was a lot of blood, right? Then wouldn't you have noticed it on somebody? You can't wash it all away, can you?"

"Depends on how much time the killer had. And on other things, too. Carter and Iris went by pretty fast, and Juno flew down the stairs. How could I tell?" And then I sat up so sharply I almost spilled my coffee. "Bullerschmidt said he couldn't shake my hand because his were still wet from washing them! And he was standing right near Parker, so what if he'd just come out?"

"Did he seem strange?"

"Stefan, that man always seems strange. Like a gigantic land mine. Like Marlon Brando playing Attila the Hun in assisted living."

"Okay, okay."

But something else had been bubbling away under all this retrospection. "Stefan. I forgot someone. There was a light on in the History Department office."

"Polly?" he asked.

"Yes, Polly," I agreed, and we put our coffee down to head for the door, Stefan obviously as curious as I was now to know what she'd seen or heard yesterday in Parker Hall.

Her unassuming pale blue ranch house was on Didier and Lucille's side of the street, near the end of the block.

As we headed down toward it, I could have sworn I saw the guy I thought was Napoleon dart around the far corner, but by the time I got Stefan's attention, he was gone. Stefan glanced at me as if he was hoping I hadn't fallen prey to hallucinations.

"Maybe it was a ghost," I threw off, annoyed.

Though Polly's house was one of the smallest on our street, the yard was as well tended and attractively landscaped as any in the neighborhood, her weedless brick path lined now with crocuses and narcissi. Polly was flustered to see us, probably because we'd never visited before. And as she let us in, her gauzy blue sleeve making a little paisleyed flag under her arm, I couldn't help thinking of that sweet elderly witch opening the door in *Bell, Book, and Candle* for Kim Novak and Jack Lemmon. The house reeked of incense, and angel mobiles hung everywhere I looked, twirling languidly above angel sculptures, crystals, candles, and other New Age impedimenta. All the bulky furniture in the small, squarish living room was covered with velvet throws in purple, crimson, and midnight blue, sucking up what light did manage to filter through the heavy dark blinds.

I suppose I shouldn't have been critical. It was probably a great room for an out-of-body experience or a Vulcan mind-meld.

More agitated than I'd ever seen her before, Polly asked if we wanted some mulled apple cider. It was an unusual choice for spring, but I said yes, since I didn't want to displease her. Stefan was silent, already in his author's mode, observing her as she swirled and rustled out of the room.

Her mild-mannered bichon frise, Spartacus, appeared at my feet, looking up with his adorable Ewok-like face. Before I could even bend down to offer him my hand for a sniff, he suddenly tore off behind me as if late for a train, but he didn't leave the room. He circled the couch and chairs and did it again and again, a silly fuzzy blur of white. Stefan smiled indulgently.

"That's what they do," Polly said, returning with two steaming hand-thrown dark mugs she set down on the tree-stump coffee table. "He's an Aries, but it's a characteristic of the breed."

I was relieved to hear that, since I had suspected that Spartacus had simply been driven mad by living with Polly.

"It could be worse," I said. "He could be into drugs, or cyber porn."

Polly smiled wanly. Just then, Spartacus stopped at her feet, panting, grinning. She scooped the tiny dog up and plopped him in her lap, where he stretched and nestled for a bit while we talked, then fell asleep. I wondered idly if Stefan and I should get a dog. Neither one of us worked full-time, so it wouldn't ever be alone for long stretches of time, which I knew was important. Would all this turmoil be easier to take if we had a pet?

Stefan launched right in after some pleasantries about the weather.

"You probably heard about Delaney Kildare?"

Polly nodded, biting her lip.

Stefan turned to me, and I took my cue, saying, "The light was on in the History office after five, so I figured you were there and might have heard something."

"That's right." Polly nodded eagerly, I guess relieved that I wasn't going to accuse her of murder.

"How late did you work?"

She shrugged. "I don't remember."

"Did you hear anything?"

She frowned, eyes on Spartacus where he snored a little in her lap. "I was filing," she said slowly. "Banging drawers. You know. Oh, and the radio was on. That new country station," she added brightly. "I just love Shania Twain, don't you?"

"So there wasn't anything unusual?"

"I like working late on Friday, it's easy to get things done," she said, somewhat inconsequentially, slim hands combing back her hair. As she did so, I realized that not only was she quieter and less energetic than usual, but she looked a bit haggard.

"Did you know Delaney?"

"Of course I knew him," she snapped, and the abrupt change of tone woke her dog, who muttered a little. "He was once a history graduate student, wasn't he? Getting his M.A.? So of course I saw him around." Spartacus slipped from her lap and started on his Grand Prix thing again.

Stefan asked, "Why did he change departments?"

Polly shrugged and told him to ask Dean Bullerschmidt. "He was involved somehow."

I was struck that the usually garrulous Polly was so close-mouthed, her reticence thrown into higher relief by Spartacus's manic activity. Stefan eyed me with the signal to leave, but I was convinced Polly was holding something back. At the door, I asked if Detective Valley got the same story as we did. "He probably interviewed you at the office yesterday."

"It's not a story!" she shouted. "I'm not a liar, and I told him exactly what I told you!"

Nixon, I said to Stefan outside on the sidewalk. It was the same as Nixon claiming he wasn't a crook. "Except she doesn't sweat as much," I said. He nodded. Letting ourselves in back home, I stopped in the doorway, key in the lock. "I'm assuming she was still there when the campus police arrived, but what if she was gone by then? What if she just forgot to turn off the light, or ran out because she was scared?"

Stefan gently pushed me inside. I disengaged the key and followed him to the kitchen, where we sat at the table. "What's your point?" he asked.

"I don't know. I can't even remember if the light in the History office was on when I left—I was so freaked out. I should have asked her, huh? But I don't think she'll want to talk to us again right now." I beamed. "Hey—maybe getting angry was a stroke of luck. Maybe she'll stop barging in on us!"

Stefan poured us some Perrier while we puzzled over why Polly had been so defensive. Stefan thought it might simply be reality. "She's a space cadet, and this is too concrete for her. A murder, an investigation." But he was smiling, and I could tell he was imagining what fictional possibilities a character like her would have in a situation like this.

"I don't see why you're not trying to write mysteries. How many authors have material like this falling at their feet? You wouldn't have to invent much at all." As soon as I said it, I realized he might think I was disparaging his fiction. I tried explaining, but it was okay.

"I know you're trying to be helpful, Nick. And maybe in a way you're right. Maybe it's time to rethink my career. If my novels aren't going anywhere, then I should write something else. But mysteries?" He shook his head. "That's just not how I see the world."

"Meaning—?"

"In a mystery, everything gets solved at the end, right? There's chaos, and then there's order. Life isn't that neat."

"But I'm not talking about life, I'm talking about fiction! You know what Wilde said, 'The good end happily, the bad unhappily. That is what fiction means.' "

He smiled.

"Wouldn't it be fun, Stefan? We could even write it together. You could do the nasty stuff, and I could do the jokes."

"There'd have to be jokes?"

"For sure. How else could you stand the grim parts?"

"Let's stick with Polly. Now, she's so out of touch, I bet that if she saw or heard anything, she might not even have realized it."

"Stefan, she's a secretary, and she must be good if she's working for the History chair. Give her a little credit. And didn't you notice how she wasn't doing any of that spirit-in-the sky crap today? No astral projection, no canals on Mars? She seemed normal, for her. And scared, or at least worried."

Stefan agreed, but it didn't lead us anywhere.

"Her dog's cuter than I remember," I heard myself say.

"You've only seen him digging up our yard," Stefan pointed out.

"Exactly. You didn't have a dog when you were a kid, did you?"

"No. I told you that before."

"Just checking. I didn't, either. Do you think we'd make good parents?"

"We might need some counseling first," Stefan mused, and at first I thought he was serious. His next comment was, though. "What makes you bring it up now?"

"I don't know. Seeing Spartacus up close, maybe. It's not as if we know a lot of people with dogs. He's cute, even though he's Polly's dog. The racetrack stuff was kind of adorable."

"I wonder if thinking about adopting a dog is connected to Jesse and Delaney dying?"

"Hey, I'm not talking about getting a guard dog."

"No, I didn't mean that. It's—it's seeing death and wanting to be more involved with life."

I thought that over a little and told Stefan it made sense. "I know it's a lot of work, and would really change our lives, but what kind of dog would you like if we got one?"

The phone rang before he could answer, and since I was closer, I picked it up.

"Professor Hoffman, it's Margaret Case—are you all right?" she asked in her friendly but formal tone.

"Sure," I said, startled, and whispered who it was to Stefan. Stefan said quietly, "Ask her how Delaney died."

I nodded.

Dr. Case was saying, "Remember I said I'd get you the number for her parents in Houghton? I tried it myself, but it's always busy."

"Oh."

"I was worried about you. I saw your name in this morning's paper. It didn't say anything about how you were—except alive."

"Really, I'm okay."

"Well, you must be used to dead bodies by now," she threw off, and I laughed for what seemed like the first time in days. I suppose her gallows humor was what kept her from running around in circles like Spartacus. Whatever its source or function, I was happy to benefit from it. I explained the joke to Stefan, who handed me a pad and pen.

"I know you're just itching to get a preview of the report on the latest death, Professor Hoffman—"

"You have to call me Nick," I urged. "Even if you want to be Dr. Case. I don't mind."

"Deal. He suffered a minor injury to the head—he was punched, and that broke a tooth. But the cause of death was massive cranial trauma." Case explained that Delaney had apparently been slammed against the wall in the men's room, cracking the back of his skull. There were hair, blood, and skull fragments on the wall and plaster and paint in the wound at the back of his head. I jotted notes down, turning the pad around so that Stefan could read.

"You're sure about his being pushed? He couldn't have fallen somehow, slipped? Or deliberately done it himself?"

"Given the impact, it's unlikely that he fell. The boy was pushed, and pushed hard. And he didn't punch himself, then slam his head into a wall. If he wanted to kill himself, there are better ways to go about it."

"So whoever did it was very strong?"

Dr. Case hesitated. "Strong, or outraged. Since there was no evidence of a struggle, no bruising, defensive wounds, nothing under his nails, surprise seems to have been a factor—"

I pictured someone coming in after him, Delaney turning. . . .

"—no matter who was responsible, man or woman. Maybe more so, if it was a woman. He was a muscular boy, but not very tall or all that big. And even though the bathroom window was open, there were no reports of a struggle, or noise, or shouting."

I scribbled some of this down for Stefan and showed it to him. "How about the time of death?" I asked, knowing that determining it wasn't an exact science like economics.

"I'm judging somewhere between four and when you found the body around six P.M."

The conversation was starting to wear me down as it brought back the horrible scene in that men's room, and the glaring, hungry crow. But I'd been so overwhelmed by the shock, by the blood, that I couldn't really recall a lot of details, so I asked Dr. Case if Delaney had been standing at or near the urinals when it happened, and if someone had snuck up on him.

"Good question. I don't think so. He had just urinated, as it turns out, but his pants were zipped and there were traces of soapy water on his hands, so he was actually leaving, I think, or about to. But that's all I can tell you, Nick. My advice? Stay out of it now. I called because I was concerned, and told you this much because I knew you'd be poking around. But really, stay out of it. Detective Valley doesn't like how you keep showing up when someone's been murdered. And he doesn't like *you*."

"What else is new?" I countered, thanking her for calling, for her concern, and for the info.

When I hung up, Stefan asked me to pour him some more coffee and nipped off to the john. While he was gone I found myself regretting not just the mess I was plunging myself into, but that I was doing it on Shabbat, a day that was supposed to be given over to rest and retreat from the outside world, a sanctuary in time. Stefan had over the years come to enjoy the meditative tranquillity, the exaltation of inwardness, as much as I did. Yet here we were, the world way too much with us. I wished at that moment that we were doing more by way of observance, had more of a structure for our one truly sane day of the week. I wished that we did more, made more of Shabbat. But how? I wasn't wild about the only synagogue in town, where people struck me as either stuffy academics or stuffy businessmen, and even the new young rabbi already seemed embalmed.

Was this longing for a deeper connection to Shabbat of a piece with thinking about a dog? What was going on with me? Was it about aging? It certainly had nothing to do with nostalgia for home, because to my parents, Shabbat was a set of strictures: no TV, no radio, no movies, no playing, no activity beyond walking to synagogue and taking part in services.

When Stefan returned to the kitchen, sat down opposite me, and said, "Tell me everything," I knew he wanted to hear about Dr. Case, and that sharing what I'd been thinking about would be bad timing. But I was tempted.

Instead I repeated everything that Margaret Case had told me, including the warning. We tried imagining what might have happened in that men's room. Someone followed Delaney in, or perhaps was already there, and attacked him. Given the lack of a struggle, we agreed that it must have been someone Delaney knew but wasn't afraid of. Obviously still gunning for Juno, Stefan argued that it must have been a woman, because that would have been more of a surprise, but I couldn't see it.

"No," he said. "Think about it. Killing him right there in Parker Hall where anyone could find you, anyone could walk in? That's so cold and calculating. Sneaky."

I went to the sink to wash out my cup and set it in the drainer, then rejoined him at the table.

"Men aren't sneaky? Come on, Stefan, use your imagination—you're a novelist! It had to be a man, because no one would notice a man going into the men's room or be surprised seeing him leave. A woman would risk calling attention to herself."

"But where are the witnesses? I can picture a woman doing it, someone daring, wild."

"Juno?"

He nodded.

"Okay, let's say she did kill him? Why?"

"Why did anyone who could have killed him do it? Bullerschmidt, Iris Bell, Carter, Benevento, Polly."

"Let's just hope Valley doesn't start suspecting *you*," I said, "if he finds out we had an argument about Delaney." At Stefan's frown, I said quickly, "Don't worry—I won't tell him, it's not important."

Stefan cracked his knuckles and leaned back in his chair. "We should invite him to dinner, ply him with wine, and while he's surprised, get him to tell us about his investigation."

"That's the kind of thing *I'd* suggest, and it would never work."

He smiled wryly. "I know—that's why I said it. You can't always be the one to have the good lines."

"So what now?" I asked. We both glanced around the kitchen as if the answer would leap out at us from the simple array of ordinary things. "Will you come with me to talk to Bullerschmidt?"

"The *dean*?"

"That's the one. Polly said he was involved with Delaney moving from History to EAR, and he was outside Parker, and he did say his hands were wet. The man's got killer written all over him."

Stefan washed out his cup. "I don't know, Nick. He's a bureaucrat, an administrator. He'll strangle people in red tape, drown them in memos, crush them with committee work—but actually commit murder? Besides, he's the dean of our college, we can't just drop in."

"I know that. But I never get to see him on campus, and besides, it would have to be an official visit. Seeing him at home is just a neighborly call."

"Bullerschmidt lives in Michigan Estates—that's a mile away."

I sighed. "Are you going to carp, or you going to help? I have to pursue this, I can't let it go and sit around forever waiting to find out what happened. But I don't want to do this alone."

He said, "Sure." And if it wasn't quite as stirring as crossed swords and "One for all and all for one," it was good enough for me.

After checking the dean's address, we set off on the short drive in Stefan's Volvo. Michigan Estates, due north of us, was an exclusive walled community with enormous, lavishly landscaped 1960s-era homes, many of them worth over half a million dollars, which is a lot in Michiganapolis since housing in the Midwest is more reasonable than in any other part of the country.

We parked at the end of the cul-de-sac where he lived so our car wasn't visible and approached the house as if expecting wild dogs to tear us apart. Faced with glossy white bricks, it was right out of a movie: large and vaguely oriental under an ominous low-slung roof with a deep overhang guaranteed to make for a sepulchral interior.

Before we even knocked or rang the oversize doorbell, one of the enormous double doors swung open to reveal Nina, the dean's well-dressed, reed-thin wife. I'd seen her at some official gatherings and decided that she was either tragically shy or deeply miserable because her mouth seemed perpetually on the edge of trembling. I could imagine that being married to the dean was as demoralizing as living in a village clinging to the side of an active volcano.

Today she looked as tormented as usual, despite the elegant aquamarine silk dress with matching pumps and a pearl torsade. We introduced ourselves and said we wished to talk to her husband.

"He can't see anyone," she stuttered. Behind her I could make out that the house was as shadowy inside as I'd guessed. But before either one of us could plead or insist, Bullerschmidt, who'd obviously been listening, loomed at the door and swept his wife aside. "Lovely of you to drop by," he said, without smiling. "Nina, bring us some coffee." He was wearing a huge smoking jacket with braid-trimmed lapels and a richly patterned ascot.

Bullerschmidt shepherded us across the marble-floored foyer right into the dark, crowded library, which looked like a Ralph Lauren Home Collection ad, complete with spaniels snoozing by the fireplace, where one log burned a bit fitfully. Sitting in one of the two club chairs opposite the nailhead leather sofa where he perched like a pharaoh, I felt suffocated by heat and clichés: the leather-bound author sets, the hunting prints, the lead crystal bottle stoppers on the Renaissance-style bar cabinet, the smug air of anglofraudulence.

More gracious than I'd ever seen him, Bullerschmidt made some small talk about various SUM matters, none of them controversial, clearly killing time until beaten-down Nina returned with the coffee, which she set on a red lacquered coffee table designed like a chinoiserie trunk. She decamped from the room as if she thought we were dangerous, closing the door hurriedly behind her.

As he poured coffee for us from what I suspected was a Georgian silver pot, I wondered why *I* couldn't be a dean making over $150,000 a year to intimidate people and produce blizzards of pointless paperwork.

The pretty cups didn't prepare me for how bitter the coffee was. Bullerschmidt didn't seem to notice, unless he liked it that way.

"Following up on Detective Valley?" the dean said pleasantly—for him. "Do you think he can't do his job well without amateur assistance?"

I felt as tongue-tied and ashamed as a tiny grade schooler called before the principal for a major infraction; what *were* we doing here?

"I know all about your previous escapades. You weren't hired for your forensic skills, you know. You were hired to teach."

Stefan tried to rescue me. "Nick was the one to find Delaney's body. It was very traumatic, for him, and—"

"—and you're trying to help him achieve what they call closure?" he said scornfully. "By quizzing all the 'suspects' on their whereabouts? Or is it just me you've come to exercise your ratiocination upon? Well, since I'm sure that our Detective Valley has better things to do than talk to the Snoop Sisters, here's my story. Yes, I was in Parker Hall yesterday afternoon, on the way back from a very late lunch with the provost in town. I stopped in Parker to use the men's room. But not the one on the third floor, or the second. The one on the first." Spreading wide his hands to highlight his bulk, he said, "I'm not in the habit of ignoring a perfectly good bathroom to climb stairs I don't have to. I neither saw nor heard anything the hysterically minded would call suspicious. Satisfied?"

Since he asked, I plunged on. "Delaney said he got you to approve funding for his becoming my TA because you were good friends." It was something of a lie, but I said it to see if it would shake him out of his elephantine composure. It didn't.

"I'm sure he was exaggerating for effect," the dean rumbled. "He made a good case for the assistantship, that's all. I'm sure *you'd* agree that he was a very personable young man. It wasn't a significant sum of money. Why shouldn't you have a teaching assistant? That way more students can take the class without burdening you. No doubt it'll be a very popular course. We are in the business of satisfying our students, or haven't you heard?" And he peered down his tuber of a nose at me.

"Oh," I said, flattened by his rhetorical juggernaut. But then I rallied a little. "Why did Delaney move from the History Department to EAR?"

"I don't know. Shifting intellectual pursuits, I'd guess."

"But didn't you have something to do with that?"

"I barely knew him," Bullerschmidt said with a sneer.

"I find all this hard to believe," Stefan said, sparked to anger by Bullerschmidt's ponderous show of contempt.

The dean said, "Mr. Borowski"—I'm sure stripping him of Dr. or Professor was both an insult and a warning—"I'll tell you what's hard to believe. That an assistant professor like your little friend here, who's just starting the tenure review process, would go out of his way on a weekend to harass the dean of his college." He put his cup down on the tray, and the gentle clink was to me like the pounding of a judge's gavel. He eyed me with open fascination, as if he were one of those eighteenth-century English aristocrats amusing himself by surveying inmates of Bedlam through his monocle.

Chastened, we sat there silently until the dean said coldly, "We're done now. You can leave."

We took him at his word. Nina Bullerschmidt stood out in the foyer, holding one of the doors open for our ignominious exit.

Our abashed silence continued on the brief ride home. Once back in the kitchen—our apparent command and control center—we did the only sensible thing. We each had a bowl of Häagen-Dazs Vanilla Swiss Almond ice cream with some Pepperidge Farm Bordeaux cookies.

12

So where did this day's inquiries leave us? We put off debating that while we made a caesar salad with grilled chicken for lunch. Stefan was in charge of the washing, drying, and tearing the romaine and preparing the chicken, while I handled the dressing, mashing anchovies into olive oil, adding crushed garlic, lemon juice, and Worcestershire sauce, and whisking it all together. We broke out the small hoard of garlic croutons I'd actually made myself one recent afternoon in a fit of Martha Stewart madness. These moments were like time portals opening up in a sci-fi film: captivating, but unpredictable and potentially dangerous. They could lead to unbridled wallpapering.

The mixing and clanking, the mild, familiar joy of working together in the kitchen, our paths weaving in and out, helped calm me after the humiliating encounter with Bullerschmidt.

"Not humiliating," Stefan corrected when we sat down to eat our Shabbos lunch after blessing the wine and the challah.

"How so?" I crunched one of the delicious, buttery croutons.

"He's lying about his relationship with Delaney."

"Of course he is. Whenever an administrator claims something's good for students, you know he's blowing smoke. Students are the very last thing they care about—protecting their butts and expanding their power is what's important." It was well known that compared to other big midwestern schools, SUM was exceptionally top-heavy with untalented but entrenched administrators pulling down exorbitant salaries. Even the state legislators had complained about it, but nothing had changed. Bullerschmidt, a junior-league Pol Pot, was a prime example of bureaucratic bloat and abuse, widely loathed for his rudeness, his overbearing presence at poisonous and often unnecessary breakfast meetings, his dreaded meteor shower of e-mail when you worked on something with him, and his persistent complaint that no one on campus was willing to work. The implication was that he was alone, slaving away to make SUM a better school.

"He's lying," Stefan repeated. "Why else would he have to threaten both of us?"

"Well, someone like that thrives on smacking people down. He's a kind of vampire; he feeds off everyone else's misery."

"But he knows he can't carry out the threats. I've got tenure, and you can claim discrimination if you get turned down for tenure."

I goggled. "Is that your failsafe plan for me? Why haven't you said anything before?"

"Because it'll be ugly, and I hope we don't get cornered. Maybe the Norton Edition will do the trick. If not, or if he's out to get you, then we can always go nuclear, right?" He held out his hands and shrugged, looking very French.

"Wow." Fighting for tenure—now, that was a new thought. I had never been given to public protests or even signing petitions, perhaps swayed by my immigrant parents' sense—out of gratitude that they had escaped the European inferno—that they should never make waves here. This was something Stefan and I shared, even though our parents were from different parts of Europe and very different Jewish worlds. He said it was fear, though, and not gratitude.

"Bullerschmidt knows we would go beyond the university and generate as much adverse publicity as possible for SUM. They're terrified of *looking* bad, not being bad."

"Good line."

He nodded. "So. How do we find out more about Buller-schmidt and Delaney?" he asked, setting down his knife and fork.

"Polly's our only hope. She was definitely not telling us the complete truth. Maybe we can squeeze it out of her."

"How?"

"Threaten to hire a psychic to jam her alpha waves?"

The phone rang, and Stefan reached for it. "Hi, Lucille. Now?" He glanced a question at me and I nodded. "Sure. We're just finishing lunch." He hung up and said she was coming over in a few minutes. It seemed odd that she had called first, since we had gotten into the habit of simply crossing the street and knocking on each other's doors.

Stefan and I put the dishes in the dishwasher, and I set water to boil to make some instant espresso with Cafe Bustelo. Lucille soon joined us at the kitchen table, where we hunched over our very sweet and strong espresso like conspirators, though I had to remind myself that she was as much a suspect as anyone else. Still, the idea of her killing Delaney when she was so fond of him seemed extremely implausible. Yet I could feel that wading through the very unreality of the situation, generating endless spirals of speculation, was helping me begin to recover from the shock.

"Detective Valley was extremely rude to me last night. That man yanked my chain," she said. "And this morning, too. He's convinced I killed Delaney, or that Didier did."

"Maybe both," I suggested helpfully.

Lucille gave us a grim smile. "Yeah, maybe both. I bet that bastard would love to nail an interracial couple for murder. You can just smell it on him."

Before either of us could ask her where she'd been the day before, she said, "I was at the library most of the afternoon, and never went back to my office, just to the lot behind Parker to get my car. I was working in the stacks, and who the hell knows what the time was exactly. I can't remember if I met anyone, so that's no alibi."

I asked, "Did you take out any books?" That would have left at least some record of when she'd been there and left. Or would it?

She shook her head, looking fretful and annoyed. "But it's crazy to think I'd kill Delaney," she said, her voice thickening, and she dragged a red bandanna from the pocket of her jeans skirt to blow her nose. "Delaney was a wonderful, kind boy. And smart. He was writing a brilliant paper on Toni Morrison's *Beloved* and Elie Wiesel's *Night*, comparing the effect of extreme deprivation and trauma."

It sounded fascinating, but I wondered if her thinking of Delaney as brilliant wasn't her own projection, and if the paper idea wasn't hers as well. Or even Bill Malatesta's—after all, he'd accused Delaney of plagiarism. Maybe it was true.

"Didier thought he was wonderful, too, all the times we had him over to dinner. Delaney wasn't any threat to our marriage," she added, as if answering an unspoken charge.

As Lucille seemed to edge closer and closer to tears, I could tell Stefan was getting uneasy. His face had taken on a kind of tense vagueness. Maybe he was thinking about how our relationship had been threatened a couple of years before when someone from his past almost came between us. "I'm going to do a little yard work," he announced. "I need to be outside."

Lucille was so wrapped up in her sorrow she didn't notice

the unusual briskness with which Stefan spoke and the way he practically fled the room by the back door.

"I was so fond of Delaney," Lucille said, shaking her head and clearly fighting back tears.

"How much?"

Her head jerked as if I'd slapped her. "We weren't sleeping together, if that's what you mean," she said sharply. But then her voice melted. "Lord, I wanted to. But something didn't seem quite right."

"He was your student."

"You think I could forget that? But he was *Delaney*," she said, sounding a little like an adolescent girl mooning over Leonardo DiCaprio. "Nothing like this has ever happened to me, Nick. It's been a hellacious year. Moving to Michigan, Didier immersed in his book, feeling so unpopular in EAR. Why I ever thought academia would be a good environment, I don't know. After all the venality in publishing, I had these romantic fantasies about a world dedicated to knowledge and learning. I should have just gone running with the bulls in Pamplona."

"I know what you mean. I've been wondering about my future here even if I do get tenure."

Lucille frowned and took my hand. "But you're a shoo-in, aren't you? If they want to keep Stefan here, they can't let you go." I pulled my hand away, and she apologized. "I didn't mean you don't deserve tenure for yourself—just that—"

I cut her off. "I know what you meant. And it's the truth. I got this job because of Stefan, even though I'm a good teacher. But no one in EAR believes that or even cares."

"At least you haven't gotten hate mail." She drained her cup and asked for more. I put up the hot water again. Thinking about what her time at SUM had been like, I understood how vulnerable she had been. Still . . .

"Has there been any more hate mail?" I asked her.

Lucille shook her head. "I suppose the brick was what it was all building toward. Oh, God, what a gross pun! Sorry." I was about to ask her something else when she went on: "Nick, you said that Delaney was my student. He really wasn't anyone's student. He's not like anyone else I've ever met. But to tell you the truth, sometimes he bothered me. I mean, something about him bothered me." Hands folded, face composed again, she seemed to be tallying it all up right there with me. "I guess you'd have to say he was seductive."

"No guessing about it! Those tight jeans—sitting with his legs wide open in that Come-to-the-Cabaret pose?"

She chuckled. "It wasn't that bad, was it?"

Was I remembering it differently now that he was dead, or had Delaney's murder freed me to recollect him with more honesty? "Yes, it was," I said. "Other people talked about it, too," I said, remembering Bill Malatesta, though he himself wasn't averse to lighting the charm incense. "The way Delaney dressed and held himself, the way he looked at people, it was too much. He probably couldn't help it. He was like a character Elizabeth Bowen writes about somewhere: 'He'd play a kitten up if we had a kitten here.' "

She frowned. "Bowen? Didn't she write *The Death of the Heart*?"

"Yes—that's the book! I read it in college."

"And you can still remember it?" She shook her head admiringly. "I'm scared of you."

I grinned and once again felt myself lucky to have found someone in EAR I could be friendly with. That is, when I wasn't suspecting her or her husband of murder.

"Nick. There was something murky about Delaney, I'm sure of it. More than just free-floating seductiveness."

"He did have a weird smile."

"Right. That smile, that smile. It was the only thing that didn't fit him well, and—"

I waited for Lucille to say more, but she looked uneasy. Should I prompt her, or let her bring it out at her own pace?

"Sometimes he said things that were—well, offensive isn't the right word."

"Things like?"

She shrugged, looking away from me. "Oh, like saying that Didier was so famous already for a book that hadn't even been published, and how that was overshadowing my career as a teacher, a very *fine* teacher. It upset me."

"Jeez." I didn't feel my hair stand on end or a sudden chill, but something pretty close to both of those. "That's the same kind of thing Delaney was trying with me. How Stefan was so well known that I was in his shadow. It only happened twice, but it made me miserable, and Stefan and I got into a nasty argument the other night."

Lucille and I stared at each other, recognition growing between us like two victims of real estate fraud or some other malicious con game.

"He wanted you to be *jealous* of Stefan," Lucille said.

"And he wanted *you* to be jealous of Didier."

"But why?"

I echoed that, and then, unbidden, I told her Delaney's creepy story about his parents, his "detective work" in ferreting out his mother's secret life.

"Shit! Are you serious? He told me I was the only person he ever shared that story with!"

"Same here," I said, realizing that we had both been victims of some obscure plan that could have hurt us very badly. "I guess it was his party piece," I mused, though that didn't at all seem to capture Delaney's smiling insidiousness.

"But why was he slinging that bullshit, if it was bull? Trying to get our sympathy? I confess, it worked on me."

I shook my head. "It put me off. And why would he need sympathy when he had his looks working for him overtime?"

"He was beautiful," Lucille agreed. "Sometimes he'd be talking, and I'd end up staring at his lips, or his hair—or something else!—and I'd miss what he was saying."

I didn't tell her that I'd seen him in the showers at the Club, and he'd been even more desirable than she knew. "But was he really smart, or were you just dazzled?"

"He got accepted into the Ph.D. program, didn't he?"

"Lucille, you know as well as I do that EAR needs a constant supply of cheap labor to teach courses the faculty doesn't want. People who won't get decent jobs when they're done, if they get hired at all. The department keeps stringing them along whether they're really capable or not—EAR can't afford not to. But forget that for now."

"Wait," she said. "Why did Delaney switch from History to EAR? He never mentioned it to me, and I never asked."

"I don't know." We sat there with our brows as furrowed as if we were on opposite sides of a very challenging chess game. Suddenly I was recalling Stefan's sleepy question from the other night: Who would want to kill both Delaney and Jesse Benevento?

"Jesse Benevento was taking a class with Delaney," I said.

"And?"

"Well, isn't that a connection? What if one of the students in that class hated them both—maybe Delaney was giving the student grief, and—and—" Lucille looked at me, but I said, "I don't know." I shifted gears. "You spent a lot of time with Delaney, right? Was there anything else about him you picked up, anything that might explain why he was killed?" I knew Valley had probably asked the same question, but I doubted Lucille felt as comfortable talking to him as she did with me. "Do you know how he was able to afford membership at the Club?"

Lucille blushed a little. "I bought it for him, since he was complaining about getting out of shape and how bad the facilities were at the men's IM." Defensively, she said, "He was only a graduate student! You know how expensive it is to join. And I felt so grateful to him because he was so warm and concerned when I told him about the hate mail. Didier was just ranting about going to the police, but Delaney made me feel better. That was what counted. He didn't get all macho on me. I hate that."

The kettle boiled, and I made her another cup of the instant espresso.

"This is pretty good. I could live off it," she murmured, taking the cup from me. "Didier plays all smooth and relaxed, but that's not the whole story. He can be mean when he's pissed off." As soon as she said it, she brought her hand up in front of her mouth as if the words were still hovering there and could be grabbed and crushed. "He didn't kill Delaney. I wasn't saying that."

I nodded.

"No, really, Nick. He didn't. He can lose his temper, but that doesn't make him a killer."

Not necessarily. Losing your temper was the first step. Lose it precipitously enough, and who knew what could happen?

"Oh, shit, Nick. You'll never believe me now."

Since she was so open, I was tempted to ask her more about her private life then, and probe a little more deeply into her relationship with Delaney, but I wasn't sure if I wanted to know anything beyond what Didier had already told me. Before I could figure out where to go next, the doorbell rang, and I heard shouting. "I'll skin you alive, you sons of bitches!"

Juno Dromgoole had come calling. Lucille and I leapt up as she started beating on the door like a Japanese demon drummer. Stefan tore in from the backyard, wiping his hands on his jeans. "I heard that lunatic from out back. Let's call the police."

But I sprang down the hall to the front door and wrenched it open, surprising Juno in mid-rant. She stalked into the foyer, red-faced, surveying me with wild-eyed disgust, hands on her hips. Lucille and Stefan warily joined us, and taking in their presence behind me, Juno cried out, "I knew it! Conspirators! You're all in this together!"

Stefan moved behind her to shut the door since our neighbors weren't fans of theater of the absurd, and I noted that even playing Medea, Juno looked sensational. She wore a tight-waisted black satin blazer over a black body stocking and silver stiletto heels, with a candelabra's worth of silver dangling from each ear and her wrists, and draping her neck.

"We're all in what together?" I asked, as we stood awkwardly by the door.

"Trying to frame me for Delaney's death!"

To his credit, Stefan turned red. He and I exchanged a wordless question: Invite her in or kick her out? I nodded to the living room, and when he reluctantly headed there, he brought us along in his wake, though Lucille and I held back from crowding Juno lest she decide to pummel one of us in her lip-trembling fury. She and Lucille settled on the couch a safe distance apart.

"Juno," I said, "Detective Valley asked me who I saw at Parker Hall when Delaney was killed. I was just telling him the truth."

"You're all trying to frame me," Juno growled. "Especially that summer stock detective. He's persecuting me. Of course I was in a hurry to leave Parker Hall early last night. I had a date, didn't I?"

"A date?" I repeated idiotically, I'm afraid.

"Yes," she hissed. "A fucking date. Does that surprise you?"

Actually, it did. I imagined her romantic life was more along the lines of a search-and-destroy party.

"Who with?" Stefan asked.

"Delaney—and he never showed up."

The three of us gaped at each other, and then at Juno. And now, despite being perfectly groomed and coiffed, she appeared to crumble. "I didn't kill him," she wailed. "I was fucking him! Why would I want to kill him? How many juicy twenty-six-year-old studs do you think I can get without paying for it?"

I whispered to Stefan, "Straight people have such strange mating habits."

Lucille eyed Juno as coldly as Alexis had ever looked at Crystal on *Dynasty*, and I was thankful we weren't near a reflecting pool or any other small body of water, because I'm sure they would have gone tumbling in.

She could kill Juno now, I thought. Maybe not intentionally, but in a building, turbulent rage. Then Lucille surprised the hell out of me. As if determined to master her jealousy or whatever else Juno's confession had triggered, she moved down the couch and drew poor Juno into her arms. Juno didn't resist, but started ululating so piteously I was glad we didn't have a dog. Lucille rocked her, and through sobs, Juno told us her story.

"I met him at that student bar in town," she wailed. "The really louche one in a basement. Earlier in the semester. There was a punk band playing, Smegmathon Gang Bang or something like that."

The image of Juno at any student hangout cracked me up, and I tried hard not to show it. She would have terrified the undergraduates.

"Delaney stood me a drink. I returned the favor. And the

next evening he called." Red-cheeked from crying, she raked us with her glistening eyes. "How could I say no? It's not as if he was in my class or anything." Lucille winced at that. "We fucked only a few times—and then he played me like a fish. He wouldn't return my calls. That's what made me so desperate this year."

Stefan mouthed, "Yeah, right," to me, as if Juno wasn't always nasty, but Lucille caught it and silently admonished Stefan.

"Busy boy. Was he screwing anyone else?" I asked. Lucille let her go, and Juno sat back away from her, perhaps embarrassed by her outburst.

Desolate, Juno said she didn't know. "But he must have been. The boy was insatiable, not just for sex, but for praise. God, it was wonderful. But exhausting. I had to tell him what a good lover he was, how gorgeous he was. How could he ever doubt it?" Then, eyes gleaming, she held her hands an improbable distance apart. "And, my dears, he was—"

"Whoa!" Lucille said. "Don't go there, girlfriend."

Juno shrunk back into herself, looking as hurt as if we'd rejected a gift she'd picked just for us. Clearly she wanted to brag about her experience as much as lament it. I was torn between morbid curiosity and disgust.

The phone rang in my study, and I went off to screen the call, aware that I hadn't played any of yesterday's messages yet. It was someone claiming to be a reporter from the *Michiganapolis Tribune.* "Professor Hoffman? I wonder if you'd give us a comment about the arrest of William Malatesta for the murder of Delaney Kildare?" I angrily grabbed the receiver, sure that it was a hoax and ready to blast whoever was calling.

"Who the hell is this?"

"Oh, you're in, professor. Great!" I recognized the voice: Brenda Bolinksy, a reporter I'd met last year. "So, any comment? Yes, it's true. Malatesta denies it, but there was some blood found on the front seat and driver's floor mat of his car, and it matches the murder victim's."

I had trouble even managing a "No comment."

"Did you know Malatesta? Was he a student of yours? Was he prone to violence? Do you think drugs were involved? Was sexual harassment a factor?"

"Brenda, please don't call me again." I was so rattled I hung up and then said, "I'm sorry," when I'd meant to do it the other way around. I lingered in my study awhile, dazed, thinking about the time just a few days before when Bill had complained so bitterly about Delaney's influence with the dean, and how he hated the way that Delaney looked at Betty Malatesta. Had there been something more going on? An affair, and Bill found out? If Valley asked me about Bill, what was I supposed to do? My recounting of that conversation would be very incriminating—I couldn't imagine having to appear in court and repeat it.

Too clearly for comfort, I could see the powerful, enraged husband slamming Delaney against the men's room wall. But why upstairs, when both of them had an office in the basement? Unless Bill had somehow chased him up there? No, that didn't make sense; there'd be signs of a struggle, and surely I would have heard something.

"Nick," Stefan called from the living room. "Are you okay?"

I trailed out to where everyone, including Juno, sat looking remarkably civilized in that calm, quiet room. I gave them the news and sat in the chair by the fireplace, exhausted.

Stefan seemed most surprised. "Bill's such a decent guy," he said.

I filled them in on Bill's complaints against Delaney and his threat, leaving out the plagiarism.

" 'Dead meat,' " Juno said with a shudder. "How repulsive."

Stefan shook his head, and Lucille and Juno reported that

they didn't know Bill at all. "Though he's rather handsome," Juno threw out tentatively. No one commented.

"I don't buy it," I said, my voice unnecessarily loud. I got everyone's attention. "Of the two of them, Betty Malatesta has a much nastier temper, trust me, and she's as hard as Barbara Bush was under all those pearls. I know Bill's athletic and he looks tough, but I think he's really easygoing."

Stefan asked me why I was finding it so hard to believe Bill had killed Delaney. "Somebody had to," he pointed out logically. "And if they found Delaney's blood in his car, who else could it be?"

"Unless he was framed."

I had everyone's attention again, but this time they all looked at me with pity.

"They had to arrest somebody," Lucille said kindly, at least granting the possibility that I might be right. "Or they'd look like idiots, right?"

I considered that, and then suddenly remembered my manners. "Juno—would you like something to drink?"

"No, darling," she said softly. "What I would like is the powder room to repair the damage from my lamentable display." She blotted ineffectively at her face with a balled-up tissue. "Which way is it?"

I pointed out to the hall. "Second door on the left," I said, and she sashayed off. I wondered how long her volcanic temper would be quiescent.

Stefan urged me to stop worrying about Bill. "And let's stop investigating. Let the campus police handle everything now, since they have a suspect in custody."

"Absolutely," Lucille agreed.

Returning to the room looking completely restored, even Juno agreed. "You can't be mucking about in police business," she said when she picked up on the conversation. "Be satisfied that it's over." Her renewed composure struck me as somewhat eerie, given that she'd been auditioning for a production of *Pride of the Banshees* just a little while before. "They could arrest you," she said. "For obstruction of justice or some nonsense. I don't trust that slimy man who calls himself a detective."

Lucille smiled at Juno.

Then, only slightly chagrined, Juno thanked Lucille for being so sympathetic. "Perhaps we can have a girl's night out sometime," she suggested. "You remind me a bit of my sister, actually."

Lucille asked, "Are you busy now? Let's have a drink. I'm sure you could use one, and I live just across the street."

"I know," Juno said without irony. "And a drink would be lovely." Juno went out like March, Lucille following. "I'll call you," she said to us.

Stefan raised his eyebrows when they were gone, and I smiled. "Oscar Wilde was right. Women only use 'sister' after they've called each other lots of other things first."

"Juno was really something today."

"Lucille was being friendly, but did you catch her when Juno said she was fucking Delaney?"

"Even if she's jealous," Stefan reasoned, "Delaney's dead, so it doesn't matter."

Remembering the flashing light on my answering machine, I told Stefan I felt up to listening to the messages now, and he headed back outside. There was a handful from various Michigan newspaper and TV reporters, one from my cousin Sharon, and a sweet one from Minnie saying that even though Stefan had assured her yesterday that I was okay, she was still thinking about me. My own mother had called, leaving her inimitable two lines: "This is your mother. Thank you."

She had never overcome her distaste for the impersonal nature of answering machines, and never left a detailed message or even let me know by the tone of her voice whether something was up or not. I decided to wait on returning her call for a while. After a chat with my parents, I often felt mildly depressed and was never exactly sure if it was me or them. Was I responding to their unstated disappointment in me, or was it the other way around? Whichever, I avoided them on the phone. In person, and with Stefan mediating the conversation, it was always much easier and more cheerful.

I did return Sharon's call, though, and when I told her that a graduate student had just been killed at SUM, she was angry and astonished. "Another murder?" She sounded like Meryl Streep shouting *"Now* a warning?" to Isabella Rossellini in *Death Becomes Her.* Then Sharon burst out laughing at the sheer improbability of it, I suppose, until I told her that I was the one who had discovered the body. She apologized frantically. "Oh, sweetie—please don't think I'm heartless! But you have to admit it's getting out of hand. Maybe there isn't enough fluoride in the water there. Your school should hire one of those PBS gurus to come do round-the-clock seminars on conflict resolution. You people need help."

"I guess."

"Nick. I don't understand why you're not writing mysteries. Look at Amanda Cross—her books are terrible, and she must make a fortune on them. I know you could do better."

"That's the problem—if I wrote something better, it probably wouldn't sell." I told her about the time that Henry James got fired early in his career because his columns on Paris for an American newspaper were too erudite. James sarcastically protested that he'd written the worst prose he knew how.

"You have a point."

"Besides, Stefan and I would probably drive each other crazy if we were both writing fiction."

"But—no offense—wouldn't writing mysteries be more fun than scholarship?"

"I doubt it. You know what I'd hate? The condescending reviews, if I got reviews. The kind by serious literary authors who announce that they don't really like mysteries or read them, but this book is good because it 'transcends the genre.' What crap! Can you imagine someone reviewing Adrienne Rich's new book and saying, well, you know, honestly, between us, I really don't have a high opinion of poetry?"

"Let me ask you something," she said with loving mockery in her voice. "By serious literary authors, do you mean people like Stefan?"

I laughed. "Guilty as charged. He won't read mysteries. And why should he? He lived a mystery growing up—maybe that was enough. Now, tell me how you are—did you see your doctor?"

"Yes, I did," she reported proudly. "And guess what, sweetie, it wasn't the cold. My hearing's just not what it used to be. I'm getting old."

Sharon was almost five years older than I, but still slim and youthful. Of course, some discreet plastic surgery had helped. But her earlier years as a model had trained her how to walk and hold herself, and that's what made the real difference, I thought. "Most American women walk like clodhoppers," she'd often said, and it wasn't until my first trip to Paris that I understood what she meant.

"Last week when Stefan and I went to a twilight movie, we were the oldest people there by easily two decades. Stefan thought it was funny, but it creeped me out."

"I know, I know. I leaf through the fashion mags, and everyone's so damned young it's like visiting another planet. And I expected my skin to change, and my hair, but I never thought my hearing would start to go this early. So much for running at the gym and yoga! Who knew?"

"Is there something you can take for hearing? You're not sure? Because there's a supplement for everything else. Stefan and I take echinacea for general health, vitamin E for our prostates, Mega-Men multivitamins, aspirin for our hearts, *Gingko biloba* for memory. I don't think I can handle any more pills in the morning."

"Are you ready for matching rocking chairs yet, and blankets over our knees?"

"Well, not quite. But it doesn't seem impossible anymore, like it used to. So, is there anything else about your hearing?"

"Not much. My doctor's sending me to an audiologist to do some tests."

"What kind?"

"I'm not really sure. It's nothing serious, though, and I already feel a lot better. Really. Thanks for lecturing me. I wish I could help you out, though."

"There's no need," I said. "It's over."

"No way. Someone was arrested. There's going to be a trial, more publicity. Much more. And even when that mess is done, it won't be finished. You were at the scene of two murders. It'll be with you a long time. That's why I think writing about it would be good for you. Even if you just journal it. Oh, God, did I just use journal as a verb? Say you'll forgive me."

"At least you didn't say 'journalize.' Now, *that's* disgusting."

Sharon went on to fill me in on the latest intrigues at Columbia University, both in the archives where she worked and in some of the academic departments. It was the usual stew of adultery, sexual harassment charges, multicultural conflict, stacked tenure review committees, professors getting drunk during the break in their seminars. No wonder Amanda Cross was on her mind.

"Two murders," I told Stefan later after we were back together in the kitchen, having some Lillet on the rocks with club soda and lime. "There've been two murders. And if Bill Malatesta did kill Delaney because he was jealous, why would he also kill Jesse?"

"Who says they're connected? Don't they say that the longer it takes to arrest a suspect, the less chance there is of solving a murder? So the campus police got Bill within twenty-four hours. And Jesse's been dead over a week." He shrugged sympathetically. "I know you hate this. But there may not be an answer to Jesse's death. There isn't always an answer."

"I don't want to believe that."

"I know."

"And I feel guilty."

Alarmed, Stefan asked, "Why?"

"Bill Malatesta sat there and told me how much he hated Delaney, how jealous he was, how angry Delaney made him feel. He threatened Delaney, and I didn't really say anything. I didn't *do* anything."

"What could you have done? Nick, please, you're not a therapist who has a 'duty to warn.' You didn't listen to someone tell you he was going to commit a crime. From what you said, Bill was just blowing off steam, right?"

"That's what I thought, but I was all wrong. I didn't listen to him. How could I miss it when it was so obvious?"

"Nick, you're no dummy. If you missed it, it wasn't obvious. It couldn't have been."

"You're just rationalizing. You're trying to make me feel better."

Stefan smiled gently. "Is that such a crime?"

I shook my head. "Of course not. But look what's happened to me. I've been in the EAR department only a few years, and I've already become insensitive to my students."

"That's not true! One student—and you were not insensitive."

"God, I just want to leave this place, get out, go somewhere, anywhere. Don't you?"

"If it's death you're running from, there's no place to go."

"I'm talking about murder, not death. I know when you approach middle age, you start hearing the sound of drums. People around you start dying. Heart attacks, strokes, aneurysms, drunk driving. But nobody tells you to expect *murder*."

"You're just feeling helpless. Being at the scene of two murders would fill anyone with fear and self-doubt."

"Stefan, I'm not having an existential crisis—"

"You got something better to do tonight?" he quipped.

He was working so hard to cheer me up that I had to at least try responding, so I essayed a smile. After all, he was the one who had recently gotten devastating news from his publisher, yet he wasn't letting it sink him. Surely I could match his effort.

I wanted to grade papers the next day to get a little ahead, so on that Saturday night, instead of spending time cooking, we warmed up delicious leftovers for dinner: turkey and sausage meatballs in a homemade tomato sauce with zucchini and green pepper, served over spinach rigatoni. We polished off a bottle of easy-drinking 1994 Gabbiano red, but I'm not sure how much I really tasted.

As we were cleaning up, the phone rang in my study, and when the message came on, I heard a frantic, tearful voice: "Professor Hoffman—Professor Hoffman—you have to help us!"

I rushed to my phone and picked it up. "Thank God you're home!" Betty Malatesta moaned. "They arrested Bill for murdering Delaney Kildare, and they're holding him without bail. I know he hated Delaney, but this is crazy! Bill just got a job offer from Amherst College—why would he throw that away?"

I didn't ask her about the blood, and she didn't volunteer anything. "You think he did it, don't you?" she finally asked, and when I didn't reply immediately, she hurled her frustration at me in a scream and slammed down her phone.

I felt tired and old that evening, contemplating Betty's terror, Sharon's hearing problem, and my own ugly and increasingly intimate acquaintance with violent death.

SUNDAY MORNING I decided I could put off grading papers for another day or two and instead spent the morning in bed reading the *New York Times*. By noon I was ready to turn with gratitude to the spring project Stefan and I had been looking forward to. We were adding a small shade garden to the backyard right near the fence under the enormous maples. It would be beautiful once it got established: a mix of coral bells, forget-me-nots, lily of the valley, violas, monarda, pink and white bleeding heart, three kinds of hosta, two dozen daylilies, and ostrich plume ferns.

I found it a tremendous relief out back to talk about nothing but the plants when we did talk. Mostly we just dug and scooped and mulched with fragrant shredded bark. Spring had definitely arrived: forsythia and daffodils were blooming in our yard and all through the neighborhood, along with ragged carpets of della Robbia–blue scilla. Birds seemed to flutter and sing in every tree and bush: plangent chickadees and shrill jays, cardinals, robins, mourning doves.

Stefan and I took frequent breaks for water and to stretch our legs, which got stiff with all the kneeling even in gardening pants. The sound of raking and pruning from other yards, of children chasing their dogs, of garages being swept and cleaned out, filled the air as richly as the smell of burning leaves did in the fall.

Time disappeared for me that sunny day until it got cloudier toward sunset. When the planting was done, we washed up almost reverentially, as if this deep and soothing contact with the soil, with growth and possibility, had somehow healed the wounds of the past few days.

And so I read the *Michiganapolis Tribune* the following Monday morning with the detachment of a convalescent soldier following news from the front. Bill Malatesta had told his story to the paper, against the advice of his attorney, and it was pretty strange. Yes, Delaney Kildare's blood was in his car, but not because he'd killed Delaney. Admitting that he was jealous of Delaney, he said that he'd argued with Delaney in their basement office at Parker Hall late Friday afternoon and thrown a punch at him. That was all.

But I knew that it wasn't the whole story; Delaney had told me that Bill had tried to punch him at a party on Thursday night. I didn't know where it'd been held, but I was sure the campus police would be hearing about it, now that Bill had been arrested.

The article also said that Bill had no idea how Delaney had wound up dead in the third-floor men's room of Parker Hall. "The last time I saw him he was alive," Bill swore, as well as that he loved his wife and was sorry this was causing her any anguish. Betty announced that she was starting a defense fund, and the article was accompanied by a very appealing photograph, along with a sober warning by the DA to the effect that it was up to a jury to decide what was true.

"It's too late," Stefan said when he saw the article. "They're spinning the murder, making Bill sympathetic, not some thug killer. They'll play the whole thing out in public. It's brilliant."

I finished my grapefruit juice. "It's dangerous," was my comment, but I couldn't work up any emotion, as if I were reading some old Scandinavian epic poem and not news about people I knew. Would the whole thing unreel with all the ghoulish media frenzy we took for granted nowadays? *Larry King Live*, celebrity attorney, sensational rumors?

❦ 13 ❧

At Parker Hall that Monday morning, a week and a half after Jesse was murdered, I found a departmental memo from Coral Greathouse in my mailbox. Delaney's family had arranged for his body to be shipped back east after it was released, and EAR was having a memorial service that very afternoon. My instinct was to avoid it, but then I thought that's what most faculty in our heartless department would want to do, and I was not ready to cast my lot with the unfeeling majority.

But deciding to go plunged me into a fog, and I know my teaching was lackluster that day. I hoped my students just assumed I was shaken by the news, since many of them seemed quieter than usual, too. Though that could have been simply the emergence from weekend excesses.

I showed up at 4:00 P.M. at the conference room of definitely unblessed memory, surprised by the number of faculty and graduate students in somber attendance. Everyone spoke softly, if at all. Even this assemblage of braggarts, egotists, careerists, and no-talents was humbled in the face of death, and that was somewhat heartening, I thought.

Like the lecture hall of an unpopular professor, the room was filling up from the back forward. Lucille sat in the very last row, and there weren't any empty seats around her, so I just shrugged sympathetically.

Juno slunk in, head uncharacteristically down, her fire quite dimmed. She sat two seats away, and I felt sorry for her. Betty Malatesta made a dramatic entrance in black blouse and long black jeans skirt. Though she always wore black, today it made her look as if she was in mourning as Delaney's wife, not Bill's. She stopped in the doorway, raking everyone with her ravaged-looking eyes, and announced, "He didn't do it." Betty glared at me, and I half expected her to berate me for not helping Bill. I wondered what dire and disgusting fate she was wishing on me.

We all looked away, furiously but quietly attempting to act casual. Betty moved to the back of the room, leaning against the wall as if we weren't good enough to sit with.

I was surprised to see Polly show up, also in dark clothing that made her seem frailer, older. She nodded at me, then caught sight of someone else, shook her head, and backed out of the room. Why was she there, and whom had she seen? I glanced behind me but wasn't sure, and it didn't seem that anyone else had noticed. Maybe I was just imagining it, given the stress of the last few days.

The mood had shifted in the crowded, uncomfortable room after Betty's announcement; maybe Polly had left because she sensed something nasty in our collective aura. I wasn't sure I believed that individuals had auras, but EAR certainly had some group psychic stink, thanks to the university administration. Over a decade back, the separate Rhetoric Department, which taught all the basic composition courses, was dissolved and its faculty moved into English and American Studies, over futile faculty protests from both departments. The budget-cutting move created a permanent rift between the two groups: The rhetoric professors were treated as inferiors, and that treatment stoked their historical resentment about low salaries and a high teaching load. This happened well before Stefan and I had come to SUM, but we were often stumbling across the wreckage of that academic cataclysm.

As the room filled up even more, I thought about Polly again. I realized that she had probably come to pay respects to a former history student, and I was sorry she hadn't stayed. Gestures like that weren't the rule at SUM—but that was speaking about faculty. Secretaries tended to be friendlier, and many of them knew more about the way their departments operated than faculty did. I often heard our own secretaries correcting misinformation professors had given undergraduates they were supposedly advising. For all her dizziness, I'd heard that Polly did her job well.

Coral appeared suddenly at the front of the room, as if stepping from behind a curtain. "We're here to honor the memory of Delaney Kildare, one our graduate students," she began, droning on like a minister at a funeral who had never met the deceased and was just working from hastily written notes. It made me uneasy to think that this would probably be what happened to me if I were to die while teaching at EAR.

Coral's remarks were very brief, and she asked if anyone wished to speak. Lucille rose, and there was a stirring in the room, as if people expected her to light into the faculty after how she'd been treated the last time we were all together. "Delaney was a student of great promise," she said mellifluously, her glance shifting around the room, settling nowhere. "He was a thoughtful writer and would have made a charismatic teacher." I was impressed by her steady tone and measured praise. If I were in her place, I might have been tempted to howl.

Perhaps Lucille was contemplating a moment like that, because she paused for a very long time, then shook her head, said "Sorry," and sat down. Around me I heard approving murmurs that she had paid respectful tribute to one of her advisees. A few other professors rose and uttered banalities, more to fill the air, I thought, than because they had something important to say. Delaney hadn't been in the department long enough to have a real history there, for anyone to tell poignantly funny anecdotes about him.

Ten minutes? Fifteen? The service was over quickly, and everyone trooped off without any real sense of grief or regret in the air. I pushed through the crowd to say something to Lucille. I didn't want to do anything ostentatious that might set people wondering about her complex feelings for Delaney, but faced with her sad, set face, I had to give her an enormous hug.

"Stefan didn't come," she noted.

"He hates meetings," I whispered. "Even ones like this." As I said it, I wondered again what I, what Stefan, was doing here at SUM.

"And he gets away with it?" she said. "Must be nice." I could understand her attitude—I often envied Stefan's ability to avoid the mass meetings, though he did do his committee work with diligence. I noticed that she had her briefcase with her. She said, "I'll see you later. I'm going home to drink as much of Didier's unpronounceable Scotch as I can without brain damage."

I took off for my office, and on the stairs, things that had been jumbled in my head started to come together. I slowed down, picturing Polly's face earlier, and when we were talking to her about Delaney, and the last time she'd been at our house, in the sunroom. I remembered how she'd become subdued when I mentioned Delaney the first time, and how she'd recently sworn she wasn't lying.

Upstairs on the third floor I was in luck. I ran into Polly

coming back from the women's room, and suddenly something started to click for me. "Can I talk to you for a minute?"

She looked anxiously around as if I had laid some kind of ambush for her and the trap were about to be sprung, but then she nodded.

"My office?" I asked, and she followed me down the quiet hallway past the History Department office and a series of closed faculty office doors. For some reason, faculty up here tended not to leave their office doors open when they were inside, so you always had to knock to find out if anyone was there. Maybe they were trying to discourage students.

When she sat down, I pushed the door to but didn't close it, so I could tell if someone was out there. I sat behind my desk and plunged right in. "Were you sleeping with Delaney?" It seemed to be the most obvious question, and one that might lead to clarity about others.

"You're crazy!" she spat, but her eyes tightened.

"Last Sunday, you were all bubbly as usual until I mentioned Delaney across the street. It didn't hit me right away."

"Bullshit." She glared at me, but she didn't get up.

"And that's why you were combative when Stefan and I talked to you at your house, isn't it? Come on, he's dead, what does it matter now?"

Shamefaced, Polly said an unexpectedly soft "Yes." But then she raised her head and looked me squarely in the eyes, and before I could ask anything else, she went on as if she'd been waiting for someone, anyone, to unburden herself to. "On and off, from last year when he was finishing his master's in history. He liked older women. At least he said he did. But he had a cruel spirit."

"Physically? Was he abusive to you?"

"Not that way, no. He was terribly sarcastic about other women. You should have heard him joke about how fat Professor

Mochtar was, and how Professor Dromgoole dressed like she was twenty years younger than she was. Not that I agreed with him," she added loyally, even though both women had been her rivals in an odd sort of way. Both were downstairs at the memorial service, I thought.

"What else did he say about them?"

She sighed as deeply as if she were a medium trying to contact her spirit guide. "That they were eating out of his hand."

"When did he tell you all this stuff?"

Surprised by the question, she said, "In bed," as if everyone shared such rude confidences there. I thought of *Dangerous Liaisons* and imagined Delaney as the contemptuous Valmont. How deep had his treachery gone, and what did he get out of it?

As if she'd heard the question, Polly said, "He liked showing off." She closed her eyes, perhaps remembering some of the very particular ways he had showed off for her, and I let her have her moment while I considered Delaney's perversity. "He told me things about other people, how he could make them do whatever he wanted. Like you," Polly said, looking embarrassed. "He told me he was going to make you take him on as TA for your mystery course. And the dean would fund the course, too."

"How was he going to do that—did he say?"

She didn't know. "He was just sure he could do it."

Well, he'd been right about the dean, but he hadn't worked his dark magic on me enough to get me to agree to take him on as my TA. But he had certainly tried—what other purpose could he have had for driving a wedge between me and Stefan? Was he planning to seduce me, too, even though he was supposedly straight, or was his game to get me to make a pass at him that he'd reject so he could have power over me?

"He also said he was going to fu—*sleep* with Lucille Mochtar, but first he had to make her depend on him completely."

"How?"

"By scaring her," Polly says. "Scaring her bad."

Oh, God, I thought, it must have been *Delaney* behind the hate mail and breaking Lucille's window with a brick. Delaney used all that to undermine Lucille's sense of security, then offered himself as savior—and more, if she wanted it. Which she did.

Polly was peering at me curiously, so I said, "The racist postcard Lucille got here—you heard about it, didn't you?"

She nodded ruefully. "He never told me what he was going to do—"

"But you knew it had to be him." It chilled me to think that I might have ended up teaching with someone as twisted as Delaney.

"I guess."

She was able to recount Delaney's cruelty without condemning him—it was a terrible sign of how besotted she'd been.

"I didn't want anyone to know about us," she went on. "Delaney made me feel so good, and so bad. It was very confusing."

I felt sorry for her, for everyone whom Delaney had come to know, including myself. I'd let him influence me, poison my thoughts not just against Stefan but against myself. As if the corrosive voice of self-doubt had assumed a human form—and what a form. Delaney had been beautiful enough to fool, to dazzle anyone.

"He was sick," I breathed.

"But he was punished," Polly pointed out. "And not in the next life, in this one."

"Wait a minute. Delaney was murdered. Isn't that extreme punishment for manipulating other people and lying to them?"

Polly shrugged. Clearly I was a spiritual Visigoth totally out of touch with the subtle harmonies of the universe.

I asked her, "Why did you act spooked downstairs? Why didn't you stay for the memorial service?"

"I have to finish up for today," she said, shutting me out completely.

I let her go and sat there puzzling over the whole situation, keenly aware that I only understood part of it. I took out a notepad and started doodling names. Delaney was in the middle, and I drew arrows out from that center to Polly, to Lucille and Didier, to me and Stefan, to Juno. Was there a pattern here, or just random malice? And wasn't there something missing? Like a reason for someone to kill Jesse and Delaney. I sat there trying to figure what that was when I heard a soft knock on the door. I looked up and jumped from my chair. "*Angie!*" I rushed to her and gave her a hug, then broke away, embarrassed by my intensity. She blushed when I told her how worried I was about her after she disappeared. Then I apologized.

"What for?" she asked, as I waved her to the student chair and sat back down, drinking in her face, relieved that she was all right.

"Dr. Case tried your number up in Houghton but said it was always busy, and I didn't try following up. It's been so crazy here on campus."

"I heard," she said. "But I'm the one who should apologize for doing a *Titanic.*"

"What?"

"Sinking out of sight. I know we should have talked about the bridge and Jesse. To straighten it out, and stuff. But I didn't leave campus because of what happened to Jesse, it was because right after he died, I got this hyper call from my parents saying we had this enormous family emergency I had to leave school for. But they wouldn't tell me what it was! I started bugging, you know? I panicked. What if my mom or dad was diagnosed with cancer or something? I wasn't thinking too straight, I jumped in my Escort and drove straight home. With only pee breaks and drive-through McDonald's stops! Over twelve hours! I thought it was the end of the world I had to deal with."

"What was the emergency? Can you say?"

She pursed her lips. "This is so not cool. Nobody's sick or dying or anything! I mean, what a waste! My younger brother, he's a senior in high school, he told them he was having an affair with his math teacher. She's twenty-five years older than him, and he wanted to marry her."

Jeez, I thought, what's the deal with older women in Michigan? Was it the beginning of a regional trend? Then something tugged at me, but I couldn't figure out what.

Now that she'd launched her story, Angie was in full swing, telling me how her parents freaked out about her brother and demanded she intervene. But Angie refused, and was so angry and mortified by her parents' dragging her away from school when there wasn't truly a crisis, she'd been too embarrassed to call anyone at SUM. She waited until the trouble sorted itself out at home, which it did when her brother failed a math exam.

"But what about Jesse? Why did you say you thought he would get himself killed?"

"We dated a few times, nothing serious, but it didn't work because Jesse drank too much and I had to drive him back to his dorm plastered each time. One night Jesse said something about knowing a secret that could get him killed. It sounded serious, not like bullshit." She blushed and started to smack her own cheek, but I stopped her by saying, "I'm not that delicate, I can take it."

"Okay. So, when I saw him dead on the bridge, I *knew* he wasn't joking. I was sure somebody was after him, and *got* him."

"So you weren't ever in danger?" I pressed.

"No way, never. *Jesse* was. He never told me why, but it had to be the truth."

She was right about that, but what could have caused Jesse's death? A drug deal? Gang violence? A cult? What?

"I gotta bail." Angie shrugged. "But I wanted to see you because I felt bad about booking like that, and I knew you'd be weirded out."

After she left, I tried Stefan at home, but the line was busy and call waiting didn't kick in, so I figured he was on e-mail. I tried leaving a message on my own answering machine, hoping Stefan might hear that if I talked loud enough, but it didn't work.

It was a little after 5:00 P.M., and I started gathering my stuff together. The copy of *Adolphe* I'd bought was still in my briefcase, which I'd left in the car all weekend, and I found myself drawn to open it. Back in college, Penguin Classics had been my passion; the bindings were so soft you never had to crack them open, and I liked the light beige paper they were printed on—somehow I never strained my eyes reading them. Each great novel had linked me through lists at the back to others, so that the year I read French literature extensively, I reeled in delight from Balzac to Zola to de Maupassant, Diderot, Flaubert. But for some reason I'd missed Constant.

I sat back in my chair, and twenty years seemed stripped from my life as I started to leaf through the introduction. And then I stopped, horrified, beginning to see what I'd left off my piece of paper mapping Delaney and people connected to him. Why hadn't I looked at this book before? I'd sometimes sneered at moments in classic mysteries where something accidentally helps a detective put a case together, something indirect but analogous. Yet here it was happening to me.

I shoved it back into my briefcase, sure I'd never have the stomach to read it now, locked up, and headed down the hall, chewing over everything I'd learned about Delaney that afternoon, and what Angie had later revealed to me about Jesse.

Harry Benevento was just locking the History office door. More good luck for me. I stopped him, asking if we could talk.

"Now?" he bristled, and I momentarily felt like a circus animal trainer unsure of his bear.

"It's important."

"Fine." Harry nodded, then let us both in and took me through to his private office, which was identical to Coral Greathouse's just a floor below but much more human and warm, filled with brilliant watercolors of Italian-looking landscapes. The office made me feel much calmer than I had in weeks, and Benevento now appeared far less formidable a man.

"Those are beautiful," I said. "So much energy."

"Thanks. My wife painted them." He pointed to the chair facing his across the wide desk and settled behind it. In his boring dark blue suit, white shirt, and orange tie, he looked like an over-the-hill anchorman at a second-rate station. "She was very good," he continued, "but never sold more than a few paintings in her life. The depression ruined her. Even Prozac didn't help."

Out of respect, I didn't comment for a moment, then I said, reaching, "And Delaney made it worse, I bet."

Harry Benevento's mouth hardened as if fiercely keeping something back, and he tried staring me down, but I felt reckless and didn't waver. Only finding out the truth about Delaney would finally purge his influence from my life. "Delaney Kildare was a very cruel boy. Or man, if you prefer." I brought this out slowly, the ideas crystallizing as I spoke them. "Probably a sociopath. That *smile*. I should have taken it much more seriously. Like something inside kept bursting through the gorgeous facade. To warn people it was all a show. Or maybe even to dare them to find out."

Benevento nodded beneficently, sitting back with a sigh and then rocking slightly in his captain's chair, inviting me to go on

as if he were a committee and I the young researcher presenting my findings. So I continued. "Delaney seemed to enjoy
pursuing women, and he probably even seduced your wife," I
said, studying his reaction, "and then strung her along. That's
what he did with Juno Dromgoole, the visiting professor in
Canadian studies."

"I know who Juno is," he said flatly.

"And your wife couldn't cope with not knowing what he
really felt about her, or if he felt anything. Maybe he even tormented her about other women he was sleeping with, made her
feel weak, ashamed, craving his affection."

Benevento snorted. "Affection? Delaney Kildare didn't feel
affection for anyone, just contempt. He used people. He used my
wife, Rebecca. All the time he was acting so charming to me,
having dinner at our house, he was getting her to write his master's thesis for him!"

I shook my head in disbelief.

"Oh, yes. She'd been a double major in history and French
at Bennington, so it wasn't difficult for her."

"But was Delaney just too lazy to do it himself?" I asked,
appalled.

"No, it was more than that. I think the idea of having the
History chair's wife secretly do his thesis for him—when I was
on his thesis committee—was just too good to pass up. Of course
I knew it was plagiarism—the writing didn't sound like his—but
when I confronted Delaney, he said he would go public about the
affair if I made trouble for him. And then he told me who did
write it." Benevento's head dropped. "What could I do?"

If I'd been feeling bold before, now I was overwhelmed by
this tangled story of grief, guilt, and shame, pondering Delaney's
need to first manipulate and then punish women. Women who
took the place of his mother? The mother who had lived a lie and

given birth to a bastard. Or was that too simple—was there something more tortured, more desperate, behind all this?

"So that's why your wife killed herself," I said, putting more of it together.

"Oh, no." Benevento shook his head. "It's Delaney who killed her."

"Delaney?" Then that meant only one thing—

"He knew how fragile Rebecca was," Benevento continued, reliving last year. "And he played with her. Destroyed her. I should have seen it coming. Delaney once told me a very strange story about how his parents' marriage fell apart, and that he was the one who precipitated it—"

"He told me that story, too!" I realized then and there that Delaney had actually been *warning* people all along what he was capable of. That he could destroy a marriage. Or more. Like Osmond in *The Portrait of a Lady* telling Isabel that he wanted her money, Delaney had dared us to see what he was planning to do to all of us. First Benevento's marriage, then Lucille and Didier, next me and Stefan. It gave me goose bumps.

"My wife committed suicide, but I still think that Delaney murdered her as surely as if he'd tied the noose himself." He squeezed his eyes shut, breathing raggedly. "Her suicide helped drive Jesse away from me, made him turn to religious extremism. It's easy enough to do at SUM. In my day, it would have been radical politics."

"Jesse was very close to his mother?"

Benevento nodded, looking somber and thoughtful.

"Do you think she told him what happened before she died?"

He shrugged. "Jesse lived on campus, but he was home often enough to know something was wrong. I'm sure he figured it out, because when he wound up in an English class this year that Delaney was TA'ing, he demanded A's for all his work, or he'd let people know that Delaney had plagiarized his entire master's thesis."

"But that would have hurt you."

"Jesse hated me, he blamed me for everything. Still, how he could have considered hurting his mother's memory—"

Yes, I thought, everything would have come out, washing himself and his parents with a foul tide of rumor and speculation—and Delaney, too. It would have finished Delaney—the degree would have been rescinded, and he would have been forced to leave SUM. The scandal would have followed him to every university in the country, so he'd have to give up academia completely, and even then, he wouldn't be safe with something like that looming in his background.

"But how did you find out about Jesse threatening Delaney? Jesse wouldn't have told you, and forget Delaney."

Benevento grinned wolfishly, his large, fat face alight with triumph. "For obvious reasons, I was suspicious of Delaney, even though he was in another department this year. After Jesse's murder, I followed Delaney around, trying to see if I could discover something. Call it a gut feeling."

So *that's* why I'd seen Harry Benevento driving on our street—it had nothing to do with Polly or coincidence. He was trailing Delaney.

"But how did you—" I hesitated.

Benevento held out his hands as if displaying himself. "How did I disguise myself? I kept as far back from him as possible, but I didn't have to be that careful. He was completely lost in himself and in his impression on people he was interested in. He left History for EAR thanks to Dean Bullerschmidt's help—but I don't know exactly how that happened. He was done here, he'd slept with the chair's wife and killed her. Time to move on," he said heavily. "I was glad to get rid of Delaney, and he didn't consider me as a threat. And he thought he was invulnerable, so he wasn't suspicious. That's how I was able to steal his backpack in the library the other night."

Letting all this out, he seemed to be feeling more relief with each sentence.

"So you were the one who stole it."

"I wanted his keys to go through his apartment for proof—of something. They weren't in there, but I got more than I needed. He kept a diary of sorts. I don't know what you'd call it. He wrote nasty little portraits of people, and recorded—fooling around with my wife, with Juno Dromgoole, even my secretary, then that Professor Mochtar. Even stalking Jesse and *killing* him, everything."

So here at last was the connection.

"Yes, Delaney murdered my son to shut him up."

Horrified, I said, "Delaney was—"

"There aren't good words for what he was. But luckily, he didn't think much of anyone except himself, that's why it was easy to kill him. He was arrogant, overconfident."

I felt my mouth go dry. What I'd pieced together was clearly true, though I hadn't seen it all clearly.

Benevento leaned down to open a desk drawer, and I froze. But he frowned and sadly shook his head as if I'd disappointed him. He produced a black-bound artist's sketchbook, the kind sold at the student bookstores on campus.

"I'd never want to hurt you, though it wouldn't have been hard," he noted.

"You're a lot bigger than I am," I conceded, oddly calm again. Then I flashed on the height difference between Jesse and Delaney. No wonder the stab wound had been up into his heart.

"No. That's not it at all. I'm not a violent man. It's this: Last year Jesse complained to me about something you said in one of your classes."

I cringed. Here it comes, I thought.

"And he showed me a letter he was writing to Coral Great-house. It would have sunk your chances for tenure; even if it were disproved or discounted, you'd be associated with something disreputable, and there couldn't be a fair hearing. You couldn't ever clear yourself. You'd be the Filthy Professor or something like that. I told Jesse not to send the letter, that it was un-Christian." Benevento grinned. "That seemed to work. I told him to pray for you instead, pray that you'd see the error of your ways."

"But *why* did you protect me?"

"I knew you couldn't have meant any harm. And my son had turned into a fanatic—look at how he got involved in the riot on the bridge, defending some stupid box of Bibles."

"And that's what got him killed," I realized. "It would have been easy to do it in the middle of a riot where no one could really see what was happening."

Benevento nodded. "His fanaticism helped him get killed," he spat. "Killing Delaney was simply an act of justice. I'm not sorry I did it. I didn't plan it, I just took advantage of the opportunity. I was working in my office late Friday afternoon when I heard someone knock on the outside office door because it was locked. Polly was still here, doing some filing, and she let someone in—I heard his voice. They were speaking low because she obviously didn't want me to hear anything, but I recognized his voice. He told her that somebody had duked him out downstairs. He was bleeding and looking for sympathy. Pathetic, both of them."

Then Bill Malatesta's story was true, I thought.

"You knew about them?"

He nodded. "I followed him once, to Polly's house."

And that was probably the night I'd seen his Cherokee speed down our street.

"So what happened when Delaney came to see Polly here?"

"I heard Delaney say he had a date—can you imagine?—but he had to wash up first. They left together, and I waited a little and found him in the men's room." He related the end of the story as unemotionally as a gas station attendant giving directions. "I didn't intend to—I told him I had his diary, and he thought it was funny. He taunted me—"

"How?"

"Never mind that. I couldn't ever repeat it."

Picturing beautiful Delaney face-to-face with Benevento, a shambling, clownish old man, I could imagine the mockery spilling from Delaney's fine lips.

"I blew up," he concluded. "It wasn't my plan." Then he handed me Delaney's diary. "It's all here in his own writing. I have a favor to ask you."

"A favor?" It was such an incongruous word to hear in a conversation filled with images of cruelty.

"Yes. Since I protected you last year, I'd like you to at least read the diary before calling the campus police and turning me in. I'll be at home. Whatever you do, I'm going to do the honorable thing. It's time."

What was that supposed to mean? I asked him, and he looked at me with some pity, as if I were very young and very naive. "My wife was driven to suicide, my son was murdered, and I've been turned into a killer. What do I have to live for anymore?"

We sat there in silence, our eyes not meeting, surveying between us the wreckage of four lives, and the lives that could have been destroyed or at least damaged: mine, Stefan's, Lucille's, Didier's. Stunned, and still wary, I agreed to take the diary home. I rose, put my briefcase on his desk, and slipped the diary in next to the copy of *Adolphe*. On another impulse, I showed him the book.

He shuddered. "Jesse had a copy with him when he died."

"Yes, it was in his backpack, I saw it on the bridge. Have you read it?"

"No, I don't read fiction, but I know it was Rebecca's favorite novel. Jesse liked having it with him as a keepsake." He looked like a hot air balloon that had crashed and deflated.

Too bad Rebecca didn't understand it, I thought, or maybe she did and was drawn to someone like Delaney because the book spoke some truth of her heart she was condemned to play out. I left, briefly wondering if Benevento might change his mind and surge after me, determined to keep his secrets to himself a little longer.

But there was nothing behind me, just silence as I began to speed down the stairs. I fled the building and drove home like a maniac, not caring if I got stopped for speeding. I burst in on Stefan, who was grinning madly. "You're going to get tenure for sure!" he cried.

But my expression must have cut him off.

"What happened?" he asked sharply, grabbing my arm. "Are you okay? What's wrong?"

"I know who killed Delaney, and who killed Jesse."

Stefan tightened his grip.

I looked around the hallway, wondering if anything would ever seem quite the same to me again, and where in this house I could possibly feel untouched by the darkness that had contaminated our lives.

"Will you tell me what happened?" Stefan asked in a low, cautious voice, as if he sensed I was on the edge.

"Sure." I followed him into the kitchen, where something wonderful was in the oven. I registered the aroma without feeling especially hungry. I set my briefcase down, pulled out the copy of *Adolphe*. "Have you ever read this?" I settled into a chair while Stefan took the paperback from me, and nodded.

"Of course. In a college French class. It's pretty grim." He frowned. "Weren't we talking about it last week in the car?"

"Jesse Benevento had a copy of it in his backpack when he died on the bridge. It was his mother's favorite book."

"So?"

"He wasn't taking any French literature classes. I checked his schedule with his adviser, but never put that together."

"I'm not following."

"Does it make sense that a religious fanatic like Jesse would be reading this? Do you remember what it's about?"

"Vaguely. It's a fictionalized version of Benjamin Constant's affair with George Sand."

"No, Madame de Staël. And? Go on."

Stefan shrugged and shook his head.

"It's the story of an egocentric young man tormenting an older woman who's crazy about him. The man's completely detached, it's like he's performing an experiment."

"Delaney?"

"Yes, like Delaney. Jesse Benevento was taking a class Delaney was teaching, but the real class was Delaney. He was studying Delaney because Delaney had an affair with his mother—who was clinically depressed—and treated her so badly she killed herself. Jesse figured it out. And *Adolphe* was her favorite book—how about that? I should have read this book right when I realized it was an odd thing for Jesse to have in his backpack."

"An affair with Rebecca Benevento? I don't believe it. Where'd you hear all that?"

I took him through the entire afternoon from the memorial service on, Stefan exclaiming more than once that he didn't believe it. He was so surprised he rose from the table and paced while I spoke. But when I got to the point where Benevento confessed, Stefan stopped me.

"You thought he might have killed Delaney—and you went into an office with him?"

"I wasn't sure. I was pursuing the truth."

"That was crazy—you're not Ken Starr trying to bring down Clinton by wiring Linda Tripp! You don't have the FBI working for you!" Stefan strode into the dining room, opened the liquor cabinet, yanked out a bottle, and returned to the kitchen with a shot glass. He filled the glass and downed it as if taking an antidote to some dread disease.

"I know you're angry, but I felt compelled to do it. Jesse was my student, Delaney was infiltrating our lives, and then *I* was the one who found him dead. I couldn't let it go, I couldn't."

"You risked your life."

"Did I? I don't think so. Benevento's a wreck, you have no idea. His wife's killed herself because of Delaney, Delaney killed his son, he killed Delaney—his life's ruined. He wasn't going to do anything to me."

"But he has nothing to lose now," Stefan had to point out.

I showed him the diary, which had Delaney's address stamp on the inside of the cover, and his signature followed by the date he bought it over a year ago. Stefan joined me at the table, and though repulsed, we leafed through it, finding more and less than we had bargained for. It wasn't exactly a diary, more a series of portraits and scenes, as if Delaney had been making notes for a vicious, satirical book. Juno was in there, and Lucille, Rebecca, Polly, Benevento. He mocked everyone and everything, like the way Polly bit the heel of her left hand when she came during sex.

Despite himself, Stefan murmured, "Good detail," and it was my turn to raise my voice. "You think he was talented? *American Psycho*, part two? You're not grading him, and this isn't creative writing, it's destruction."

"Sorry. I forgot what he was doing—"

Then we both got very quiet when we read a chilling passage about *us*: "Stefan and Nick are so smooth together—like ice skaters with perfect lines. I can't wait to do a Tonya Harding on them."

I felt a strange mix of pride and fear, and slipped a hand into Stefan's.

"What was he going to do?" Stefan wondered.

"Try to break us up, somehow."

As we read on, we learned that Delaney had apparently also seduced Iris Bell and more secretaries than just Polly.

"How'd he have the energy to screw so many women?" I muttered, still shaken by his sick tribute to us.

Stefan said simply, "He was twenty-six. Remember twenty-six?"

"Sort of. But I was never bitter."

Stefan sighed. "I was."

We broke off when the timer rang. Suddenly I wanted to eat the world. But a wild-mushroom lasagna would do as a substitute. We ate quietly, gratefully, glad to be together and safe, but I felt threatened by the presence of the black book that lurked on the table like a cackling witch in a cartoon fairy tale.

"Tell me again how you figured out it was Benevento?" he asked when we were stacking the dishwasher.

"When you write," I said, "don't you see a pattern emerging from disparate details?"

"That's part of it, yes."

"Okay, then. Delaney was in History, but he switched departments, which is pretty unusual. Why? Benevento's the chair of History. His wife committed suicide last year. There was trouble between Benevento and his son. Could have been the son blamed his father for her death, but what if there was something else? Delaney liked older women in this department—why should History have been any different? And then there was Jesse's copy of *Adolphe*. I didn't realize how important it was, but it suggested a motive once I realized what it was about." Then I smacked my forehead. "Delaney told me his favorite Wharton novel was *The Mother's Recompense*—and that's also about an older woman betrayed by a younger man! How could I miss that?"

Pouring dish soap into the receptacle and snapping it shut, Stefan closed the dishwasher and started it. The quiet chugging seemed to mirror his musing about what I'd explained. "I don't think I would have come to the same conclusion," he said as we moved back to the table. "My money's been on Didier lately."

"The wronged husband? That's always a popular selection, except he wasn't wronged, since they hadn't slept together, and even if they had—"

Stefan shook his head. "I still don't believe he's that open."

We read on in Delaney's diary and found a passing reference that stunned me: Delaney had slept last year with Serena Fisch, the EAR professor on sabbatical whose courses were being covered by Juno.

"Serena!" I said. The former chair of the once-independent Rhetoric department, fiftyish Serena, dressed like one of the Lost Andrews Sisters. It was hard enough for me to imagine her out of costume, let alone in anyone's arms.

"Maybe—" Stefan said, putting it together, "maybe that's why Serena was a little strange last year." Serena was always a little strange, but I knew what he meant. Reading further, we discovered Delaney's connection to Bullerschmidt, or at least what he had written down about it. Who knew how much was accurate? Delaney described going to the dean, asking for a guarantee that he'd be accepted into the EAR department for his doctorate, with a teaching assistantship to boot.

"Unbelievable chutzpah," I practically yelped.

The dean made a deal with him: Delaney would keep his ears open for any scandal about Coral. For the first time that evening, we both laughed. Dirt about Moral Coral? She wasn't any Jimmy Swaggart with a secret scummy life—which is exactly why the department had elected her chairman almost unanimously.

But if Delaney found anything, Iris Bell would be the dean's candidate to replace Coral, who'd have to resign. Iris and Carter Savery, deeply embittered it seemed, were also "working for" Dean Bullerschmidt.

"Why would he write that down?" I asked Stefan. "Why would he write any of it down? It's crazy."

"The same reason he told Polly what he did: bragging. Can't you see him poring over this like pornography?"

"Jeez, if I were a thug like Delaney, I could use this to get tenure. Wait—tell me what you were saying before about tenure?"

Stefan grinned. "It never rains. . . . Just before you got home, I heard a call on your machine from Verity Gallup. She's got a Wharton project she wants to get rid of. I picked up the phone and took the details. It's an introduction to an English edition of *The Glimpses of the Moon*."

"Get out!" Verity was another major Wharton scholar who'd lost interest in her subject, and *Glimpses* was one of my favorite late Wharton novels.

"Don't you want to know what she's offering?" Stefan said. "It's the same deal as Jones. You get the advance, $1,000, and your name's on the book with hers. That's *two* books you'll have coming out."

"Edited books," I had to point out, aware of the status distinction between those and a monograph, which was a narrowly focused obscure work buzzing with modish words like *relativize*.

Stefan was insistent. "Two more than you had last year, or the year before, or—"

"Stop, I get it. And you're right, my chances for tenure are much better now."

"You sound disappointed."

"Does tenure matter? Do I want to stay here? Do we?"

Ever practical, Stefan said, "Let's worry about that after you get tenure, okay? You can do both projects in the next year, and Verity said that she and Jones would write you strong letters for your tenure file."

I looked down at the loathsome diary and shoved it across the table away from me.

"Polly must have known more than she told me. She was protecting Delaney," I said.

"That would make her an accessory. Just like us."

We mused over this until I said, "Holy shit! Bill! Bill Malatesta—we have to turn this in right away to prove he's innocent, but look at all the people who'll be devastated when this comes out. What do we do?"

"There's no question about it. We have to call Valley. It's our civic duty."

"Our civic duty?" I mocked. "You want us to uphold the values of Western civilization?" I shook my head. "You mean the same civilization that threw your parents and your uncle into concentration camps, and would have killed them if the war had lasted any longer? *That* civilization?"

We stared at the diary where it lay on the table.

"The honorable thing," I quoted Benevento. "He said he'd do the honorable thing. Suicide. So do we turn Benevento in and guarantee a horrendous trial, humiliation, and at least life in prison? Or let him kill himself? You know that's what he meant."

"It's not our choice to make," Stefan contended. "You have to call Valley right away, give him the diary, and tell him everything."

I knew he was right. Valley had given me his card once, and I dug it out of a box of business cards in my desk drawer and called his direct line at campus police, but got a dispatcher instead who told me he wasn't available.

"Listen—I have crucial evidence that will free Bill Malatesta! I have to speak to Detective Valley right away."

"We appreciate good citizenship," the cool voice replied, and I knew I was being "handled" as if I were claiming that Elvis had killed Delaney. Frustrated, I left my name and number, repeating that it was urgent.

"So we'll have to wait until he calls," Stefan said.

To distract ourselves from the coming bombshell, we caught *Executive Decision* on cable, and all my tension disappeared as I watched people in far more desperate straits than I was. Not exactly schadenfreude, but close.

Valley hadn't called by the time we went to bed, and though Stefan fell asleep easily enough, I didn't. Around 1:30 A.M. I slipped down to my study to call Sharon, who was never upset by late-night phone calls. I told her about talking to Polly and Benevento, and the diary, and that I was struggling to understand how Delaney could have created such a vile and disastrous set of circumstances.

"Nick," Sharon advised, "forget the motives, forget the psychology. Some people are just *bad*, and that's all the explanation there is."

I found this sensible, and oddly comforting.

TUESDAY MORNING WAS no less dramatic than Monday night. We got up very early, and when Stefan brought in the papers, he unfolded the *Michiganapolis Tribune* and stood motionless in the kitchen, reading aloud to me a story headlined PRO-FESSOR ASSUMED DEAD.

Harry Benevento's parked car—with the motor still running—had been found up north on his Lake Michigan–front property last night. Footprints led from the car down to the water, and police were assuming that he committed suicide because he left a signed note confessing he had killed Delaney Kildare.

Stefan tossed the paper onto a counter. "We know the rest," he said wearily.

"But why didn't he wait to hear from me?"

"He probably knew you'd have to call the campus police. He was just buying some time, I guess."

Stefan made us an omelette with shallots and cheddar cheese, which we had with whole wheat toast and Cross & Blackwell orange marmalade, hashing over the news.

"It's some kind of ruse," I insisted. "Benevento's probably alive somewhere. The car was left running. Why? To attract attention, to wake up neighbors, to make people think he drowned himself." When Stefan challenged that, I admitted that I wasn't sure how Benevento had worked the footprints.

"So what if he *is* alive?" Stefan asked, forking up the last of his omelette. "Would you want to live with his memories, and try to start over somewhere else—at his age? Let it go, Nick. Now it really is over."

I shuddered as if physically ridding myself of some specter and nodded reluctantly. "But what about the diary?" I asked.

He shrugged. "If we don't hear from Valley by noon, we'll just drive over to the campus police building and leave the diary for him with a note."

"You're right. I don't want it in this house, either." Now I wished that I hadn't called Valley and had just burned the diary in our fireplace, even if it meant destroying evidence. Benevento's suicide note would have cleared Bill Malatesta, and that's all that really mattered.

Perhaps following my thoughts, as he often did, Stefan said, "It has to come out."

"God, you sound like a dentist!"

"No, seriously. It has to, but my guess is that the murders are so sensational, people won't focus on the sex as much."

I disagreed. "Look at what's happening in D.C. with Clinton. This stuff here is going to end up a movie-of-the-week, and Juno will want to play herself."

He smiled. "Who should play us?"

"Oh, that's easy: Alec Baldwin and Ben Affleck."

"But which one plays me, and which one plays you?"

Feeling generous, I said, "Does it matter?"

EPILOGUE

But fame was a long way off. The first stage for everyone was infamy. After Bill was released, he sued the campus police and SUM for wrongful arrest, and President Littleterry settled quickly so as to hush it up. Details of Delaney's diary leaked out to the press, and national magazines and newspapers spun SUM as a cross between Sodom and Gomorrah and the Wild West.

The governor ordered a commission be set up to investigate the whole mess. There were calls for pretty much everyone involved to resign, even attacks on our half-wit president for letting it all happen. I think at one point if SUM's campus had been razed to the ground and salt sown in the earth so that nothing would ever grow there, over 50 percent of Michiganders would have applauded and volunteered for the work themselves, or at least chipped in some cash.

TV shows both in-state and across the country framed the story in predictable ways, depending on their views and whom they could snag as talking heads. Some billed it as "Sexual Degeneracy Rampant," others as "The Crisis on Campus: Liberalism Run Amok," and of course there were endless variations on

"Devil Men and Spurned Women." Larry King did three separate shows, alternately agreeing with Pat Buchanan, Gloria Steinem, and Dr. Joyce Brothers. For a while the all-news stations gave it as much play as Clinton's various troubles.

Stefan and I resolutely said, "No comment," to every call and query, even the day several news trucks were camped out on our street to try pressuring us or Lucille and Didier to talk. Stefan's agent was annoyed, assuring us he could build on the publicity to leverage a juicy book deal all about the scandal.

After a few weeks of bluster and outrage, and swarms of pseudojournalists infesting SUM's campus, the imbroglio seemed to fade away completely. Juno, Lucille, and other women Delaney wrote about had been uniformly portrayed as victims of a cunning, sick seducer preying upon them, so none were professionally damaged. Juno even seemed to relish the publicity, though Lucille talked to me and Stefan about quitting. While Bullerschmidt's chances of becoming provost were over—as an administrator, he was supposed to be scandal-free—his position was still enviably secure. He denied everything Delaney had said about him, and who could say he was lying?

It turned out that the man I'd seen in front of Lucille's and Didier's house was suspicious *and* dangerous, but not Lucille's brother-in-law. He was actually Merle Flockhart, Polly's sadsack ex-husband, and had been checking out the street and her house; he tried to break into her house one night and was spotted by one of our insomniac retired neighbors, who called 911. Flockhart had a blackjack on him, which he tried to toss into a hedge, but he said he only wanted to "talk to" Polly.

Stefan wouldn't let me claim I had been even one iota right, because when Lucille saw Flockhart's picture in the *Michiganapolis Tribune*, she hooted at me, "You thought that was Napoleon!? There's no resemblance at all."

"They're both dark-haired."

"And they're both white. End of story."

In an odd way, all the tumult seemed to cheer Stefan up, even though there was continued bad news from his agent about placing his novel. Stefan was a "prisoner of his numbers." Other publishers balked at picking up someone they considered a failure, even when they were enthusiastic about his new book. "You'd be better off as a first-time novelist," was his agent's sad comment.

Yet Stefan was happy. Perhaps because after the recent nightmare, he could shout like D. H. Lawrence, "Look, we have come through!" Or perhaps it was the wonderful spring we were having, with not even many of the typical "partly cloudy" days that were endemic in Michiganapolis.

My situation at SUM had improved considerably. Since I had "braved the killer's den," as one paper told it, and secured important evidence that I passed along to the campus police, I had surprisingly earned a compliment from Coral Greathouse, who told me I "handled myself with dignity." Given that I was suddenly in Coral's favor, Stefan insisted that Iris and Carter were unlikely to scotch my tenure chances, since they'd been publicly painted as scheming against Coral.

We were talking about this one Sunday a month after Harry Benevento killed himself—or disappeared—when the doorbell rang. Polly? Lucille and Didier?

Stefan went to the door, and I heard his startled, "Sharon, hi!"

Disbelieving, I followed him to the front door, and it was indeed my cousin Sharon, looking tired but as graceful as ever in a fawn linen pants suit and mocha cashmere scoop top. Stefan took her Chanel bag and small Louis Vuitton suitcase, and when I hugged her close, I whispered, "Boyfriend trouble?"

"Trouble, all right."

I took her out to the sunroom, sorry that she hadn't been to visit us here in over a year—when we saw her it was usually in New York. "This house is so beautiful," she murmured, looking out into the backyard, "so quiet. I forgot." I had filled a vase with branches cut from our lilacs, and Sharon leaned over them, breathing in deeply. We made pleasant conversation about her flight until Stefan brought us all iced tea and we sat down, Stefan and I looking at her expectantly. Her supernal elegance reminded me more than ever of Lisa Fonssagrives, the classic Dior model of the 1950s.

"I couldn't say this over the phone," she began. "I haven't even told my parents yet. Remember those tests I said I had to schedule?"

I nodded.

"I don't want you to worry, but the hearing's gone in my left ear, almost completely, and I'm having these strange little twitches on that side of my face." She ran a lovely index finger in a line from her forehead to her jaw as if we could actually see the problem. "It's pretty definite that I have a brain tumor—it's called an acoustic neuroma?—on that side. They say they need to operate, fairly soon, and one of the best neurosurgeons east of the Mississippi for this is at your medical school."

Stefan and I both said, "*Here?*"

The words "brain tumor" shrilled inside me like a car alarm.

Sharon nodded. "So I came out to consult with him before I decide what to do, exactly."

We all smiled inanely at each other as if contemplating a picnic. Then Stefan moaned a soft, "Oh, God." I heard him but couldn't speak. Sharon reached over and grabbed my hand. "It's a benign tumor, but it's still growing. It has to be stopped, some- how."

I had to ask what I didn't want to. "What are the chances . . . with the surgery?"

"Pretty good, actually, but I'll lose all hearing in that ear, and I may have paralysis on that side of my face, too. You know, like Bell's palsy?" She was being very brave, but as I began to cry, she did, too, and we fell into each other's arms, while Stefan clumsily tried embracing both of us.

Sharon broke away when she started hiccuping, and got herself under control. She pulled some wadded tissues from her jacket pocket. "Of course, there are doctors in New York who could do the surgery, but when I checked out all the experts around the country, I figured that I'd be better off here, with you guys."

Once again, Stefan and I spoke at the same time. "Why?"

"Call me superstitious, but you have to admit, nobody ever dies of natural causes when you're around."